CHASIN' JASON

a novel by

Jane Chambers

JH PRESS
P.O. Box 294, Village Station
New York, N.Y. 10014

First Edition, January 1987

Cover design: Nancy Johnson, Aenjai Graphic Studio, New York City

Back cover photo: Beth Allen

LIBRARY OF CONGRESS CATALOGING IN PUBLICATION DATA

Chambers, Jane, 1937-1983
CHASIN' JASON.

I. Title
PS3553.H258C4   1987   813'.54   86-21456
ISBN 0-935672-13-3

Chasin' Jason

"If God created us in his own image, we have more than returned the compliment."

Voltaire

ONE

THERE'S a stray cat in this church, come up from the basement, I imagine. He may have been driven out of hiding by the shouts and chanting outside. He swishes his flanks as he circles me—more curious than cautious. I think he smells my fear. He puffs up proudly as though he believes that he's the cause of it. His eyes are glittering gold nuggets in the moonlight and I see no compassion in them. Perhaps he knows that I'm the prisoner here, not he. He turns his nose up at me and struts into the shadow of the pulpit where he sits smugly, meticulously cleaning his right front paw— watching me intently, though, I can feel. And I could swear— but of course, this is pure folly—that I heard him mutter scornfully, "You fool."

This church is large and haunted by shadows which hover in the corners and creep slowly along the walls. I seem to see a medieval priest spilling across the floor. No, maybe it's an Aztec princess or a Druid or a pill-box hatted clergy of the Renaissance. As the moonlight dwindles, then increases in intensity, my bloodless visitors change form.

I have watched the moon crossing the sky tonight. She moves so slowly, sliding her feet beneath her gown, trailing mist behind her. She is haloed by her own light and as euphoric as a bride but she's no virgin. Through the blue stained glass of the vaulted window, I can see she's far too tranquil.

The pews here are scalloped with the imprint of thousands of shifting shoulderblades and buttocks. I trail my hand along the seats and think a man sat here, a heavy man, his wife beside him. Tracing the rump-marks, I believe I can recall the asses that once warmed these pews.

"Takes one to know one." It is the cat's voice but, of course, I'm hearing things. A woman destined for execution is likely to hallucinate, I reassure myself. I must keep my mind off it. It is sorrowful enough to die this way, so soon, but to die mad is unthinkable. Facing my death might be easier were I to suddenly become unhinged but it would be a coward's way to go.

"There's nothing to it. Ask a cat. We die nine times."

I didn't hear that.

This oval indentation in the pew is smooth as satin, smaller, deeper than the others. Perhaps it was a child's place, a squirming child who, unable to see the minister above the nodding adult heads, kept turning to watch the Sunday morning light up the stained glass portrait of little Jesus in the Temple. That portrait fills the north wall of this church and even now, at night, it is the most poignant of the windows. Young Jesus, his face long and narrow, his arms and ankles frail and white, has thrown his hands toward Heaven. His hair is long and yellow and falls past his shoulders to disappear into the dark folds of his ruby robe. I have never seen Jesus depicted in a brightly colored garment but perhaps here the people cherished beauty before fact. His robe is red as blood and, with sunlight on it, takes your breath. The money-lenders, cloaked in greens, blues and purples, are cowering and crawling down the steps, looking back across their shoulders fearfully as young Jesus casts his eyes and voice to God. Jesus' eyes are sapphire blue and too large in proportion to his face. The moneylenders, even as they're driven from their place of business, clutch sacks of golden coins beneath their arms. Perhaps a little boy sat in this place here, craning his neck to see Jesus in the sunlight, hypnotized by the boy Christ's ability to speak directly to the Almighty and to forthwith cast evil from the world. Or perhaps in this rural area where the labors of farmers and fishermen have always been greater than their earthly rewards, the boy's eyes were locked on the glitter of the moneylenders' gold.

I hear the cat moving. The aisle between the pews is dark as a grave. I stay still, breathing softly. Cats like to swipe at moving objects in the dark.

Perhaps this small, deep indentation in the pew wasn't made by a child at all but by someone old and wizened, sharp-boned, hunched, brittle frame made heavy by pain and the pull of gravity sucking her each moment closer to the grave. She spent the hour long service staring down at her sore feet, toes gnarled inside muddy, scuffed boots, dreading the moment when the organ sounded and she had to rise with the crescendo and begin her arduous walk home.

The cat leaps suddenly into the pew. He curls into the indentation.

Before me is the altar, a hulking monument. It writhes with angels. They are crushed together in their small space, elbows and knees entwined, eyelids squinted to better hear the music of their horns and harps. One angel rises above the rest, lips parted as though singing. The figures are carved deeply in the black wood and moonlight catches in the crevices.

Oh, what I'd give right now to hear the strains of some old-fashioned music, familiar, comforting. I sing. My voice is strained and weak. The sound loses volume in this cathedral.

I'm as corny as Kansas in August

High as a flag on the fourth of July...

We're dancing in the dark
Til the tune ends
We're dancing in the dark
And it soon ends...

Whenever I feel afraid
I hold my head erect
And whistle a happy tune
So no one will suspect...

...in the wonder of why we're here
Time hurries by
We're here
And gone.

...I'm afraid.

Blue moon.
You saw me standing alone
Without a dream in my heart
Without a love of my own
Blue moon...

I've got a blue moon of my own through this stained glass window. I can't stop looking at it. It's the last moon I'll ever see.

The cat is at my legs. He strokes my ankles with his flanks. I tell him that I have no food to give him. I speak to him aloud as though he can understand. As I look down at him, he appears to be gray but that may be the way the moonlight colors him through the stained glass.

I'm using the sacramental table as a desk. It has a niche carved in it for the wine bottle and a shelf below to hold the Holy Host. Between the shelf and tabletop, cobwebs are so thickly embroidered that I took them at first to be a doily. Caught in the intricate design are tiny white specks, carcasses of dead flies, perhaps, or crumbs from a long-ago communion.

The cat weaves in and out my ankles. I read somewhere once that a starving cat will eat a human being. This cat does not appear to be that hungry. I expect the basement of this church is full of rats.

"Only thing tastes worse than a muskrat is a human. I had a cousin tried them both."

A cat is talking to me. It's come to this.

I would scream but they're bedded down outside and I don't want to wake them. They said they'd execute me at sunrise but they have no sense of time. Wakening them now might hasten the event. I haven't tried to sleep myself. At sundown, a small girl was allowed to enter the sanctuary and bring me a blanket. She whispered so rapidly that I'm not sure she was speaking English. The best I could make of it, she was saying Louis ordered her to bring the blanket to me. I grasped her wrist and tried to question her but the young man guarding the door, his pistol jammed into the waistband of his cut-offs, motioned her out. They don't want me to talk to anyone.

The blanket she brought is thick, heavy—I believe it's handwoven out of rope. A single zigzag stripe runs down the center of it like a streak of lightning. Orange. Smells of honeysuckle. Perhaps they use flowers here to dye their fabrics. I may be thankful for this blanket before sunrise. I can feel the temperature's dropped even now and it's still early evening. It seems pointless to sleep. I haven't slept in two, or is it three?, days now although at one point, I did lose consciousness.

This afternoon when they were rallying outside the eastern window—it depicts Judas and the Roman soldier, their hands clasped around a sack of gold—there must have been a fickle wind. Sometimes I heard the voices clearly, so raucous and enraged that I pressed my hands against my eyes. Then suddenly the sound would fade and disappear and just as suddenly blast back again, as though someone were idly fiddling with the tuner on a radio. Only one voice remained constant. When the wind took all the others, this single voice boomed. Bone weary and shaken as I am, he seemed to shout "My Will Be Done" and for a moment, I believed God was finally speaking to me.

Maybe this cat is not real at all but a spirit which belongs to this old church. No, he purrs too loudly to be a ghost. He is rubbing his cheek up and down the calf of my leg.

"Stop flirting with me," I admonish him. I say it more to hear myself than to stop the activity of the cat. In fact, physical contact with another living creature feels good to me right now.

"Jeez. Just like a woman. A fellow tries to be friendly and she thinks he's coming on to her." The cat leaps to the table, bats my ballpoint pen out of my hand and swats it to the floor. He pounces on it as though it were a mouse but when he takes it in his mouth and discovers it is plastic, he spits it out and stalks away, tail high in disgust. He doesn't go far. At the edge of the shadows, he turns and sits. His eyes glow, the last coals in a dying fire. My fear has created such tension in this sanctuary that I can feel the air moving in jagged waves. The cat seems oblivious to this. I'm clutching at each passing second, desperate to hold time still. He seems to languish in its forward movement as though his time were endless.

I'll name him Solomon.

I haven't read a newspaper or heard a newscast since my arrest. If anyone knows where I am now and what has happened to me, I'm sure the federal attorneys are filing for my extradition but the Jasonites won't wait around for legal remedies. They yield to no law but God's. Maybe God will stay their hands the way He did Abraham's. I haven't lost my faith. On the other hand, I haven't prayed for deliverance. I'm trying to accept that God has nothing to say to me. If that sounds flippant, it isn't meant to be. God knows how I mean it. God and I have a long history of one-sided conversation.

Solomon has found a spider in the cobwebs beneath this table. It looks dead to me, its legs curled to its belly but Solomon pokes it as though it's living. He wants it to recognize me, to scamper off terrified or spin and bite but it falls on the floor instead. Persistent Solomon claws at the crack.

I am spending these last hours of my life writing in a book. I found it in the vestry of this Church. The paper is yellow and brittle; it breaks off along the edges when I turn a page. The volume is bound in leather so dried that it looks and feels like cardboard. One side only of each page has been written on—it lists the names of parishioners back to—the early entries are barely legible and the ink's turned faint yellow. From the flourish of the penmanship, I'd guess two hundred years—maybe three. Toward the back of the volume, the names are entered in brown ink, then blue, then black and, on the last page only, in ballpoint pen. The ballpoint ink is streaked as though someone dashed water on it. Paging through this volume, it would appear that a lot more people were seeking God in 1700 than in 1980.

I'm glad there are no mirrors in this sanctuary. Even fully coiffed and spanking clean, I never much liked reflections of myself. It's the curse of my life that I'm an ordinary looking woman. Once, shopping in a discount store on Third Avenue, I discovered that my hair was the color of bulletin board cork. Henceforth, I could write in those little blanks on driver's licenses and insurance forms, *color of hair:* cork. As though my scalp were a bulletin board on which passersby could post messages. COME HOME, ALL IS FORGIVEN.

My eyes are not completely blue but not always green and sometimes, if it's raining, they are gray. I have, on occasion, been introduced to the same person three times at a single party and the person smiles each time and shakes my hand heartily with no notion at all that he/or/she has seen me before. I would make a good spy.

Once, in an effort to look singular, I had my hair cut short and permed into an Afro. The people who always recognized me, did. "Goodness," they said, "something has changed about you, have you lost weight?" The people who never recognized me, didn't. Those who know me intimately—but there are none of those left now, I'm afraid—would know I have a mole on my left breast and just the tiniest bit of a wart in my hairline. My front two teeth are capped. A TV newswoman must have perfect teeth, the camera glorifies defects.

It would be easier to tape record these thoughts. I've spent most of my working life with tape and video. I'd forgotten the drudgery of pushing a pen across paper. But there was no time to grab a tape recorder when Jason and I ran—it seemed as though half of the population was behind us, chasing Jason. And there is something about the holding of a pen, of forming letters on the page by the motion of my fingers, that gives my thoughts indelibility. Perhaps I've seen tape recordings degaussed too many times. Pass the recorded human voice across a tiny magnet and, in a fraction of a second, it is gone forever.

I'm surprised the Jasonites let me keep this pen. It was in my jacket pocket and I know they searched the jacket but when they returned it to me, the pen was still there. They must have overlooked it.

It's unlikely anyone will ever read what's written on the backs of pages in this old ledger. The Jasonites will probably pull this old church down and chop it into firewood. Still, there's the off chance that someone (perhaps that little girl who brought the blanket, she had a kind, inquisitive face) will find this book and spirit it to safety. I'm not sure there are any publishers in business now that the power system's failed and currency is useless—but perhaps this book will be passed among the few remaining unbelievers and give them some perspective on how the Second Coming came about.

TWO

'LL be executed tomorrow morning. Daybreak, they said—
although the Jasonites are noted for sleeping late. They say
I sent Jason to his death. I didn't sell him out for money; I'm
not like Judas in the window there, his fingers reaching for
the gold. The only remuneration I received was my regular
weekly salary and, while I'm paid to ferret out the truth, that
had very little to do with Jason's death. And further, in this
instance, I've withheld the truth for twenty years. That's not
why they're executing me, however. If it were, I could justify
their wrath.

I started this whole damned thing. The Jasonites consider
that my one redeeming action. I suppose that's why they
permitted me a trial instead of executing me on sight. I
pointed out that, in the Bible, Jesus Christ instructed his
disciples to let Judas go unpunished. The Jasonites considered that. It brought the whole mock trial to a dead
standstill for an hour and a half. When we reconvened, the
Jasonites announced there wasn't much truth in the Bible

anyway and, given my relationship to Jason, my crime was greater.

I was the beginning and the end. I had good intentions but as Grandma used to say, the road to Hell is paved with those.

At the outset, let me make it clear that I never intended Jason to die. At my trial the Jasonites said no one loved anyone as deeply as they loved their Lord. I believe my love for Jason transcended theirs. Jason was my son.

Solomon has discovered the blanket. He is concentrating all his efforts on one strand in the hope that when he pulls it free, the rest will follow. I call him sharply by name. "Solomon." He is unaccustomed to the name; perhaps mine is the first human voice he has ever heard. He perks his ears, fixes me in his yellow stare, then leaps into my lap, rolls onto his back, embraces my hand with his paws and licks my palm with his sandpaper tongue. He is placating me with acts of love.

Jason used to do that, too.

If it were not for me, Jason would be pulling rickshaws in Seoul, ridden with lice, poverty and ignorance. He might, in fact, be blissfully content. My Grandma, a schoolteacher, claimed no one should seek more education than they need to just get by. She believed knowledge is a burden and allowed no books but a dictionary, an encyclopedia and a Bible to be kept in her house. "If the Bible's the only book God wrote," she said, "the devil himself might have authored the rest."

If I'd left well enough alone—oh, hell, who knows? Maybe it would have ended up the same way. Someone else would have adopted Jason. What's meant to be will be. God works, as they say, in mysterious ways. I can testify to that.

In this, my last epistle, I must deal with facts. Keep reminding me of that, Solomon. I tend to wander off sometimes; I am addicted to theorizing. Whether *it was meant to be* or not is totally irrelevant.

Solomon dips his nose between his paws and peeks up at me.

Josephine Mary Caldwell. That's my real name. Grandma had it first. Born Advent, Georgia, 1936. Daughter of Walter and Ruth Caldwell, I came into the world three weeks later than expected weighing eleven and one-quarter pounds upon arrival. I was bald as a billiard and my mother swaddled me in pink so everyone would know for sure I was a girl. My father said I looked like a monkey. My Grandma vowed I was the ugliest newborn she'd ever seen though she reluctantly admitted that I got better looking as I aged. I resembled no one in the family and I walked and talked so early that my mother complained she'd never really had an infant to look after.

My father was an electrician and an alcoholic. My mother was a cashier and a saint. They grew up during World War I, the roaring 20s and the Great Depression. They witnessed the rise of Freud, the magic of Einstein, the miracles of autos, radios and airplanes.

"To understand the Second Coming, Solomon, it's necessary to understand me."

Solomon, draped now on my shoulder, bats at the ballpoint pen I'm tapping on the table. "Slow down," he's saying, "Take it easy." Ah, but Solomon, I have so little time left, don't you see? "Then use it well," he advises, purring against my cheek, "Fill it up."

The moon is near a half-arc in the sky but Solomon is right, there is some time left.

"If you catch me jogging, Solomon, holler."

"You places your bet and you takes your chances," Solomon retorts and leaps from my shoulder, gouging my flesh with his claws as he propels himself toward the altar. He lands with a thud, sits on the slanted podium and cocks his head in my direction. When I lift my pen, he dismisses me and cleans his paws. My blood, no doubt, on his claws.

When was the last time you opened up to someone, God?

Joan of Arc? Jason swore he talked to you, but we both know that was a lie. God, it would be very helpful if you'd burn a bush—or part the Potomac during Cherry Festival—something.

Are you still up there?

Breaker, breaker, this is Josie, virgin mother, calling the Big Boy, do you read me? What's your 10-6, good buddy? I believe I'm about to be heading up your way.

The moon moves slowly, the shadowy clerics on the wall lean toward me. They're curious. Closing in. Outside, sleepers turn restlessly in their bedrolls. I can hear the rustling of pure goosedown against polyvinyl fabric.

A dog barks. Solomon rises, arches.

I have so little time left.

I can't wait any longer, God. With or without your help, I've got to forge ahead.

THREE

I HAVE no prenatal memories. Sourball was my nickname the first six months of my life. It's written in white ink beside my baby photos in the family album—*Sourball and her Easter Basket, 5 wks. old, 1936; Sourball sees her 1st sand castle, smashes it, 16 wks. old, July 1936;* etc. I learned to walk before I laughed.

My mother was a product of her time. In the early pages of the same family photo album is a snapshot of her in diapers and an Army hat, dangling a small American flag in her chubby hand. Written in white ink beside this photo is the legend, RIGHT IS MIGHT! It is printed doggedly in Grandma's hand and the ink spattered in some spots casting a flurry of dandruff-like dots across the black page. Next to that photo, there is a newspaper clipping—a picket line of suffragettes. They carry picket signs and look worn out. One states EQUAL RIGHTS FOR WOMEN! Another MARCH OUT OF HIS SHADOW! OPEN THE POLLS TO WOMEN! CLOSE THE BARS TO MEN! Grandma, unmindful of the camera, is standing near the end of the line. She appears to be picking her front tooth with her fingernail. A picket sign is propped against her hip. It's homemade—a piece of cardboard strapped to a tree limb. In Grandma's printing, it is lettered RIGHT IS MIGHT! Several small children sit on the curbstone grinning at the photographer. A blotch of white ink obscures two of the little faces. One of them must be my mother.

They tell me that the southern economy blossomed during Prohibition and that Advent, Georgia had more stills per capita than any place below the Mason Dixon. At any rate, next in the scrapbook there appears a photo of my mother at 16 with bobbed hair and a flapper dress, perched coquettishly on the rumble seat of an old Ford. She is gaily displaying a flask of homemade hootch. The caption, in my mother's delicate penmanship, says PETE'S OWN BRAND. BET HE'LL GROW UP TO BE THE GOVERNOR! Across the page, a grinning teenage boy dressed in his Sunday best, straw hat cocked over one eye, saddle shoe up on the running board of the same Ford. Beside that photo, Mother has written PETE and drawn a heart around his name.

The next two pages of snapshots are taken on a college campus. Mother, cloche hat, fringed dress, dancing with a skinny boy in white pants and a striped shirt. He also has a predominant Adam's apple. I imagine that it bobs in rhythm with the music. CUTTING A RUG WITH ROGER. A photo of a muscular young man standing ape-like, smiling broadly, wearing a girl's dress and high heels. CRAZY WILLIE. BOYS WILL BE GIRLS! Mother on the shoulders of two laughing young men. CONQUERED THE WORLD TODAY! ELECTED SOPHOMORE CLASS PRESIDENT! 1929. WHO SAYS GIRLS AREN'T EQUAL? There are no more college photos after that. Just the front page of the Advent Tattler, folded in quarters, one quarter pasted to the scrapbook pages; when opened up, the headline reads DEPRESSION DEVASTATES SOUTH GEORGIA. There's a photograph of a peanut processing plant, boarded up. Another of a group of men sitting by the roadside, baskets of pecans at their feet. 5¢ A Basket, says the sign. One of the men appears to be trying to hail a passing car. In the right hand column, there is a picture of a college campus, stone buildings gleaming in the sun, bright-eyed boys and girls hurrying to class. COLLEGE CLOSES says the sub-headline. Beneath the photo, *Advent Christian College closed its doors June 30, 1931, after ascertaining seventy per cent of its enrollees would be unable to return next fall. Ruth Baldwin, President of last year's sophomore class, expressed the students' regrets at not being able to continue their pursuits of higher education. "It's this depression," Miss Baldwin stated, "We all have high hopes that it will soon be over and we can return to our classes at Advent Christian." Miss Baldwin is the first girl to be elected to the position of class president in the fifty-two year history of the college.*

On the next page of the scrapbook, another clipping from a newspaper. The photo reveals Mother, standing dutifully before a filing cabinet, dressed in a conservative business outfit. She wears roller skates. The headline says FILE CLERKS SKATE BETWEEN DEPARTMENTS AT MOORE PRO-DUCTS. ONE GIRL CAN DO THE WORK OF THREE.

Next comes an 8x10 glossy, a professional portrait of my Mother and my Father at their wedding ceremony. The composition is poor and the newly married couple stand just left of center. Mother wears a light-colored dress, embroidered at the neck and hem. Her pocketbook is draped over her arm. In her hand she holds a single white rose. My Father stands beside her, grinning at the camera. His thumbs are hooked in his pockets and he appears to be rocking jauntily back on his heels. He wears a white dress suit and vest, a carnation in his lapel and a red rose stuck in the band of his straw hat. My mother is smiling shyly at him. They both look slightly surprised. Beside this photograph, in white ink, Mother has written MARRIED WALT, FEBRUARY 6, 1935, ADVENT CITY HALL. At the far right, in the background, a stubby figure appears ghostlike through the darkness. It is out of focus but I can tell from the rigid stance and the thick arms firmly crossed over the chest, it's Grandma.

Though she talked a good game about the Bible, God, Devils and the Fires of Hell, Grandma hadn't much use for religion. She hadn't much use for learning, either, and she'd taught school most of her life. She refused to attend church services claiming that somebody had to cook the Sunday dinner. She retained her letter of membership in Advent Baptist Church because it assured her of a free plot in the cemetery.

Mother and Grandma had a lot in common, I guess. They both revered the miracles of modern science and abhorred all bodily functions. They believed in authority. The President was right and was accorded respect. In our household, Mother was the authority. Grandma was retired authority serving as consultant.

Mother and Grandma thanked science for packaging biscuits, slicing bread, inventing Tampax, frozen dinners, rayon, TV and vacuum cleaners. They were devoted consumers and expressed faith that within the century women would be able to order babies at Walgreen's. They foresaw a world without need for kitchens or bathrooms. One pill a day would supply all needed nutrients and create no resultant gas or waste. They were mesmerized by space flights but agreed that science should commit itself to pressing domestic needs. These domestic priorities were: (1) human reproduction without intercourse, pregnancy or lactation; (2) sustenance without mastication, digestion or defecation; and (3) a new and better male animal, devoid of external genitals and low on testosterone, male hormones being responsible for crime and war and male genitals ugly as a chicken's neck.

My father was a dapper man. He always wore a straw hat, generally stuck a flower in the hatband. His shoes shone like patent leather and he wore silver cufflinks shaped like catfish which his father had won in a casting contest at the 1901

World's Fair. Father preferred pin-striped suits and always wore a vest. Even when he was working at his trade he wore his dress suit to the job and home again.

My father, a licensed electrician, had no talent or instinct for the job. He was afraid of voltage. He wore rubber shoes with rubber inner soles when he worked and never touched a wire unless he had on two pairs of heavy-duty rubber gloves. He tacked tire treads on the steps of his ladder. He sweated when he worked, from nervousness, and kept a headband tied around his forehead so the sweat wouldn't drip onto a hot wire and short-circuit it and him. Most days, he never made it to the job site, having been waylaid by the flashing neon sign at the GATOR BAR & GRILL.

Eventually, my father took to growing hot peppers and asparagus in Grandma's flower bed and, evenings, he'd sit on the steps alone in the moonlight sharpening knives and eating one hot pepper after another. Sometimes he drank tabasco sauce directly from the bottle. He had a wooden box filled with knives of all sorts and kept them sharp as razors. Everyone pretended not to notice it. One night, while I was in the living room with Mother and Grandma watching Liberace on TV, my father plunged six inches of a twelve inch blade into his abdomen just below the ribcage, puncturing three organs. At bedtime, my mother sighed and went to the front door to call him in. She found him lying in the flower bed, bled to death.

My father had no interest in God. He viewed church-going as women's business. He referred to the minister as that old fairy but I never heard him protest my being hauled off to Advent Baptist every Sunday.

Solomon is standing up beside me, his head in my lap. I can feel his motor vibrating against my thigh. His claws dig in just above my knee. Even so, I am beginning to trust that he wouldn't harm a fly.

"Wrong," Solomon corrects my thought. "I've killed many a fly in my day. I'm a champeen fly-killer." He pins his ears back and revs up. The sound is amplified in the chapel and seems to echo back from the shadows. The ghosts of clergy past are purring at me.

I was eleven when I heard my mother's sharp exasperated sigh. I peeked out the front window and saw my father lying on the sidewalk. His flesh was yellow in the moonlight. His mouth was open as though he'd just thought of something that he wanted to say and was waiting for an opening in the conversation so he could interject it. His eyes were open but there was no life in them, not even the reflection of the moon. If I said he looked sad or peaceful or angry lying on that sidewalk, I'd be making it up. He just looked dead.

Ever since I can remember, there was an incessant hum in our house like a radio that's lost contact with the station. The sound grew higher, shriller that night and for the days and weeks to follow. It pressed against my skull, trying to get inside. I knew that if it touched my brain, I'd go crazy like my father. I fought it all the time. It hummed against my skin. It skimmed my body the way low voltage does when you press your finger on a faulty light switch. I've gotten used to living with the buzz.

A police car arrived first, followed by an ambulance. The lights flooded our front yard like a county fair. Neighbors peeked around the edges of their window shades. Uni-formed attendants rolled the corpse onto a canvas stretcher and carried it down the sidewalk to the ambulance. One arm dangled. Fingernails scraped on the sidewalk. The ambu-lance pulled out, siren blaring. The police came in the house to fill out forms. They laid the papers on the coffee table, forms printed in red ink, and asked to use a fountain pen. My mother rummaged in a kitchen drawer. I ran to my room and produced a pen, trying to be helpful. Grandma sent me straight to bed.

The next morning, I went to Sunday School and sang in the choir for the early service. Grandma cooked Sunday chicken and greasy green beans. I might have thought I dreamed my father's death except that after dinner I went out front and found the whetstone in the flower garden. There was a trail of blood the length of the sidewalk, a serpentine line of evenly spaced drops. My mother hosed down the walk.

"Say Daddy had a heart attack."

My mother made the funeral arrangements in the same defensive tone of voice she used to fend off creditors. There was no service. I'd heard her purchase a casket over the telephone and inquired as to what had become of it. She said they burned it when they burned him. Some of the ashes in the urn were the casket's, some were my father's. I couldn't tell the difference. They let me throw a handful of dirt into the grave and it landed directly on the urn which wobbled several times, then toppled. It was sealed and nothing spilled out. Grandma gasped.

My mother took a night job selling Lusair Cosmetics door to door. Daytimes, she cashiered at Colonial Drugs like she'd always done. I joined every club at school and stayed until they locked the doors at five. Monday nights, I babysat at church while the Young Baptist Mother's Club met. Tuesday nights, I went to choir practice. Wednesday nights, I attended Prayer Meeting. Friday and Sunday nights I went to Baptist Youth. Thursdays and Saturdays still depress me. My mother's dissatisfaction thundered when she walked.

We moved shortly after my father's death. We always moved twice a year so it was no big upheaval. In the spring and summer, we lived in big houses on a lake; in Fall and Winter, when the tourists descended like geriatric birds to bask in winter sun and bathe rheumatic joints in the healing water of Advent Spring, we moved into a cramped apartment downtown, located one flight above a flashing sign. Until I was thirty-five years old, I never collected more possessions than I could fit into a car trunk.

I'd like to go back now to Mrs. Williams' Sunday School class when I was two or three, the time God spoke to me and I didn't have the sense to listen.

Solomon's stretched across my feet. I feel him breathing. Slow and gentle, warm. This room is growing colder.

FOUR

SOLOMON, who has lived in the basement of this church a month, a year, perhaps a century or two, was the runt of a litter of twelve. His father was a travelling man and made no provision for his progeny. Solomon's mother had insufficient milk to feed her litter and little Solomon had to bite his brother on the tail, sometimes hard enough to draw blood, in order to get access to a tit. Before he was fully weaned, his mother, out hunting rats in the overgrown field behind this church, was ensnared by an unemployed weaver, father of six himself, and was slaughtered for Sunday stew. Solomon insists I bring this up to illustrate that every family has its problems and the only purpose of recalling them here is to serve as a reminder that the more questions life poses for a creature, the more likely he is to scratch wildly for the answers. I believe there is some truth in the adage that a rejected child will become a criminal, an actor or a preacher.

My earliest recollections are of conversations with a cat, a dog and an alligator. Long before I could make myself understood by other human beings, I had lengthy inter-changes with non-verbal creatures who wandered into our various backyards. The neighbors' bulldog had made strenu-ous efforts to converse with the Almighty to no avail, so he told me when he peeked into my baby carriage as I lay sunning by the lake. He had come to the conclusion that the higher power, so to speak, was a sham and agreed with Einstein that if, in fact, He existed at all, He had no time to fool around with us. This realization made the bulldog grumpy and Mother began to shoo him from me because he growled and snarled into my carriage. Actually, his growls and snarls were directed at the heavens, not at me, but my mother had no way of knowing this and I, who didn't speak, had no way of telling her. She reported him to his owners who chained him to a tree where he grew progressively so depressed that he took to sleeping in the direct sun and stopped burying his bowel movements.

The alligator sunned itself daily on the bank. When I began to toddle, I encountered it by accident, its snout and tail half buried in the grey sand. My mother, had she known, would have suffered cardiac arrest, for there had been a newspaper report that very Spring about an alligator kid-napping a colored baby in Gainesville, Florida. That is, the alligator allegedly seized the child in its jaws and dove toward what observers believed to be its nest. The child rose to the surface several minutes later, a scratch mark on its leg, but none the worse for wear. PICKANINNY ESCAPES GATOR'S BELLY read the headline in the Advent Tattler. A travelling freak show hired the child and displayed him sitting in the giant open jaws of a plaster of Paris alligator while a somber man, dressed like a minister, speculated on the Biblical meaning of the event. Later, when the child himself learned to speak, he sat in a plaster of Paris throne sprayed gold, his rapidly vanishing battle scar accentuated with mercuro-chrome, and told awe-inspiring stories of the minute he spent in the gator's stomach.

My mother knew a gator lived in the lake beside our house but she'd only seen it once and then she'd snatched me up and run inside to telephone the police. The police responded although they admitted they had no S.O.P. for dealing with alligators. There were men in Advent who could wrassle a gator to the ground with their bare hands and gave demonstrations on hot Sunday afternoons in summer, but gator wrasslers were always Negroes and there were no Negroes at all on the Advent police force. As luck would have it, by the time the police arrived, the gator had ambled back into the water and disappeared beneath the scum of algae on the shoreline. This particular gator, as I came to know, had no interest in fooling around with humans. She considered us a noisy nuisance, a generally inferior and rank-smelling species, irresponsible and devoid of morals and, to sum it up, ascribed to my Mother's and Grandma's philosophy about keeping to one's own side of the street. The gator only spoke to me because I practically tripped over her. I was barely toddling at the time and could not make four forward steps in succession without falling to all fours. The alligator hadn't ever encountered a human quite as small as I was—and being that small, I still found it easy to communicate with her although my life-experience was so limited that I had little to say. She asked me if, new as I was, I recalled my heavenly creator. I told her I remembered nothing much until I started cutting my first tooth. The gator claimed to be two hundred and seventy-one years old, and had come to the conclusion that we each are God. The gator didn't call it EST. She called it *I*. The strongest *I* will conquer, she said. I was aware that I was not a very strong *I* so I left her to her own devices. She made off with my teething ring which I accidentally dropped on the sand. She said her baby was cutting molars and needed a pacifier worse than I did.

One gloomy day when I was propped up against a pillow on the porch, I saw the gator inching slowly up the lawn. I could hear the grass bend as her belly slid across it. She approached the bulldog chained to the oak tree, and observed him with curiosity. They may have had a conversation to which I wasn't privy but the bulldog didn't seem alarmed. He didn't bark or run. They stared at one another for a long time and then the gator lifted her belly resolutely from the ground, her legs went rigid and she opened up her jaws and swallowed the bulldog. The bulldog's owners were outraged by the incident and for several nights, my father and the bulldog's master sat in a rowboat on the lake, guiding a flashlight in lazy circles across the water, shotguns cocked across their laps, seeking revenge. The alligator never surfaced and may be living still for all I know. I was never put in the backyard to sun again.

When I began to speak, I lost this ability to communicate with dogs and gators. To this day, however, it appears I can converse with cats. This surprises me as much as it does Solomon. The first and best friend I ever had was a feline, a Tom, missing one ear and half his tail. He was reared to be a housecat but he had no tolerance for inside work and took to sneaking out the window of the small apartment where they kept him and returned only to request a bowl of chow when the rats in the adjacent alley ran low. My mother often left me sitting on the doorstoop of the building while she went shopping in the market next door. It was during these times of waiting that the cat and I became close friends. He had no name. Cats don't give each other names. People give each other names and name cats, dogs and birds, as well, our personal identities being as elusive as they are. Solomon is very patronizing about this and claims even to like the name I've given him, saying it reminds him of the sound a female makes just before he mounts her. When I was one year old, I had no need for names. I didn't, in fact, know my own.

This cat had looked for God on rooftops, in gutters and in alleys, in restaurants and movie houses, in bars and brothels, in fields and lakes, and had concluded that God must reside in the ocean. It was the one place that the cat had not yet looked. The ocean was a fifty mile walk from Advent and the cat worked out every day preparing himself to make this journey. He ran the circumference of the town, once in the morning, once in the evening, every day, especially in the rain as he knew that he had to overcome his fear of water if he was to locate God in the ocean. This bravery was his undoing. Running in a rainstorm, he caught cold and while his resistance was low and I consoled him, he contracted diptheria and passed it on to me. I was hospitalized and after some weeks in an oxygen tent, recovered. The cat, so I heard its owner tell my mother, met God on the tar roof of our building. The odor had drawn attention to his remains.

The cat was the first true Seeker that I ever met. A true Seeker never gives up like the bulldog did or accepts an easy answer like the gator. A true Seeker seeks until, if he does not find God, he finds death. Long after my conversations with the remarkable cat passed into the dark recesses of my maturing mind, I could recall his devotion to the search. The cat had looked everywhere but one.

Whenever I'm near an ocean, I listen intently. I've dunked myself beneath a wave and stayed down long as I could, straining to hear. God has not uttered a single salty word so far.

"He was yellow, Solomon, a yellow cat. And he was closer to finding God, I think, than any creature I've ever known."

Solomon yawns, very slowly, exposing the perfect pinkness of his mouth. He directs his attention to his back left paw and cleans it compulsively.

Jason was not a Seeker. Jason, like the gator, had his answer. I have thought and thought about the *I* and about Jason's personal sense of divinity and I've asked myself if I, too, am God and if I've been searching all my life to find myself.

Jason didn't speak aloud until he was nearly four years old and then he spoke in sentences. I read stories to him every night to encourage him to talk; like my mother, I was peeved by his slow development. When he finally uttered his first words it was to interrupt me. I happened Christmas Eve as we were sitting beside our small tree, Jason in a lotus position, elbows on his knees, chin in hand, round black eyes locked on mine. I was reading aloud the story of the birth of baby Jesus.

"I remember that," Jason said.

Why shouldn't he remember that? I'd read the story to him every Christmas for four years. I whooped with joy because at last he'd spoken. I seized him, squeezed the wind out of him, kissed him sloppy wet and begged him to keep talking.

"There was a goat," he said after he wiped his mouth dry. "It nibbled at my toes. It wanted hay. It was hungry. It always ate at that manger and I was in its way."

Jason had seen goats. I took him to the Children's Zoo in Central Park every summer weekend. A baby goat once chewed the hem of his blue jeans. "Goat," I'd repeated then, hoping Jason would utter his first word, "goat, goat, goat, goat." Jason seemed delighted but his lips remained sealed.

That same Christmas Eve, delighted with his sudden ability to speak in sentences, I taught Jason a song.

Away in a manger, no crib for his bed, the little lord Jesus lays down his sweet head (Jason listened intently but didn't join in. I sing so poorly that it's possible he couldn't follow my tune.) *The stars in the heaven look down where he lay, the little lord Jesus asleep in the hay* ("Sing, Jason, sing," I encouraged him and pulled him on my lap. Reluctantly, he hummed.) *The cattle are lowing, the poor baby wakes but little lord Jesus no crying he makes, we love you lord Jesus, look down from the sky...*

"That's the only true part," Jason interrupted brusquely. "I never cried. Never."

Jason rarely laughed, either, even when I swang him high above my head and blew bubbles against his pudgy tummy. His dark eyes would open wide but there was no fear in them. And no joy. I was a sourpuss at that age, myself.

Jason's hair was thick and black. I had to trim it every week, it grew so fast. His eyes were not just warm dark brown, they were ebony and shone as though they had a light behind them. He was an easy child to rear, obedient and quiet, seemingly devoid of prankishness and idle curiosity— the kind of child about whom a mother says "He's such a pleasure. I hardly know he's in the house. He never gives me any trouble." Which wasn't exactly true, even when he was younger and still living with me. I worried constantly about his reading and writing skills. He had none and showed no interest in developing them. Every school year until he dropped out in the tenth grade, Jason was required to take remedial reading and he never passed it. At twenty, Jason could barely write his name and was dependent on his Apostles to read road signs.

I read the Bible to him aloud the years that he was six and seven. He claimed it wasn't true. "The Bible," said Jason, "was written by men for men. It has nothing to do with God and me." The only destructive childhood act of Jason's was when he shredded the Bible which I'd received for ten years of perfect Sunday School attendance at Advent Baptist Church. He tore the pages into minute scraps which he flushed down the toilet, chapter by chapter, book by book. He was a painstaking, patient boy, even in a tantrum. He didn't stop the toilet up. "Now men are free to think again," he declared on the last flush, "God is so much more complicated than that." Had Jason lived, he promised to lead us all to a state of consciousness in which words would not be necessary. Jason believed words, more than anything, stood between us and God.

The Jasonites had not gotten the hang of non-verbal communication before Jason's death and we don't, in fact, know that Jason could do it since there was no credible adult who could testify that Jason conversed with him non-verbally. The Jasonites tell stories about the time Jason presumably spoke with a herd of stampeding elephants and convinced them to alter their course around, instead of through, the Jasonite's African campsite. It's been said that Jason spoke to apes and snakes and turtles and that sometimes they cooperated with his wishes and sometimes they continued doing just as they pleased. "But that's the nature of living creatures," Jason shrugged. All the Jason stories are passed from mouth to mouth because Jason never willingly allowed anything to be printed about him or his works. He forebade the writing down or recording of any of his ministry and consequently, the focus of the Jason stories changes depending on whether a camel driver or a U.S. Steel executive is telling them.

That Christmas Eve when Jason spoke his first words, he also pointed to a color plate of Jesus in the Bible and asked, "Is that supposed to be me?"

"That's Jesus Christ, the son of God," I replied.

"I never looked like that," Jason said. "I've always been a roly-poly." He poked his tummy and almost, but not quite, smiled.

I didn't take it seriously, of course. I laughed, still overwhelmingly delighted that my son could speak at all, and hugged him. "Well, sweetheart, you've got the right initials for it."

Jason Caldwell.

He dropped his last name when he went into the streets. I named him Jason because I thought he'd be a Seeker, too, like me. I didn't know he'd be the Sought. I still don't know who Jason was although I diapered him, bottle fed him, raised him and loved him wholly. For a few years, I considered myself a believer. I was the first Jasonite, the original Apostle.

That same Christmas Eve, I went to bed and lay awake most of the night, half-listening as I always did for any cough or sound of distress from my son's room. Near morning, I drifted off and awakened with the memory that sometime, somewhere, I'd read that when Christ came again, he'd be born of the yellow race.

Jason slept soundly in his youth bed. He'd kicked off his covers and his Roy Rogers pajama top had come unbuttoned. I brushed his thick hair off his forehead and bent down to kiss him. He was slightly wet from perspiration and he smelled pungent as any normal little boy. his eyes were tightly closed and his thick lashes accentuated the sharp slant of his cheekbones.

I didn't go off half-cocked. I observed Jason closely through the growing years. I never encouraged his claim to divinity. I waited. I watched. Every night I prayed for guidance.

And from heaven came silence.

"Solomon, do you suppose they'll shoot me tomorrow? Or hang me? Will it hurt? I don't think I'm afraid of death but I know I'm terrified of pain."

If there is no God, then Jason is dead and gone forever.

Before Jason spoke, when he was still small enough to be washed in a bathinette, we played a little game. He pointed to a place on his body, made a gurgling sound and I, my hand covered by a yellow washcloth that looked like a duck, would attack the spot with soapsuds, washing and tickling him at the same time. He'd point to one ear and then the other, happily bubbling spit between his lips as the ferocious duck scrubbed both ears squeaky clean. He'd point then at his neck, his nose, his nostrils. Jason was painstaking in his attention to detail. His penis wiggled like a fat earthworm when the duck snared it, swallowed it in soapsuds, then regurgitated it spanking clean. Jason would roll onto his belly then and present his plump buttocks as the final target. On one or two occasions, his stoic little face erupted in giggles as the soapy duck burrowed between his cheeks to clean his anus. The Jasonites say he never had an erection in his life. As his mother I know this: his genitals *looked* perfectly normal although when he was freshly washed and still wet, his buttocks shone like chunks of burnished gold.

I'm ambivalent about Jason's divinity. I saw him do things that were startling: he snapped his fingers once and what appeared to be four million cockroaches departed our kitchen cabinets and marched out the crack beneath our front door. They invaded the Super's apartment en masse and caused such a commotion that the building management agreed to hire a monthly exterminating service, an expense they had been systematically avoiding up to that point. On the other hand, Jason sometimes said things that sounded to me like pure nonsense.

God loves fat people best because they're easier to see.

The nonbelievers swore Jason used drugs or dispersed some type of nerve gas to attract his followers to him. This wasn't so. There was an aura about Jason, a body halo that glowed with serenity and wisdom. Sometimes it was actually visible to the naked eye (golden yellow or a white so pure that it was almost blinding) and other times, one just sensed that it was there.

It is an odd thing about motherhood. A mother wants her child to be a little brighter, a little better than the neighbor's kid—but not so much brighter, so much better that he sets himself, and her, apart.

"You can forget this calling," I reasoned with him. "Maybe it's all in your head. I'll arrange for you to see a shrink. Maybe I can somehow find the money to send you to vocational school."

"How can I forget that I'm the Son of God?"

"Take a vacation from it," I replied, "come home and get some sleep. You'll feel better in a week. We'll work it out."

My eyes are scratchy, my thoughts muddying one into the other. My shoulders ache, my fingers throb around this pen.

Solomon springs onto the table, plants himself right on the page. "You have to keep writing," he reminds me, "there isn't that much time. You don't have a whole lifetime ahead of you, you know, so move your ass."

"All right, Solomon, all right. Just let me put my head down on the table for a minute. I promise I won't go to sleep."

FIVE

I DID not intentionally lie to you, Solomon. Honest to goodness, I didn't. I didn't mean to drop off like that." I don't have a watch. The Jasonites made me remove it, the Judge crushed it with his heel. God does not live in hours, they say, but in sunrises and sunsets. From the movement of the moon—about half a foot—I'd say that not much time has passed. I didn't even dream. You'd think I'd have one last dream, wouldn't you? I've always been a champion dreamer—Cecil B. DeMille productions, technicolor, casts of thousands, so thick with images and allegory that Dr. Binbaum kept a file of them with the intention of putting them together in a book.

For instance, I once dreamed that I was Lana Turner's daughter and, dressed in dazzling white, I won a tennis tournament against little Shirley Temple. I dreamed my fingernails were made of graphite and the points kept breaking off. I dreamed my mother kept me in a jar and when she removed the lid, I fizzed up and spilled out the top. And, of course, I have the traditional Seeker's Dream in which I lease an apartment and when I move in, find a dozen secret rooms no one knows about. The closet door opens onto a Grecian garden; behind the 1920's bathtub a sliding wall parts to reveal an artist's loft; a trap door in the kitchen floor exposes a sprial staircase which descends into a perfectly appointed Victorian parlor. I'm afraid to use these rooms, terrified my landlord will find out they're there and raise my rent accordingly.

The garden goes back a thousand years in time, its marble sculptures depicting people who seem to be familiar to me. The sun is fierce and blinding bright, the stone benches almost too hot to sit down on. In the center of the stone patio a lifesized marble angel pours clear blue water from a vase into a pond of water lillies. This garden is located in an atrium, closed in by walls on four sides and open only to the heavens.

The artist's loft is in Germany, I think, or Scandinavia. There are vicious mountain peaks visible outside its one large window. The space itself is sparse and naked. The floor is pitted, worn, the walls cracked and peeling yellow paint. There are heavy tables and a work stool. There is no illumunation except that natural light which penetrates the grimy window panes. It is raining outside and the room smells damp. It is a place for doing things, accomplishing. One couldn't pass the time there.

It is the Victorian parlor that I covet uncontrollably. Long and narrow, its celing is high and domed. A six foot brass chain supports a massive, sparkling crystal chandelier. When I press the light switch tiny nuggets of gold gleam through the crystal. There is a chair rail circling the walls and fancy moulding borders the high ceiling. The trim is mahogany, thickly varnished, so deep brown in color that it has a yellow sheen. The walls are unpainted plaster, soft and dusty to the touch; they leave powder on my fingertips. There are ornate mirrors on the walls, framed in heavy gold gilt. Rich, dark oil paintings line the wall behind the stiff-backed velvet sofa.

The paintings depict shadowy meadows and open, raging seas. The cushions of the sofa and the chair are stuffed with goose down. On the oak floor there is a single Persian rug. The background of the rug is creme and the design, in green, depicts the Tree of Life. I'm afraid to use this room. I can't afford to pay a higher rent.

More than once, I've dreamed that I am looking at the ocean when I die. I can't see the water from this church but I can smell the salt air, Solomon.

When Jason was eleven, I asked him if he ever dreamed. He had a hard time understanding what a dream is. I'm not sure he was ever clear about it.

"When you go to sleep at night..."

"Yes," he said, his round black eyes peering somewhere beyond my soul...

"Like a movie you made up inside your head..."

"Yes," he repeated but seemed to have no understanding of what I was getting at...

"A little story, usually about yourself..."

He closed his eyes as though that might help him have a dream right then and there...

"Sometimes the stories don't make a lot of sense..."

He opened his eyes quickly. "Are they scary stories?"

"Sometimes."

"You wish it would hurry and be over?"

"More often than not."

"But you can't make it stop until it's finished?"

"That's right. Or unless someone shakes you and wakes you up. Maybe the phone rings."

"And somewhere way back you know all the time that it can't hurt you?"

"It's just a dream."

"Even though you're scared, you know you won't really get hurt?"

"That's right, because sooner or later you're going to wake up."

—36—

"Yes," Jason said, and nodded.

"Well, honey, have you ever had a dream?"

"This is a dream."

"What is?"

"This." He pressed his forefinger against his pudgy belly.

"You? This life?"

"Yes." He sighed. "It can't hurt me. Sooner or later, I'll wake up."

Jason, Jason. I hope it was true. I'd like to think you're playing now on the grassy fields of heaven. I know you always said that heaven has no grass, no ocean, no towering locust trees to shade a summer day. "It's much more complicated than that," I can hear your voice saying it, impatiently, "and you could understand it if you'd just stop thinking." Well, I've never been able to stop thinking, Jason, though I tried. Forgive me if I picture you running pudgy-legged through the tall grass. I mean well. And however faulty the image may be, I picture you with love.

I hope Jason was the Son of God.

They say that over half the world are Jasonites now. The national economy has virtually collapsed. Only a few strongholds remain. Jason's serenity appears to be contagious. Scientists, in their rush studies to fight the Jasonite invasion, have been unable to isolate a virus. Like the plague, serenity spreads quickly, apparently air-borne. Some theorize it is emitted from the nostrils of Jasonites or perhaps contained in sputum. Others claim it's a hypnotic which somehow leaks from the souls of Jasonites and exits through their placid eyes. Any nonbeliever who has lost his family to the Jasonites will testify that all it takes is for one single Jasonite to walk through town. If someone doesn't destroy him quickly, he'll leave with half the population.

"It's not a matter of morality," Jason insisted, "it's not a matter of what pleases God. Until you return to your nature, God is irrelevant. You aren't in touch with Him nor He with you. You are like goldfish imprisoned in a tank, flapping your fins and puckering your lips to entertain your Master who isn't even in the room. God doesn't live in rooms. He abhors walls and goldfish tanks."

I have never understood a single one of Jason's metaphors.

It pained him, even to the very end. He'd come home for a night and wedge his body between the safety rails of his youth bed and say to me, with such deep sorrow in his voice:

"How am I ever going to make you see? Your head is in a box. God hates right angles."

I believe somewhere along the line, Jason gave up the hope of making any of us see. "Don't question. Just follow my example. When you have done what I do, then you'll understand."

We're all dangling now, quivering from time to time. Our images must flicker through his mind, wherever he is now. We are the faint and fading memories of his interrupted dream.

Sleep again, Jason, and remember us. You only led us part way on this mystic journey. You have left us in a dark place and we're frozen here in fear.

That's how it was that Sunday morning in Mrs. William's Bible Class. I was two or three. I wore a pink coat with yellow flowers stitched on the collar. It had a matching hat and my mother tied it so tightly around my head that I had difficulty hearing and was unable to move my jaw. Mrs. Williams allowed no parents to audit Bible Class. She said children behaved badly with their parents present. I wouldn't allow Mrs. Williams to remove my coat or hat and backed up to the wall, pressed my fanny into the comforting warmth of a metal radiator and stood there, furious, my eyes closed. Mrs. Williams read the story of Sodom and Gommorah. We understood very little of it but the tone of her voice was sufficient to set us to trembling. Mrs. Williams encouraged questions from her students.

"But before they lay down, the men of the city, even the

men of Sodom, compassed the house round, both old and young, all the people from every quarter; And they called unto Lot and said unto him, Where are the men which came in to thee this night? Bring them out to us so we may know them."

"Do they want to come out and play?" asked a boy on the far side of the room.

"Precisely," snapped Mrs. Williams, "and raise your hand before you speak, Raymond."

"And Lot went out at the door unto them and shut the door after him."

Raymond raised his hand. "So the people inside wouldn't escape?"

"No, silly," squealed Nellie Lee, who tee-heed and curled her hair with her finger, "Lot doesn't want the people outside to come in."

"And Lot said, I pray you, brethren, do not so wickedly." Mrs. Williams could make the word wicked sound wickeder than anyone I've ever heard; it made the skin behind your ears cringe.

"Why was it wicked to ask the men to come out and play?" Raymond raised his hand after the fact. "I ask if Billy Perkins can come out and play nearly every afternoon."

"Because," said Mrs. Williams, "they had evil intentions. And what are evil intentions, children?"

"When you think bad stuff," Nellie Lee answered pertly, "but you don't do it."

"Somebody catches you before you get a chance to do it," added skinny Winnie, who later became a trusted friend of mine.

"Lot said Behold now, I have two daughters which have not known man; let me, I pray you, bring them out to you, and do yet to them as is good in your eyes, only unto these men do nothing; for therefore came they under the shadow of my roof."

"How come," asked Raymond, raising both hands, "the

girls could go out to play but the boys couldn't?"

"Because, the bad men outside are going to hurt them and it's better to hurt girls than boys," replied Nellie Lee in a tone of voice that implied Raymond had gone daft.

"Of course," said Raymond, "I know that."

"The angels," continued Mrs. Williams, jerking her head forward as she read *"smote the men that were at the door of the house."*

"Smote?" Raymond raised both hands and stood up.

"Killed them dead," answered skinny Winnie, "dead as doornails."

"I knew that."

"Sit down, Raymond."

Raymond sat down.

"Smote the men with blindness, both small and great; so that they wearied themselves to find the door."

"They smote the little boys, too?"

"Sit down, Raymond, Raise your hand when you want to speak."

Raymond raised his hand. "I thought the angels were supposed to be the good guys."

"They smote the bad men," Winnie explained as patiently as a four year old can.

"And little boys!" Raymond was incensed.

"You better watch your step then," Winnie replied, "you don't want to get smote. I saw you stick your Mama's hatpin in that toadfrog's eyes."

My legs hurt, my rump hurt but I was too terrifed to cry. I stood bug-eyed, pressed against the radiator, staring at Mrs. Williams as if she herself were capable of smoting.

The Lord said Escape for thy life; look not behind thee."

If I'd had any feeling in my legs I would have made a run for it.

"And The Lord overthrew those cities and all the plain, and all the inhabitants of the cities and that which grew upon the ground."

It was like the fires of hell," Winnie yelled triumphantly, "everything burned up!"

"Bad people always burn up," Nellie Lee added ominously.

There was a pain from my shoulders to my ankles and a funny, smoky smell about me. Tears filled my eyes but didn't fall because I was too frightened to blink.

"But," and Mrs. Williams' voice trembled with the drama of the story's end, "Lot's wife looked back from behind him and she became a pillar of salt."

I screamed bloody murder.

She had to peel me off the radiator. The back of my pink wool coat was soldered to the cast iron, the tender flesh of my calves was clinging partly to me, partly to the radiator.

"Didn't you feel the heat?" Mrs. Williams was angry and hysterical. Never, but never, had a child in her care come to physical harm. "Couldn't you smell the burning of your flesh? Couldn't you hear the hiss? What's the matter with you, child? You got no feelings? You gone deaf?"

"God always speaks with fire," Winnie announced.

"Is that right, Mrs. Williams?"

"Precisely, Raymond. How many times do I have to tell you to raise your hand before you speak?"

"If she'd just been listening the way she's supposed to," Nellie Lee piped, "God was telling her to move."

"Is that true, Mrs. Williams?"

"Precisely. Sit down, Raymond."

My legs were bandaged for a month and while I lay supine staring out the second storey window watching the neon sign flash DR PEPPER DR PEPPER DR PEPPER, I thought about what Mrs. Williams said. I watched a robin build a nest in a black oak even though the wind was blowing hard and when she laid her eggs and a twister came up and splattered them onto the sidewalk, I figured she hadn't heard God either. I started listening hard, then, but if God ever spoke to me again, I missed it.

Jason says our whole concept of God is wrong from Go. "It's like jamming up a computer so it's rocking and squealing and telling a little child that it's a hurricane. It's not a hurricane, it's just a jammed up computer. The hurricane and the computer don't have a single quality in common. Your God isn't God. He's just your God. He's got nothing in common with my Father."

"Then God is beyond our understanding," I said.

"No," Jason screamed. "Can you see a hurricane?"

"Yes." I never knew what the devil Jason was talking about.

"You can see God, too."

"God is a hurricane?"

"No, God isn't a hurricane. God is God. You can't see him because you don't look."

"Is he in the ocean?"

"No. People who say they see God in the flowers and the fields and the oceans and the winds are full of bull. God is God."

"Does God look like a person?"

"Oh!" Jason moaned and held his round face in his hands. "It's like trying to teach multiplication tables to a mouse. You have to be naked to see God."

"You mean, take off my clothes?"

"Oh, no. No, no. That isn't what I mean at all."

Before Jason, I had many different concepts of God. There was the God of Mrs. Williams who was a vicious terrifying thug; there was the God of Mother and Grandma, a frail and filmy apparition in a white lab coat bending over a stainless steel table, pouring steaming liquids beaker to beaker inventing test-tube babies; there was the capricious God of my Bible Youth Group who took perverse delight in striking down your natural urges; there was the jovial but temperamental God of the tent revival shows, a good old boy unless you crossed Him, then he turned meaner than a rattlesnake. There was the unbending, paternalistic God of

Advent Christian College who told me that no female was worthy to stand behind a pulpit. I always pictured him as John Wayne. And there was the white-gloved God who lived in Boston. I encountered Him when I met my husband who was studying for the ministry at Harvard. His God never did a day's work in His life.

Jason said that all of our human depictions of God were pitiful. Sometimes they made him angry. When I showed him a photograph of Michelangelo's Hand of God, he announced that we were egotistical, willful, deaf and blind and it was beyond his comprehension why God bothered with us at all. From the way Jason talked most of the time, I got the impression that God didn't, in fact, bother with us much.

"Sense is what's keeping you from finding God. God makes no sense. You think of sense as something good and desirable. God thinks of sense as senseless. Actually, God doesn't think of sense at all. It would never cross God's mind. Sense would be as foreign to God as God is to you. Lord, Lord," Jason would cry and look wildly about the room, "there's a terrible communication problem down here."

When I failed as revivalist and was rejected as a minister and had enough insight to recognize that I could not stomach the day to day rejection of a writer's life, I turned to TV. It is there, in the peacock colored studio of News 3 that I've earned my livelihood for twenty years. Of course, twenty years ago the studio was not peacock colored for we had no color equipment then and very few viewers had color receivers. We had just begun to use videotape and were awed by the miracle of electronic editing.

The first ten years I was at Channel 3, we had an anchorman named John Joyce. John had been with the station since it was AM radio. He was as much a part of News 3 as the elusive leak in the studio skylight. And just as cracked and grimy. We were resigned to him and expected him to last fully as long as the building did.

John Joyce was flustered, titillated and embarrassed by

the advent of mini-skirts, irritated, puzzled and grumpy about civil rights, infuriated, threatened and enraged by revolutionists and flower children. His attitudes rang out loud and clear on-camera and we had many viewers who regarded John Joyce as the Voice of America. John had the good newsman's talent for reading the most innocuous copy and by the set of his jaw and the tilt of his eyebrows letting viewers know exactly how they were supposed to feel about it. He was a master at the non-verbal editorial.

One afternoon, during the set-up in the studio before the six o'clock newscast, old Arnie, our director, suffered a heart attack. He was in the booth with Reidy, his assistant, at the time but Reidy was sleeping off a four-martini lunch. The cameramen were in the studio setting shots—each had a fist on the leather grip of his camera, each had one scuffed shoe resting lightly on the dolly; the headsets gripped their ears like muffs and a pencil-thin mike swept around their cheek like a fairy's hand so their slightest whimper could be heard by Arnie in the booth.

"Two," Arnie said and Cameraman Two, hearing his name called through the headphones, nodded. "Stay with John's head and get ready to pan right to the weathergirl. Can you do that without losing focus?"

"Can't," Cameraman two replied, trying it, "I'll have to switch lens."

"Oke," Arnie sighed. "I'll cut to the Three then and I'll come back to you on a long shot of the girl and the map. I'll lose you right after the film clip when John says Haight-Asbury will never be a family neighborhood again. One, you've got Roger at the sports desk. I'll switch to you. Josie, give Roger something intelligent to say there while Two changes lenses."

I was leaning against the water cooler on the south side of the studio. The big glass bottle was sweating on my upper arm. "Okay, Roger, say the last time I was in Frisco..."

"I've never been to San Francisco," Roger called.

"Who cares?" boomed Arnie's voice over the studio loudspeaker, "Who the fuck cares anyway?"

Those were the last words Arnie ever said. We didn't know that he was dead for several minutes. Roger spoke to Arnie through his neck mike. "Arnie, you're making me look like a goddam idiot. I'm a jock. I don't comment on the news. You're going to blow my image. Why can't you stay on John with Two and let One get the weathergirl?"

There was no answer. All of us immediately assumed that Roger had once again overstepped his bounds and pissed Arnie off.

After a moment or two of dead silence in the studio, Roger unsnapped his mike and stormed to the control booth to demand an answer. He found Arnie slumped across the board, his finger hooked around the dissolve switch. The dead weight of Arnie's arm was pulling the switch and above Arnie's head, on Monitor One, the NEWS 3 logo was undergoing a slow dissolve to black.

A brash young Ph.D. from NYU was hired to replace Arnie. Fober, the new director, had his doctorate in Communications. He also had a beard and a broad liberal streak. None of the above set well with our anchorman John Joyce.

John Joyce didn't set well with young Fober, either, looking and acting as he did like Fober's father, a Con Ed executive. Fober wore ragged blue jeans and a burlap shirt. His blue jeans were embroidered and the rear pockets replaced with lace handkerchiefs.

He got rid of John so cleanly, expeditiously and without leaving a single self-incriminating clue that it was only upon reflection that I figured out what happened. Fober set the cameras slightly lower, week by week, and raised the lights an inch or two each day. John, who prided himself upon being a journalist and not a TV performer, never looked in the monitor. He considered preening an act unworthy of a hardnosed newsman. By the third week, Fober had John so starkly shadowed that he looked like Dracula. Then Fober took to changing the film clips so that when John's editorial-izing tone of voice was making it clear to viewers that we ought to fly over Saigon and drop a bomb big enough to finish off the whole thing, the film clip on video was showing our viewers the shattered bodies of infants and children who'd been caught in crossfire. Two months of Fober's clever direction of News 3 and the station manager's mail quadrupled with demands to take that hawk John Joyce off the air.

Fober hired Sam Dowdy to replace John Joyce as News 3 anchorman. Dowdy was longhaired, lanky and very hand-some, an actor not a newsman, so easy on the eyes that he offended no one. He could read copy perfectly so long as it was on the cue cards. He had no ability to improvise, however, and I fell victim to his long blank-eyed silences when I co-anchored the news with him for three years.

It was the apex of the women's movement and the feds and the FCC were squeezing TV stations to put ethnic and female faces on-camera. The station manager auditioned for several months, looking for a Negro woman with a Hispanic surname. I lasted three years as co-anchor because I really didn't want the job. I didn't care how I came across on the air. I always disliked on-camera work although during my twenty years at Channel 3, I hostessed the women's show and co-anchored News 3. For one hideous year, I was cast as Happy the Witch on Panda Playhouse every weekend morning at 7 a.m., live. This entailed rising at five a.m., riding in an empty, dangerous subway car to the studio, donning a bright red wig with turned-up pigtails, a polka-dot moo-moo and matching witch's hat, elf shoes with bells, straddling a broom to which a Mattel VVRROOM motor had been attached and with the help of the magic special effects machine, appearing to fly over the greater New York area singing Up in the Air Junior Birdmen. I introduced cartoons, traded quips and insults with two surly puppets named Peter Panda and Silly Goose and sold vitamins by putting velcro smiles and frowns on a blue pillow called Charlie Chocks.

Most of my years at Channel 3, I wrote news. That's what I did best. My idea of a really terrific news day was one in which nothing happened. I could sit at my typewriter eight hours, occasionally writing poetry, sometimes reaching over to the UP machine and ripping off seventeen inches of prepared copy. On such days, the wire services contained such stories of human interst as: LONG LOST SISTERS FIND THEY'VE BELONGED TO THE SAME BRIDGE CLUB THIRTY YEARS. NATALIE SANDSPUR AND ROSEANN GREENE WERE BORN IN CHICAGO IN 1911 AND PUT UP FOR ADOPTION. EACH HAD BEEN TOLD THAT SOMEWHERE THEY HAD A TWIN SISTER BUT ATTEMPTS TO RECONCILE WITH ONE ANOTHER HAD DEAD ENDED. BOTH SISTERS HAD GIVEN UP THE SEARCH. LAST WEDNESDAY MORNING AT A MEETING OF THE GOLDEN YEARS BRIDGE CLUB IN NORTH MIAMI BEACH, NATALIE HAPPENED TO MENTION THAT SHE HAD A TWIN SISTER WHOM SHE'D NEVER SEEN. ROSEANN, NATALIE'S PARTNER, CRIED OUT IN SURPRISE. AFTER COMPARING BIRTH DATES, THE TWO WOMEN FLEW TOGETHER TO CHICAGO WHERE THE CENTRAL ILLINOIS ADOPTION SERVICE ASCERTAINED THEY WERE ONE ANOTHER'S MISSING SIBLINGS. ROSEANN HAS MADE ARRANGEMENTS FOR HER DECEASED HUSBAND'S BODY TO BE MOVED INTO THE GRAVESITE RESERVED FOR NATALIE. NATALIE WILL TAKE THE GRAVESITE NEXT TO ROSEANN SO THAT THE SISTERS CAN BE BURIED SIDE BY SIDE. I preferred such stories to bombings and assassinations which require a lot of legwork and phone followup.

We must have sent out the mobile unit a hundred times to capture Jason's ministry on film or tape. The Jasonites would not let recording or film equipment near their lord but we devised many different ways to get around that. We put cameras in baby carriages, hid them on rooftops, carried them in umbrellas. One of our film crew built a beer belly in which a camera was concealed, the lens peeking out the naval. He strapped it to himself and got right up on Jason as he was speaking. There was nothing on the film when it was developed.

When I first adopted Jason, I went right out and bought a Polaroid so I could record his childhood as he grew. I thought I just didn't know how to operate the camera. After having been shown by a dozen different helpful people and still no success, I figured that I bought a lemon. Three years in a row the public school photographer sent a note home with Jason explaining that he must have accidentally exposed the negative of Jason's school shot and that he hoped for better luck next year. Jason could not be photographed but I didn't accept that as fact for many years.

"Solomon, why is it so hard to believe in things we can't see or explain? We are such pragmatists, we human beings. We have to touch it with our fingers, see it in black and white."

"Stop seeking," Jason used to say. "Don't think. What you're seeking is already in you."

"But that's not reasonable, Jason," I argued, "I am not happy and I have not spoken to God although I often don't think."

"No so," replied Jason, "you always think. It is your undoing."

"Do you mean faith, Jason? Are you talking about faith?"

He wrinkled his nose quizzically. "Picture your brain as a slop jar. Upend it. Rinse it out. Set it on a stump out in the field to dry in the sun. God will settle in it like a genie in a bottle."

You can imagine the reaction of rational, educated people to Jason's ministry. Nobody was convinced by verbiage to become a Jasonite. It was that aura of Jason's and the total serenity that overcame those in his presence, as though the millions of thoughts in each mind were instantly reduced to one or two, perhaps a dozen, essential under-standings.

"They allow themselves to be and so they are."

I almost got there once or twice. I could almost touch the feathery edges of serenity with the fingers of my mind the way one is almost able to slip back into a pleasant dream.

"There is not a natural question in the universe," Jason said. "God never heard a question until He came on man."

I'm afraid that ten or a hundred years from now someone will remember Jason's ministry and look down their nose. Lucy Dobdaughter, Assistant Station Manager at Channel 3, always looks down her nose at me. She has a Ph.D. in History, a Masters in Communications, a certificate of achievement from Mid-Manhattan Plumbing Institute and a paper permitting her, should the occasion ever arise, to serve as a midwife under the supervision of a medical doctor. Her name was originally Dobson but she changed it legally as a political statement against patriarchy. When she comes into a room, she perches on a table to make her taller than anybody in the room. She cannot speak unless she's looking down on you. Lucy sneers loudly. For Lucy, it is not enough that she succeed, everyone else must fail. Pay no attention to her, we tell each other, anyone that arrogant must lack self-confidence. Inside Lucy Dobdaughter is a frightened, insecure woman desperately reaching out for acceptance and love. In our hearts, though, we don't believe a word of it and everybody scatters to psychic shelter when Lucy enters the newsroom.

Lucy, of course, is an unbeliever and flat-footedly gallops through life, her long arms swinging with her stride, knocking over anyone who gets too close to her. She has written and published a book attacking Jason and in it she states that she would prefer death to serenity. She also states that the human animal is superior because she communicates. Lucy always uses the female pronoun when she's speaking generically.

"It may come as a shock to Lucy Dobdaughter but the Second Coming is more important than she."

"Thanks, Solomon."

He nestles on the slanted top of the altar, his head dangling off the low end.

"The blood is going to run to your brain," I warn him. "That stimulates thought."

"Better than running to my ass," Solomon retorts.

I am tempted to stand before that altar tonight and speak aloud to the thousands of spirits who once worshipped here. God wouldn't let me preach in his church officially, although I filled in twice for the Advent Baptist Minister when he had an emergency appendectomy and the church board couldn't afford to pay the fee for a replacement minister. In Mrs. Williams' Bible Class, I once said that it seemed to me that God just didn't like girls at all. "I know that," Raymond responded.

Jason never seemed to notice gender. He frequently confused the pronouns, referring to a she as he or vice-versa. He said, however, that God had a reason for creating genders in the first place but it had nothing to do with rank or power or special interests.

"For human reproduction," I said with certainty.

"No," Jason replied. "You could reproduce yourself. God had it set up that way for a while. It didn't work out. There was no reason for any of you to get together. You just sat around in your isolated caves, reproducing exact replicas of your-selves and thinking you and yours were best."

"God makes mistakes?" I was horrified.

"Nobody's perfect," Jason shrugged.

The night's nearly half over now. It's cold enough to wrap that blanket around my shoulders. I can feel a draft coming from somewhere. I spit on my finger and hold it up. I think the breeze is coming from the window over there, the Judas window under which the Jasonites are sleeping. I'm going over to take a look. "Solomon, do you suppose that window opens somehow? Perhaps there's a possibility I can escape?"

Where would I go? The world is mostly Jasonites and

those who aren't are Lucy Dobdaughter. Nevertheless, I'd like to live and so I'm going to explore the possibility of escape. My legs are stiff. They need stretching.

"Walk with me, Solomon? You've a keen nose for ferreting out small exits." Like my husband George who disappeared from our marriage so many times that I once accused him of slipping out the mail slot in the door.

S I X

THE Judas window doesn't open. There is, however, a crack in it. Not exactly a crack more specifically, it's a separation. Beside Judas' bare left foot, diagonal from his index toe, there is a coin which has presumably spilled from the bag of gold being handed to him by the Roman soldier. The lower edge of the coin has parted company from the lead which solders it to the surrounding glass. If I pushed hard, placing my thumb in the center of the coin, I could likely dislodge the piece totally—but what would that accomplish? The hole would not be big enough for me to escape. Solomon couldn't even squeeze through it to go for help. Actually, Solomon hasn't offered to go for help and since we're in the middle of a Jasonite settlement, I doubt there is any help to go for.

So I've wrapped the blanket around me. I can feel the weight of it on my shoulders and it seems to pull me down but I'm quite cold now so there's no choice. I stood beneath the Judas window for a while, peeking through the crack.

there is no sign of life out there at all. I presume the dark lumps on the grounds, thousands of them, are Jasonites in bedrolls. They sleep without tossing and, according to Jason, without dreaming. If you are a Jasonite in the truest sense you have already passed from this dimension into a perpetual dream state. What we call dreams, said Jason, are the natural landscape of the mind.

I preached tonight. Behind a real pulpit, in a real church. I pretended that my childhood ambition had not been thwarted, that I was a real minister with a real flock. I wrapped this blanket around me like a bishop's robe and I spoke to the seekers of the past: they filled the empty pews, buttocks to buttocks, and leaned forward to hear my words. To assuage my nervousness, I spoke directly to Solomon who was sitting in the third pew right of the aisle. I pictured him, as my public speaking instructor at the Hollywood Playhouse had suggested, in underwear. Solomon in jockey shorts was such a bizarre image that I lost my nervousness. When I confessed to Solomon how I'd pictured him, he said I'd robbed him of integrity. He's still pouting in the vestry, curled into the corner of the second shelf.

The spirited parishioners didn't seem to mind listening to a woman preacher. They hung on every word and were so silent I could have heard a pin drop.

"Seekers," I addressed them, "we are gathered here tonight because we are imprisoned in this chapel, imprisoned by the four stone walls, the massive stained glass windows and even more tightly imprisoned by our minds. We would like to believe there is a Second Coming, wouldn't we? We would like to believe that God so loved the world He sent His only begotten son. We would like to know once and for all, proof positive, that God sees us, knows us by name, delivers us from evil. But God sends us no sign and Jason gives us no proof and we are not spiritualists. God endowed us with a brain and we strain to use it, if not fully, at least to the limits He allows us."

"We who are gathered here tonight don't have egos large enough to believe that we are God and yet we are apparently possessed of too much ego to accept the divinity of Jason and acknowledge and submit to the requirements of the Second Coming."

"Jason says the fires burn hottest for the Evangelists. On the other hand, Jason also says that's just an allegory because there is in fact no such thing as hell or hellfire. There is in fact no such thing as fact. Truth is, in its broadest sense, beyond our comprehension. It's almost enough to make a Seeker throw in the towel.

"Yet we Seekers hang on, century after century, world after world. We know there's something more; we know it the same way a baby knows to suck and swallow, to wince and cower at the sound of thunder. We just can't prove it. We can fertilize an egg and, with some red plastic and vinyl tubing, construct a beating heart that keeps a calf alive and enables it to walk year after year on a rubber treadmill while we probe its veins with syringes and monitor its blood pressure. We can sprinkle clouds with salt and make it rain in Utah, drive a rod into the sea and suck up fuel oil from the middle of the earth. Yet a thousands babies are born every year with three or more nipples distributed evenly in two lines down the torso. Not to mention the thousands of vestigal toes and fingers and tails that are snipped off in delivery rooms before proud Mama sees her newborn.

"There was the case, not many years ago, where a vagina erupted in the armpit of a normal adult male. Perhaps that's the way it once was, like Jason said. With a penis between our legs, a vagina under one arm and two rows of healthy nipples, we'd be self-sufficient.

"There was also a case, I remember, where several teeth broke through the flesh of a young man's belly as though they'd been lost in a time warp and appeared at last where they expected the mouth to still be. That case occurred in the late 1950s, I believe, and the attending medical physician called in a dental surgeon to extract the teeth. Blue Cross-Blue Shield would not cover the extraction.

"In God We Trust if we could prove that He exists."

There was silence for several minutes in the church. At last, the snoring of a Jasonite seeped through the broken stained glass window. Solomon mewed softly, growled in his throat and lunged with one paw at a passing moth. He missed.

"Amen," I said. "Amen anyway."

You may wonder how I have knowledge of the bizarre medical situations I spoke of during my sermon. For twenty years, remember, I have had access to the wire services, tippity tapping twenty-four hours around the clock, spewing forth miles and miles and miles of feathery gray paper filled with peculiar items designed to take up space between the news releases. These human interest fillers, as they are called, are seldom used on air or printed in newspapers because, for the most part, they offend our deep respect for logic. "We are not fools," say we. "A vagina in his armpit, indeed. Who on earth would believe that?" So we never included such items in the news script.

The wire service also reported virgin births. There seemed to be several of these every year. Once, when I was hostessing the women's show, I interviewed a renegade priest who told me, in our pre-session interview, that he had seen dozens of virgin births and believed in the ability of a woman to reproduce herself. Furthermore, the church required that he exorcise the devil out of these virgin mothers using the hair of pregnant oxen, bat's wings and his own sanctified warm urine. He declined to repeat this statement on the air.

The one claim to virgin birth that everybody heard about was Donellen's, the Korean prostitute who testified that she gave birth to a baby boy when she was eleven years old. She said she turned the baby over for adoption to the Save A Child Agency. To be perfectly honest, Jason looks rather like

Donellen. When I adopted Jason, I was given papers that stated FATHER UNKNOWN, MOTHER UNKNOWN and I fantasized that some sweet Korean girl who hadn't known the facts of life gave birth, alone and frightened, in a patch of bamboo and abandoned the result. Jason and Donellen are both short, stocky, roundfaced, dark-haired, black-eyed, still, I tend to believe she's just a glib opportunist and has no blood ties with my Jason whatsoever. She certainly wasn't doing him any good, saying he was a mental case and should be institutionalized. For all I know, Donellen may be in the employ of what's left of the U.S. Government. They've classified Jason as National Enemy No. 1.

One could certainly guess that Donellen's claim to be the Virgin Mary is self-serving. She never came face to face with Jason and I'll warrant she'll make a fortune from book and movie rights to her life story. I should never have let her get my dander up.

But I'm a mother. I was threatened. Jason was my son no matter who he claimed his father to be and I think I was flattered that if Jason was the Son of God, God had selected me. I didn't take well to being deposed by Miss Donellen, she of the cork stack heels and four inch dangle earrings.

There was even a period of time, early on in Jason's ministry, when my absent husband George tried to lay claim to fathering Jason. It was absurd, of course, George looking as Irish as Patty's pig. It also would have profited George nothing. Who cares who Jason's father is if Jason's father is not God? It took George several months to figure this out, however, and he made a general nuisance and spectacle of himself before he did. George always leapt before he looked. I believe the School of Divinity was right in its assessment that George didn't have what it takes to be a preacher although at the time they dismissed him from the school, in his final year, I was angry. Partly because George was so devastated, partly because I wanted to be married to a minister, not to an unemployed actor which is what George became.

I'd never been accepted in Divinity School because applications from women were dismissed summarily. I'd dropped out of Advent Christian when they made it clear that there was no role for me in any Baptist Church except unpaid positions like teaching Bible School or advising the Baptist Youth. My counselor at Advent Christian encouraged me to seek a fine young man among the students who were preparing for the ministry. Being a preacher's wife, she assured me, was a gratifying thing and anatomy is destiny.

No matter. I dropped out of Advent Christian at the end of my sophomore year and determined I'd become an actress. I liked to preach and acting was as close to that as I could get. I had read somewhere that the theatre was the pulpit of the people. I liked the sound of that. Much to the consternation of Mother and Grandma, I immediately got a scholarship to the Hollywood Playhouse, a private acting school in California. I won a scholarship by reading John Brown's Body very loudly. The talent scout commented that I had a remarkably good Southern accent.

Mother and Grandma were dismayed when I packed my suitcase and boarded the Trailways bus to Hollywood. They had a suspicion that the devil audited classes at the Playhouse.

At the Playhouse, the boys got first choice of the courses which most interested me. I waited a semester to get into Directing I and nearly two semesters before a seat opened up in the Essentials of Dramatic Writing. I loved to write plays although the instructor, Mr. Potter, repeatedly advised me it was not a woman's field.

"Playwriting," said Mr. Potter, "is like mountain-climbing. It requires a bold sense of adventure and the courage of one's convictions. There are no important women playwrights. Lillian Hellman is the exception who proves the rule."

"If I can't write for the theatre, I can write for movies," I argued. "Look here at this History of Motion Pictures. It lists a hundred women who have written screenplays."

Mr. Potter tapped his finger along the column of names. "Ah, but, Josie," he explained, "these women worked for the big studios in the 1920s and 30s. Why in those days, Josie, screenwriters were glorified secretaries." Mr. Potter then leaned back and lit his pipe as though he's satisfactorily answered my questions. He took a hearty puff and expelled the smoke toward the open window. It was golden outside and the sidewalks simmered. Squat palm trees lined the curb, basking in the sun. The day looked so full of hope and promise that I felt like leaping from the window onto the perfectly manicured lawn and singing Hooray for Hollywood.

"Each to his ability," Mr. Potter nodded. "Screenwriting is big business now."

"And women can't write screenplays because it pays too much money? Mr. Potter, I can't make sense of that."

"It's a dog eat dog world out there." Mr. Potter pointed with his pipe to the placid, lazy brick street lined on both sides with pastel stucco houses. "No woman wants to get involved with that."

Mr. Weber was my instructor in Directing I. He was a middle-aged man and so effete that the boys, behind his back, called him Auntie Gus.

"There are only two women in the world who are directing," he declared loudly, "one of them owns her own theatre in Texas and hires herself. The other is Margaret Webster who..."

"...is the exception who proves the rule," I sighed.

"Sorry," Mr. Weber said. He touched my shoulder briefly then pulled his hand back as though he'd been stung. "Well, that's how it is, Josie. A man won't take direction from a woman."

Mr. Weber, during my annual Career Prognosis, offered several alternatives to me. Career Prognosis was a big moment for a Playhouse student. At the conclusion of each school year you were called into the theatre and sat on stage as each of your instructors evaluated you out loud. On the basis of this event, a student might be cast in the Senior Project, sent on an interview with an agent at William Morris or be uninvited to the Playhouse for the following year. We all lived in fear of being uninvited. To be uninvited meant you didn't have a single salvageable shred of talent.

"We have decided," said Mr. Weber, "that you can be an actress, an agent or a gossip columnist."

In the Channel 3 newsroom, there is a junior writer by the name of Ginger Grosswoman. She is a fan of Lucy Dobdaughter—Lucy doesn't have friends, only fans—and in an effort to secure Lucy's respect, changed her name. It seems to me, however, that Lucy still sneers at Ginger Grossman/or/woman and I have a feeling that Ginger, who is very short, may feel the daggers of that sneer even more painfully than I do. Ginger's Achilles Heel is that she elicits and assimilates gossip with the speed of a computer and feeds out pages of print-out every day. She takes every piece of information as Gospel, regardless of its source, and considers it her responsibility to act on it. She has been known to stop speaking to people for several years because she heard something from someone that may or may not be true.

I don't have anything nice to say about gossip. Like sneering, it ought to be a capital offense.

Having turned thumbs down on becoming a producer, an agent or a gossip columnist, I had no theatrical choice but to act. I wasn't bad at it nor was I brilliant but I worked here and there, summer stock, coffeehouses, off-Broadway and one Broadway play which closed on opening night. I might have kept it up until I reached my thirties and I might have finally earned a living at it. But Jason happened and I couldn't starve a kid to death so I could pursue a career I hadn't wanted in the first place. That's when, at the urging of Dr. Binbaum, I settled down at Channel 3.

At the Hollywood Playhouse, or Gayhouse as we often called it, there was a whole lot of sex going on. There was a whole lot of sex going on at Advent Christian College, too, but sex was in the closet there. According to good Baptists, that is where sex belongs. At the Gayhouse, it was lying on the sidewalk, sparkling like a brand new toy in the California sun. My previous experience with sex had been limited though not through choice. Everybody in Advent was as Baptist as I was. The girls in Advent High School had cardinal rules that governed necking. First date, shake hands; second date, kiss; third date, kiss incl. tongue; fourth date, above the waist, clothes on; fifth date, above the waist, clothes off; sixth date, touch his penis through his pants. That was the limit unless he asked you to go steady. Then you were allowed below the waist, clothes on. If you were engaged, you could do below the waist, clothes off so long as his genitals weren't within spraying distance. But woe betide you if you broke up after that. You were besmirched, despoiled, used goods and hadn't a chinaman's chance of marrying rich unless you moved to another town.

Not so at the Gayhouse. The more experienced you were, the more you were in demand.

Jason says that God places no restrictions on sex whatsoever, that, in fact, God thinks no more about our sex lives than he does about our dental cavities. Sex is irrelevant to God and, like clipping our toenails, has no bearing on the status of our souls. God, says Jason, is interested in much more important matters. It's only man who is fascinated with sex and when a man nears godliness, this interest peters out. The Jasonites appear to have no sexuality. In fact, it's often difficult to tell the boys from the girls. But, as Jason said, we were originally all one gender anyway and God isn't interested in how and when and with whom or with which gender we couple up.

I don't know if the Jasonites copulate in order to reproduce or not. I've never seen a pregnant Jasonite. I've never even seen a naked Jasonite. For all I know, the woman may be capable of parthenogenesis or the men may be sprouting vaginas in their armpits. Apparently it's all the same to God.

With all the fooling around at Gayhouse, I technically remained a virgin. I'd done everything else in every conceivable arrangement but I refused penetration, not out of fear nor on moral grounds, but because I didn't trust a single guy I knew to use a condom properly and I had a funny feeling that I was Fertile Fanny.

So on my summer vacation after my first year at Hollywood Playhouse, I returned to Advent, Georgia, hymen intacta and joined up with a band of singing revivalists who were touring tent shows in the South. We called ourselves God's Children and I sang alto and preached part of the sermon for 5% of the nightly take. We generally collected $200.00 a show and sometimes did three shows a day, seven days a week. During the summer, I earned my tuition for another year at Gayhouse.

The services held by God's children could be compared, I suppose, to a circus or a rock and roll show. They were certainly noisy but I have more than a little holy roller in my soul and I've always been a firm believer in making a joyful noise. We travelled on a reconditioned school bus, spraypainted white enamel with golden sunbursts on the sides and rear. We also had a plywood sign, white with brilliant yellow letters: HERE WE ARE! GOD'S CHILDREN COME HOME AT LAST!

There were four of us and our manager, Mr. Angel. I'm sure that wasn't his real name but he signed our pay-stubs, Gabriel Angel. Mr. Angel was a tall, gaunt man with a large hooked nose. Grandma said two things about him when she met him. One: He'll never run in from the rain for the want of an umbrella, and Two: He hasn't seen the good side of seventy for nearly a decade. Mr. Angel was old but he was lively. And he could hear everything you said even when you were whispering in the back of the bus. He couldn't always see the middle line of the highway but the bus was so brightly painted the oncoming cars saw us and skidded onto the shoulder.

Our tent was designed to cover up the lights that made haloes seem to appear around our heads and to conceal the tape deck which played organ music as backup to our singing. We all preached part of the service. Leroy and Raymond (yes, the very same Raymond from Mrs. Williams' Bible Class) were the main preachers. I was the only girl and so I couldn't preach alone. Mr. Angel said the audiences would complain unless I could prove that I could lay on hands and heal or perform miracles. My preaching partner was an eleven-year-old named Maloney. Maloney had bright red hair and a pale complexion which caused people to ask if he was mulatto. Maloney didn't talk much except when he was preaching beside me at the pulpit. Then I could hardly get a word in edgewise.

When Jason's ministry began, one of the first churches to dissolve and follow him was Advent Calvary whose minister was Rev. Maloney Taylor. I don't think to this day (I'm assuming Maloney is still living and wasn't massacred in the wars against the Jasonites) that Maloney knows I'm any kin to Jason. When I knew Maloney, he considered me a pushy girl who had a lot of gall to get up in front of the pulpit when I knew that God was offended by my presence there. Even if Maloney were among the Jasonites who are camped outside this church tonight, I doubt that he would recognize my face or name. Maloney never did think much of me.

The summer of God's Children was about as close to heaven as I ever got in this life.

It was an illusion, I expect, like when I opened in my first and only Broadway play and got applause on both my exits and a final ovation loud and long enough to support four curtain calls; I began composing my acceptance speeches for the Tony and the Oscar. When the reviews came out just after midnight, Kerr said I was an obnoxious ingenue; Watts observed my role could have been more efficiently handled with an offstage phone call.

Humility has a rancid taste but once you get it down, it's like hot grits on a winter morning. Sticks to your ribs a good long time.

Jason was always humble. Well, you might say (Lucy Dobdaughter would certainly say) why shouldn't he have been humble? He was fat and couldn't write or read, never earned a nickel in his life. By all the standards we hold precious, Jason was a bum.

Ah, Lucy (and I'm fantasizing that I'm looking up your narrow sneering nostrils as I say this), Jason was good. In the long run, Lucy's nostrils, good is all that counts.

"Right, Solomon?"

Solomon has got a flea. It's nibbling the left side of his belly and he is much too busy to listen.

Jason was a bundle of goodness, so solid and so strong that evil couldn't touch him. It was goodness that killed Jason.

SEVEN

THE moon outside seems to be growing larger or perhaps moving closer to this church as though she's lost her footing in the sky and is falling slowly, painlessly, the way one rolls softly and pleasantly down the damp grass of a hillside in the springtime—on the other hand, she may be wandering of her own accord. Perhaps my bridal moon got cold feet on the way to the ceremony and is coming home to mother. Her aura has grown, too, as she seems to approach me and her light fills the Judas window with such whiteness that it pales the stained glass. The gold coin appears to have been miraculously alchemized into worthless, tarnished silver.

I think the moon is running away from home. I did it countless times in Advent, Georgia, hiding behind bushes and in deserted privies while my mother sat in a police car and uniformed officers prowled vacant lots and fields with broad-beamed flashlights. I was a champion runner-away-from-home-er. If they'd given prizes in my age group I would have won hands down. I ran away from home so often that frequently my parents didn't even know it. Sometimes I'd run away from home as many as three times a day but not finding what it was that I was looking for, I'd be back before they missed me.

Jason never once attempted to run away from home. When the time came, he left for good but I never had to call the police or sit up nights staring out our west side apartment at the carnivorous waters of the Hudson, waiting and wondering where my boy was.

Jason had a lot of human qualities. He wasn't always sweetness and light. He grew irritable with me, with all of us, especially when it seemed that we just couldn't, wouldn't understand.

He was never much of a talker but he had an affinity for numbers. He could count, add, subtract, multiply and divide by the time he was six. I thought I had a genius on my hands. In school, he had no trouble with chemistry and actually seemed to enjoy physics. He refused to learn the symbols for chemicals but he could identify them with a sniff and frequently performed successful experiments before the teacher handed out the instruction sheet.

Jason's interest in mathetmatics so encouraged me that I asked Martha, who worked in the bookkeeping department of Channel 3, to make up little puzzles and quizzes for me to take home and so further encourage Jason's knowledge of numbers. He was only eight at that time and I still had hopes he might give up his calling and go to college. I thought he had the stuff to be a CPA.

Martha was as tall as Ginger Grosswoman was short but they had one thing in common: gossip. Martha was the voice of the first floor, Ginger of the second. The boys in the mailroom said it was hardly necessary to route ALL STAFF memos through the building so long as Martha and Ginger worked there. Tell either one of them anything at all and it spread through the building like Drano in a septic system.

Ginger repeated all items, big and small, regardless of the

source, whereas Martha was more discriminating. She only repeated items with a sense of tragedy, a comic highlight or a moment of breathless drama in them and, like a cranky slot machine, she didn't accept wooden nickels. There were certain people who had, in Martha's judgment, proven unreliable and she turned a deaf ear to their stories. If one of these unworthies had shouted Fire, Martha would not have even scrambled for her pocketbook.

The main difference between Martha and Ginger Gross-woman was that Martha never got the gossip straight. If she told you that Herb Lewis in Production fathered a brain-damaged child, that might mean that Sol Lucas in Film fathered a brain-damaged child or that Herb Lewis, who had a brother-in-law with multiple sclerosis, fathered a perfectly healthy set of twins. There was just no way of telling so most of us regarded Martha's gossip as our fiction for the day.

Jason seemed to enjoy the mathematical puzzles Martha created for him. He worked without a calculator or slide rule and could, by running his forefinger along a line, compute angles in degrees. Martha, who had once dreamed of following in the footsteps of Albert Einstein but had been distracted by marriage and the birth of four daughters, was so fascinated that she begged to meet my son. Jason would have no part of it. I cajoled and pleaded, wanting to show him off to the Channel 3 newsroom, to no avail.

"It will hurt you later on," he insisted, "and I don't want to hurt you. I never want to hurt you."

I had no idea what he meant until, years later, news and wire services were full of Jason's ministry and the prevailing attitude then, at the beginning, was that a lunatic had been let loose from Central Islip. He was the butt of office jokes and stores on 42nd Street sold posters that depicted Jason naked (a drawing because Jason couldn't be captured on film) with a tiny little erection trying to peek out from under a pendulous belly. In the first place, Jason's belly was not pendulous. And Jason never showed a prurient interest in anything.

I do know Jason wouldn't hurt me. Jason never wanted to hurt anybody. He'd be heartbroken if he could see me now, imprisoned in this church, awaiting execution. He would be dismayed that the Jasonites are executing anyone. Jason told us that death was nothing to fear, just another state of being, and so the Jasonites believe they aren't hurting me, just removing me from their world. I've become an air pocket in their smooth flight to serenity.

Jason hated the term Savior and never referred to himself as that. "Man is his own savior," he said, "I'm just the son of God." Jason also grew irritated with references to the second coming. "It's completely inaccurate," he complained, "I've been here two hundred seventy-four times." Jason had a deep respect for numbers and accuracy.

"When did you first come, Jason?"

"A trillion forty-two years ago but that won't calculate with time the way you count it. You started counting much too late. Besides, time doesn't move forward."

"It doesn't move forward?"

"No."

"Does it move backward?"

"It doesn't move at all."

"The past and the future are happening now?"

Jason heaved a sigh. "Time is a state of being."

"I don't understand that."

Jason held his head in his hands. "I know." There were tears in his eyes. "Sonofagun and doggone," he said. "Am I ever going to get the hang of this?"

"When was the first time, Jason?"

Jason pressed his index fingers against his eyelids as though that helped him to remember. Or perhaps he was sliding around in time, I don't know. "It was at the beginning, of course. There's ocean over that place now. I didn't have a name. Nobody spoke. It was wonderful. The best time of them all. Communication was total, complete. God was everywhere, in everyone."

"They could see God?"

He shook his head without removing his fingers. "You never see God. God is just there. There were no buildings then, no books to wall Him out. It was easy." Jason smiled and removed his fingers. "It was easy for me. The next time, it was harder. They were sharpening knives and killing animals and one another. They talked. Not like you do but it was language just the same. It wasn't quite as hard to break through as your words are but it was a whole lot harder than total silence had been. They got it, though. Finally, they got it. But after I left, they got to talking about it and putting names to it and building buildings to it."

"And the next time?"

"I don't want to go through all of them," Jason snapped. "It'll take all night. You wouldn't understand it, anyway."

"Please, Jason. Talk to me. I'm trying hard."

"I'll just hit the high points. There was Oowow. They'd started naming babies then. Oowow was black as coal. She mothered sixteen children and had them tear the temples down. They got it and kept it for a while but then they sent out missionaries and told the yellow and red tribes that God was a a woman with black skin."

"Is He? She?"

"You missed the point, just as they did."

"What is the color of God's skin?"

"God doesn't have skin," Jason hissed.

"I'm sorry. Go on."

"There were several other times—a lot of other times—but they were of no great importance. In one of them I got gored by an elephant while I was still a toddler. And there was Guah. Guah was born a prince. The King was the meanest sonofagun I ever met. You'd think those people would have been overjoyed when I deposed him and had his castle razed to the ground but they got stirred up as hornets. They tied me to a raft and pushed it out to sea. Jonah didn't get eaten by the whale but Guah did. Then, of course, there was Abraham, Jeremiah, Elijah, Deborah, John, Jesus. I think I'm leaving someone out."

"The Bible is true, then?"

"Oh, Margaret, Sitmanda, Lucante, Roget."

"Jason?"

"Ramond, Lucinda, Elijay, Mettepolis."

"Is the Bible true?"

"Hirrida, Achto, Namaholata, Francis."

"Jason!"

"The Bible describes the perceptions of one family of man living in one part of the world during what is, in the overview, a minute span of time. Although, as I've tried to explain, time doesn't span. Time is. Oh, dear." Sigh. "The danger of the Bible is that it provides easy answers to man's questions. I never asked a question until I met a man. Questions, questions, questions, man's voice rising at the end of every sentence. It's contagious. Next thing I knew, I asked a question, too. I raised my voice to God and asked Why Man?"

"But the incidents in the Bible, did they really happen?"

"Your Bible is not enough and yet, being not enough, it instructs mankind to look no further. Becoming Godly is really easy but you have to start off on the right foot. Ask no questions of man. Accept no answers from man. You can't reach godliness travelling in a pack. Every seeker must come alone."

"Why can't I get this, Jason?" I could feel a headache trembling above my eyebrows, getting ready to take hold.

"You revere the accomplishments of mankind more than you long for godliness. You can't have both. They're mutually exclusive. The accomplishments of man inherently require management and labor, investment and profit; of themselves they create inequality of life. I chased the money-lenders from a temple once but I realize now that it was just a waste of time. They were back in business before sundown. I could have bombed the banks this time but it would have no lasting effect. I've learned it's useless to change the structure. I have to change the man. That's where your revolutionists are off the track. It is not your system that must be overthrown. It's man himself."

"I don't understand, Jason. I can't understand what it is that you want us to do."

"Follow me," he replied simply.

"How can I follow you?" I almost screamed it. "I don't know where you're going!"

Shortly after that conversation, Jason took to the streets again. The next I heard he was travelling toward Alaska. I worried. It was the dead of winter and he'd left without taking his overcoat and scarf.

In the next weeks after that I began to have a strange new dream. It was so brilliantly real and filled me with such wholeness and joy that I'd wake up smiling broadly. Yet I never could remember it except that there was yellow in it— gold—the color of the sun.

"Solomon, Solomon. Do you suppose I saw God in my dreams?"

"Don't strain your brain," Solomon advises. "You'll have answers soon enough. The moon is on the wane."

"Solomon?"

"Solomon?"

"How can you go to sleep at a time like this?"

EIGHT

I FEEL dreadful. My stomach is cramping. There is no bathroom accessible to me from this sanctuary. I just went to the massive twin doors of the church, arching twelve feet into the air, six inches thick at least and covered with reliefs of sinners being tortured in the most hideous manners. Heads roll, limbs fly, mouths are open in death screams, spears impale sinners like shishkabobs. And overseeing it all is the vengeful bearded God of Abraham. He looks self-righteous, smug, even gleeful at the sight of carnage. He sits on a throne which, though ornate, is too small to encompass Him. His robes are blowing in a mighty wind and disappear off the edges of the doors as though the artist is showing us that God is too large to be contained in such a picture. In God's right hand, toy-sized, is a small figure I take to be Jesus Christ. On each of the twin doors there is a legend, the letters fitted into the form of an oval, so that when I approached the door the two eyes glared at me, each proclaiming JUDGMENT DAY.

The guard outside must be asleep. I knocked and

knocked with the brass cross which hangs beside the door but got no answer. Perhaps the door is just too thick for sound to penetrate it. I hurried back to the Judas window and peeked out at the sleeping bodies. I considered hollering through the crack beside Judas' gold coin but thought better of it. The Jasonites might not take kindly to being awakened. I don't want them to get started on tomorrow's work too soon.

In the vestry, behind some tattered choir robes, I found a pan made out of metal of some kind. A tin collection plate? It filled the bill. I didn't even mind squatting. It felt rather natural. Perhaps I'm closer to becoming a Jasonite than I have thought.

I have always been peculiar about my bathroom habits. I've been known to excuse myself and walk to the nearest ESSO station if nature calls when I'm entertaining guests in my apartment. In Advent, Georgia, everybody turned on all the faucets when they entered a bathroom so the thundering sound of running water covered any human noise.

My husband, George, once farted onstage but it was unintentional and George, upper crust Bostonian that he is, refused to take a curtain call.

I met George after my second year at the Gayhouse. I had written to Mr. Angel about summer work and had gotten a reply that God's Children wouldn't need my services. All preaching would henceforth be done by Maloney, so Mr. Angel wrote, because there had been complaints about a girl behind the pulpit.

I then sent out a dozen 8x10 glossy photographs with a neatly typed resume stapled to the back of them. The photograph was what we in show biz called a composite. It had four photographs on the same page, each depicting the actor as a character of some sort. We took a six week course at the Gayhouse in how to select photographs for a composite and how to assemble a resume in such a manner that it would tantalize a producer. On my composite, I appeared as an old woman, a drunken prostitute, a happy housewife gleefully holding up a dirty rag and bottle of Mr. Clean, and as a sweet young ingenue.

Eleven of the twelve theatres sent rejection letters within two weeks. Downhearted, I boarded a bus to the heart of Hollywood and applied for summer work at Woolworth's. I thought Woolworth's would leap at the chance to hire someone like me. I had four years of schooling beyond high school and I was reasonably attractive, well kept and well spoken. There was a line waiting outside the door marked Personnel and after a half an hour wait, a pleasant young man came out and handed us each a piece of paper and a pencil. It was a Woolworth's policy, he said, to test all applicants. He blew a plastic whistle which signaled us to begin. I whipped through Page One of the test. It consisted of multiple choice answers such as (A) We ain't got none. (B) Not my department. (C) I'll be happy to ask the manager for you. Page Two, however, was a different kettle of fish. A sense of doom descended on me. (1) One Jolly Jawbreaker weights 1¼ oz. Jolly Jawbreakers sell for 50¢ a pound. A customer wants 30 Jolly Jawbreakers...

Back at the Gayhouse dormitory, I telephoned the twelfth theatre, the one which had not yet responded to my picture and resume. The Director, Mr. Harris, answered the phone. Children were crying in the background. Several times during our conversation he turned from the phone and screamed. He explained that Kissing Rock Theatre, located in Kissing Rock, South Carolina, isn't really a theatre at all. It's a large tent with a platform for the actors. The audience is seated in folding chairs donated by a local church.

Mr. Harris remembered my composite and resume and had, in fact, once seen a performance of God's Children although he couldn't remember which one of them I was. He was interested in knowing if I was related to the Caldwells of North Carolina. His wife had a second cousin who had married a North Carolina Caldwell. I said I didn't believe I was although my father had once mentioned having kin in West Virginia. Mr. Harris offered me a job as leading lady of his company. The pay was room and board and twenty dollars a week. He said that he would have liked to send me bus fare but that his budget simply couldn't accommodate any additional expense and if push came to shove, Mrs. Harris could be recruited to act as leading lady as she had been the previous year and that would cost him nothing at all but did present a baby-sitting problem as they had four children and the nearby church camp wouldn't keep the children after five p.m. Threatened, I informed Mr. Harris that I also wrote plays and happened to have several unproduced one-act plays that he could do and save money. I explained I was aware of the expensive royalties one has to pay to get the rights to perform a Broadway play. Mr. Harris said that was one of the advantages of Kissing Rock, South Carolina. No one from Broadway knew their play was being done there.

This left me with the problem of getting from Hollywood to Kissing Rock. My mother responded to my request for a loan by saying she'd had enough of this show business nonsense and thought I had, too. If I'd just say the word, she could line up a job for me as assistant teller at Advent Trust and in that event she could probably scrape together plane fare for me to return home.

Manny Meyer was a student in my class at the Gayhouse. You may have heard of him. For a number of years, he was a popular comedian. When Jason began his ministry, Manny, deeply opposed to the Jasonites, gave up show biz and returned to work alongside his father in the family company. Meyer Co. designed the small airborne craft which are used offensively against the Jasonites. These Green Flies, as they're called, painted to resemble foliage, are wingless and nearly soundless. They are quite small and manned by one soldier, curled into the cockpit like an embryo. Armed with splashes, a nuclear device also invented and manufactured by the

Meyer Co., they release radioactive gases which mutilate all life in a five mile radius. There are rumors that, in the jungles where the splashes have been dropped, natural vegetation and wild life is mutating in bizarre ways. They say that the limbs of trees are no longer reaching toward the sky but are aiming down and burrowing beneath the soil, dislodging massive stones and creating tunnels into which the wildlife is retreating. Someone claimed they saw an opossum without legs which slithered like a snake.

When I knew Manny Meyer at the Gayhouse he was a very small person, no taller than a ten-year-old boy, loud and pushy, as small people tend to be; he was at the same time funny and obnoxious.

Manny owned a Thunderbird, a car which in 1957, came equipped with automatic social status. Manny's father didn't think any more of show business than my mother did and demanded that Manny earn his Gayhouse tuition by working at the Meyer Co. every summer. He assigned Manny to the nastiest jobs in the hopes that Manny would give up and accept the offer of a $30,000 a year executive position. So, every summer, Manny was relegated to shoveling aluminum shavings, filtering and cleaning motor oil, or laying on his back on an assembly line tightening one screw in the belly of each plane as it moved over him. These assignments only served to strengthen Manny's love of show biz.

Manny had no luck with girls. Much of his comedy routine was about the predicament of short men in this particular regard. "Other guys," said Manny in his act, "look deeply and longingly into a girl's eyes. I look into her nipples."

Now, the Meyer Co. plant happened to be located in North Carolina, not too far from Kissing Rock. I knew that if I asked Manny for a ride to Kissing Rock, he'd get his hopes up. I was no great looker but I was female and that was enough for Manny. His expectations had a low threshold. I didn't want to sleep with Manny, but I needed a free ride to

Kissing Rock.

Manny didn't bring the subject up but he must have made assumptions because the first night on the road, he pulled into a motel, wiggled his eyebrows like Groucho Marx and rented a single room with a double bed. I should have protested then and there—but (1) nice girls didn't bring up sex unless they intended to do it because the very mention of the word was reputed to give boys something known as blue balls and then it became the responsibility of the girl to relieve their pain; and (2) I didn't have a dime with which to rent a room for myself. There is no back seat in a T-bird so it was sit up all night outside or sleep in Manny's bed.

Manny emerged from the motel bathroom in white silk pajamas. They were still creased from the package and the price tag hung from the left sleeve. They were several sizes too big and Manny, his teeth gleaming, his breath smelling of Listerine, his fingernails and toenails gouged clean, his hair slicked neatly back, put me in mind of an infant prince viewing his legacy for the first time. He was breathing through his mouth and he kept his hands clasped tightly together and pressed them against his crotch. He sat carefully on the edge of the bed and waited for me to enter and exit the bathroom.

The only sleepwear I owned was a pair of baby dolls which my mother had sent me as a birthday present. They were yellow cotton bikini panties and a sleeveless, scoop-necked pullover top which only descended as far as the hipline. My mother never intended me to wear them in mixed company. I went into the bathroom with my suitcase and picked through it until I came up with brown bermuda shorts and a sweatshirt with the sleeves cut off.

Manny looked dismayed when I emerged.

Even so, he pounced on me, darting like a frenzied ant, first at my head and neck then dashing down to nibble at the frayed hem of my bermuda shorts, back up again, diving beneath the sweatshirt and encountering my full-line Playtex bra. I could have heaved him to the floor or pinned him to the wall with one hand. I did nothing, hypnotized the way one is when watching the workers in an ant hill. To and fro, up and down, right and left, He had gotten one of the four hooks on my bra when I took action. I rolled over on him. He was helpless, one hand snared in my bra-hook, the other crushed between our bellies.

"I can't do anything in this position," he wailed.

"Can't anyway," I answered. "I'm a virgin."

"Cock tease."

"Don't blame me."

"I'm paying for the gas. It's my car."

"I'll send you the money."

"Kiss it?"

"Huh?"

"Some girls like to."

"Who?"

"None of your business."

"You got blue balls?"

"You never did it?"

"Not all the way."

"Gee."

"You?"

"Nope."

"Want me to say we did it?"

"Would you?"

"Sure."

"You know what, Josie?"

"What, Manny?"

"You're a real nice girl."

"Thanks."

Having shared our deepest secrets, Manny and I became friends. We corresponded for many years. He remained a virgin until he fell in love with a girl even smaller than he was and, the last I heard of them, they were still happily married. They came to dinner at my apartment many times when

Jason was still a tyke. It was Manny who said of Jason that if he were me, he'd drive out to New Jersey and look for a stream with bullrushes.

At Kissing Rock, the actors and the crew all lived together family style in a big farmhouse. Behind the farmhouse was a field which had been overturned and packed down to serve as a parking lot for the audience.

The tent was pitched beyond this parking lot. Mr. Harris had purchased it second-hand from Ringling Brothers. Three hundred people could sit under it. There was no natural windbreak in the field and the tent top held rainwater like a reservoir. On stormy nights, Mr. Harris rang a bell and the cast and crew leapt from their beds and raced to the rescue of the tent. The women sat on the edges of the tent to hold it down and the men climbed ladders and bailed out the canvas roof.

It was impossible for a couple to make love secretly in the farmhouse where we lived. We learned to recognize the sound of one another's barefooted steps in the midnight hallway and most of us could identify which bedroom door was opening by the pitch of its squeaks. As a family, we all became concerned when we heard Beverly's footsteps and Karen's door for several nights running. George determined that all Beverly needed was the love of a good man. He set out to find one for her. Beverly had no knowledge of this and was surprised when a tall burly man in a blue suit arrived backstage one night to announce that he was taking her dancing at the Shake and Rattle Club. Beverly didn't own a dress—or if she did, she hadn't brought it to Kissing Rock since she was employed to dress sets and hang lights and spent a good deal of time on twenty foot ladders. Beverly told him to get lost. He was insulted and threatened to punch out George. George had encountered this travelling salesman at the laundromat in Lumberville where the salesman was servicing detergent vending machines. While George did his laundry he convinced the salesman that he could set him up with a terrific girl who was hot to trot. The salesman had driven forty-six miles from his home in Columbia to Kissing Rock on a perfectly good Saturday night and had paid money to sit through Time Out for Ginger. The man had expectations.

George took Beverly aside and spoke of trust, friendship, responsibility. He mentioned perversity, the devil, judgment day and hell. He told her the story of Adam's Rib and quoted at length from the Bible about the role of woman. Beverly, verbally battered, acquiesced. Mrs. Harris loaned her a silk dress and spike heels. Beverly teetered on them but she clung to the salesman's arm and managed to make it to his car. Karen watched and wept copiously. George, victorious and righteous, sat up on the front porch until three a.m. and came to my bed pleased as punch that Beverly had not returned yet.

She arrived the next morning during breakfast. She had to pass through the dining room to get to the staircase that led to her room upstairs. Her flesh was pale white and there were strawberry hickeys on her neck. She carried Mrs. Harris' spike heels in her hands. She tried to tip-toe through the dining room, staring at the floor, but George stood up at the breakfast table and led the company in a round of applause. Beverly broke into a run, took the stairs three at a time and locked herself inside her room. George thought she was recovering from having been deflowered and tenderly, thoughtfully, made a sandwich for her and set it by her door.

At midnight that night, we heard Beverly's bare footsteps and Karen's door. George was so frustrated that he wept in my arms.

I remember George's embrace. He had a sharp bone in his elbow which always got me in the curve of the back of my neck and caused a temporary paralysis of the left side of my face as though I were afflicted with a stroke. Immediately after making love, George rolled onto his stomach to protect the lil' fella—as he affectionately named his penis, sometimes bouncing it gently in the palm of his hand and regarding it with wonder. George rolled onto his stomach as a learned response. Once never satisfied me but it satiated George. For me, once was like jogging in place—a warm-up for the run. George, however, put his all into the initial effort and was dismayed that his all was not enough for me. Post-ejaculation, he regarded my still swollen, aching vulva with dismay. George claimed I allowed my concentration to wander. George said I approached sex as I did writing—I insisted on a first draft. He said marital love was a sacred and profound act like prayer, and I profaned it by my demands. In retrospect, I can see that George was right about a lot of things but not so many as he thought.

Tonight in this dank church, I find myself pining for George. Sharp elbow or not, his arms were comforting. They provided a thicker shield between me and the world than this blanket does. I would like to hear George snore right now. If I could hear that tremulous wheeze followed by a honk, I believe everything would be all right. Solomon is trying to oblige by making a shallow snorting noise as he sleeps but he can't compete with George's snores. George was the champion. His inhales tossed the mattress like a ship in stormy water and his exhales, forceful as an autumn wind, set the bedroom curtains quivering. At the end of each exchange, he honked like the impatient horn of a Model T. In bed with George, I always knew I was not alone.

I stopped writing here and lifted Solomon into my arms, holding him against my breast and shoulder as though he were an infant. I buried my fingers in his fur and absorbed the wetness of his nose with my cheek. He remained limp and trusted me to hold him tightly for a minute, then he squirmed and wiggled, pushed for freedom and in doing so, clipped my cheek with his claw. I pressed my finger on the spot until the blood stopped but it still smarts. Solomon leapt a good distance from me and sits there now, his back to me, regarding the wall with intense interest. "You don't fool me,

Solomon. You're not studying the wall at all, you're rejecting me."

"You're so intense," Solomon retorts, "you're always grabbing, clutching at me."

"I need you, Solomon. I love you."

"Need and love are mutually exclusive," Solomon sniffed and padded to the vestry, out of my sight. "Pick one," he called back through the archway.

Jason said much the same thing. "Love has no fingers, draws no boundaries."

"Impossible," I argued. "The very act of love is to draw someone into yourself."

"That's cannibalism."

"Well, what is love, Jason," I demanded. "If love is not sex and love is not romance, then what?" I saw the balance of human life teetering on this very point.

"Let go," Jason instructed.

"Let go? Let go of what?"

But Jason was finished with that discussion. He closed up like a clam, his mouth a tight and slightly curved line. Jason didn't want to get dragged into the whirring and useless machinery of human intellect.

Solomon is curled up on a shelf like a fetus, his chin tucked in the cavity above his ribcage, his paws sheltering his eyes.

George, George, I wish you were sitting here now. We could have a crazy contest, the way we used to. Sitting up in bed, our backs against the wall; you'd painted the bedroom with sandpaint to cover up the cracks and it skinned our flesh on more than one occasion. I can almost feel the prickles now against my shoulderblades, the heat of your fingers on the back of my hand, your thigh against my knee.

"I'm crazier than you," I'd start.

"Oh, no, I'm crazier than you."

"I'm afraid of cold showers in the morning. They shock my brain and make me think I'm going to short-circuit."

"My naval is going to come untied and my intestines will fall out. I wash my belly-button with a Q-tip carefully."

"I hate it when the dental hygienist cleans my teeth. She's going to yank my caps off."

"I never clip my toenails short, I'll lose my sense of balance."

"What if a bug crawled on my pillow and into my ear and through my sinuses and up my optic nerve and into my brain? I'm afraid of a mosquito bite on my cortex."

"What if you sat down on the toilet to take a dump and there was a snake in the bowl, come up from the sewer system?"

"What if it slithered up your rectum?"

"Or up your vagina, through your cervix and nested in your womb. Weeks later, you'd give birth to a slither of snakes."

"A slither?"

"A clutch?"

"A gangle?"

"Whatever. A bunch of them."

"Would you have to raise them as your own?"

"What if an airplane crashed through the window of this bedroom?"

"Or a truck careened into the first floor, smashing the support beams and causing the entire building to collapse."

"Suppose the steering wheel of the car came off in your hands."

"Or your eyes rolled up in the back of your head and locked there?"

"What if you looked up in the sky and saw a giant set of teeth with braces on them and realized that the earth was just a kid's dollhouse?"

"A tick might imbed itself in your testicle."

"Or on your nipple."

"What if you breathed in a baby bumble bee and it grew up in your lungs?"

"I'm afraid of Alka-Seltzer bubbling inside me."

"The hair on my head protects me. The longer it is, the more protected I am."

"There is always a chance that my cock is going to be melted out of shape by a hot vagina."

"Or fall off inside."

"Yes."

"Or keep growing, growing, growing until it impales me and comes out the top of my head."

"I look under the bed every night."

"I check the closet, kick the clothes."

"Some people may possess a supernatural ability to hate you to death. You never know who has it and who hasn't."

"Never go barefoot in the dark."

"Sometimes I cry at sudden sounds."

"I cry at Lassie."

"And commercials."

"I weep at bravery."

"For bravery?"

"At it."

"I cry for love."

"I glance up the rooflines before I walk down a block. Snipers."

"Falling bricks."

"Glass."

"Yes."

"One day I will find a battered envelope in the gutter. It will be floating unnoticed in a stream of trash and debris. It will contain a million dollars cash and no one else will claim it."

"What if God is looking at us right this minute?"

"What if He isn't?"

"You're crazier than I am."

"No. It's a draw."

And then, having reduced ourselves to the lowest single common denominator, we'd make love. And George was satisfied or so he said. I was not.

The moon is high enough now to light the ceiling of this sanctuary and I see things there I haven't seen before. It's made of pressed tin, I think though it's been painted dozens, maybe hundreds, of times and the images which were hammered into the tin are blurred and, in some places, obscured completely. Staring at it, I believe it was meant to represent the universe—or the heavens, as man saw it in the 1700s. There are stars and moons—there is the goat, and over there the dippers, and that's probably Orion just above me although much of his outline has disappeared beneath the layers of peeling paint. If I lay down on the first pew, I could see the sky as Gulliver might have seen it—the brilliant layout of the heavens made small in proportion to my greatness. I dare not lay down, though, for any reason. I'm afraid to sleep.

Would it make any difference? If the world were suddenly to disappear from my mind and I were wakened when this sanctuary is bright with sunlight and warm again? If I were seized from sleep by two Jasonites, each grabbing one of my arms, and led out to the square, made to stand naked in the yellow sand under the blistering rays of sun and, before I'd fully regained consciousness from my deep sleep, my innards blasted by machine guns? I don't know if Jasonites possess machine guns. Or if they plan to make a spectacle of my death. Perhaps one of them will just sneak into this church at daybreak and strangle me with a stocking.

Am I important, Jason?

Jason doesn't answer any more than God does but I'm so familiar with the tone of Jason's soft voice that I can hear it, anyway.

He says, "Probably not."

"I refuse to accept that, Jason."

In my imagination Jason sighs, "Oh, well, your loss."

I am willful and enangered. "No," I say, "that's God's loss."

"Ut-oh," comments Jason.

"Ut-oh? What does that mean, Jason?"

But Jason has disappeared. He hates questions.

I'd give anything for an ice-cold Coke right now. I'll swallow hard and think about crushed ice. Tiny slivers that fill my mouth and quickly melt against the heat of my parched tongue.

Imagination is a marvelous device. Cool liquid trickles down my throat now. I swallow and feel refreshed.

The first summer I lived in New York, I was married to George. We couldn't afford an air conditioner and if someone had given us one, we couldn't have plugged it into the antique 110 wiring of our tenement apartment. When it was ninety-eight degrees outside, George and I stood naked in our living room and pretended we were pine trees in a storm. Our boughs became heavy with the slanting on-slaught of rain, our trunks soaked and chilled, our needles fluttered with the bitter wind. We trembled, shivered, swayed until our roots snapped and we collapsed across the floor. George and I could sleep with a blanket on the hottest nights.

NINE

IT'S very cold in here now. Thinking about being a pine tree in a storm has chilled me to the bone. I've pulled this blanket around me as tightly as I can. Only my hands and eyes are peeking out from under cover.

George used to sleep with the blanket wrapped around him like swaddling clothes. He'd cover up his eyes as well, leaving only his mouth visible, gaping and honking like a fish deprived of water. I complained so frequently about his snoring that he took to laying a pillow on top of his head. At first, I worried that he'd suffocate but he didn't and the pillow seemed to muffle the sounds that rolled out of his throat. I harrassed George to the point that he volunteered to be a guinea pig for the sleep research center at Columbia University. He packed his bag and moved into their laboratory for two nights. They sampled his blood and X-rayed his respiratory system. Finding him in good health, they tucked him into bed, placed sensors on his forehead, temples, Adam's apple and chest, connected him with tubes and wiring to a monitor, focused cameras on him and filmed his sleep. At the end of the weekend, George returned home waving his discharge paper triumphantly. George didn't snore either of the nights he spent at the research center. It seems I'm the only one who ever noticed George's snores. His mother swore she had never heard him and neither had his sister with whom he shared a bedroom until he was of high school age. George claimed no girlfriend had ever shaken him by the shoulder out of a sound sleep the way I did night after night.

I borrowed a tape recorder and secretly placed it under our bed. When George drifted off, I pressed the record button and lay for a half hour grinning gleefully as sounds of eardrum splitting dimensions ricocheted off the walls of our small bedroom. The next morning at breakfast, I greeted George with the recording. He puffed up like a rooster and said the noise on that tape could not have been produced by him. It sounded, he said, like the subway station at rush hour and he had no assurance that I was playing the recording at the same volume at which it was recorded.

George was the first person I saw when I arrived at Kissing Rock, S.C. Manny had planned for us to arrive at the theatre mid-afternoon. That would give me time to settle in before I began rehearsing the next day and would allow Manny to get back on the road and travel several more hours toward Raleigh before dark. There were no signs to Kissing Rock, however, and we didn't know to look for Lumberville, the nearest town, so we overshot the turnoff and drove north for two more hours. About five p.m. we began to see signs heralding the North Carolina line and we pulled into the first Howard Johnson's to ask directions.

I asked every customer in Howard Johnson's if they were heading anywhere near Kissing Rock but no one was. Manny suggested I hitchhike and I, proud and offended, strutted to the roadside and stuck out my thumb. Manny licked a double scoop of orange sherbet and watched me through the window of Howard Johnson's. A pickup truck stopped right away. It was driven by an emaciated man, bald, toothless, with skin leathered from exposure to the sun. He spat when he spoke and his accent was so thick that I, a native Southerner, only understood snatches. I said Kissing Rock several times and he nodded amiably as though he were going directly to the place. He got out of the truck, approached my suitcase to toss it into the cargo bin beside the hog he had tied in there. At that moment, Manny came running toward me yelling, "Okay, all right, you win!" He grumbled with self-pity all the way back to Kissing Rock.

It was dusk when we arrived, past suppertime. The farmhouse sprawled across the clearing, its neo-gothic silhouette slightly warped by settling. In the upstairs bedrooms, lights glared like rhinestones against the royal purple sky. The front porch ran the length of the house, supported by massive columns once painted white, now chipped and peeling. The porch light, a single yellow bulb screwed in the clapboard wall, cast a tremulous spotlight across the porch swing. Gnats splatted suddenly against the windshield of Manny's T-bird as though a massive hand had hurled them at us. Manny flipped on his windshield wipers and buttered the glass with carcasses.

"God damn," Manny cursed, "I can't see where the fuck I'm going."

That's when I noticed George. He was the only human being in sight. He sat alone on the porch, idly pushing himself back and forth in the porch swing. Illuminated in the yellow spotlight, he was as unreal and unknown as the first character onstage when the curtains open on a play. His high school letter sweater, snagged and moth-eaten, was draped across his shoulders. He wore khaki workman's pants, so new the horizontal creases were visible along the legs, and a madras shirt carefully laundered so the colors bled into each other. His penny loafers were brand new, the coins shiny. As I was later to discover, George couldn't look unkempt, it was against his nature. He tried valiantly to adopt the bizarre, untidy look preferred by actors but never succeeded. With the exception of his high school letter sweater, George's clothes never looked broken in.

He was balancing a playscript on his thigh and glanced down at it occasionally as he spoke his lines out loud. He looked up briefly when we slammed the car doors, cast an appreciative glance at the T-bird and wagged one finger in salutation. His sandy hair looked golden in the porch light and his Irish face was broad planed and open. George has pouty, sensous lips with charming little puckers in the corners. I instantly sensed magic although he didn't even glance at me when I stepped up on the creaky porch. He kept his eyes closed and continued to recite his lines as though I weren't standing three feet from him, staring. He would not be distracted from his work. I snapped my fingers but George didn't look up. Manny took the snap as an indication of my impatience and he hurried to remove our suitcases from the T-bird and shot nasty looks at me. I continued to stare at George; gnats swarmed around his head but nothing seemed to penetrate the thick wall of his inner world. I couldn't see the color of his eyes but I guessed that they were green; his eyelashes curled against his cheek. He had dimples in both cheeks and one slightly off-center in his chin. His eyebrows were thick and tangled. Later I found out that he sometimes put vaseline on them and combed them with the fine teeth of his pocket comb, to no avail—like the southern kudzu vine, George's eyebrows stubbornly adhered to the paths that pleased them. He seemed to me to be a large and intense leprechaun. And he was *my* George, from the moment I saw him.

My breathing quickened but my heart didn't pound noisily. My knees didn't tremble. I didn't spend the rest of the evening thinking about him, longing for his embrace, although I recall peeking out the window twice to assure myself he was still there. In fact, I didn't see him again until after breakfast the next morning.

Meeting George was as if, while working a complicated jigsaw puzzle, I suddenly discovered that I'd left a piece inside the box. Just looking at it, I could see that it was going to fit; that once inserted, everything else would fall right into place. I felt an enormous sense of destiny about George, quite calm and sane, nothing like books tell you that you feel falling into love. It was no chance meeting on that porch. God had a hand in it.

I heard George's voice the first time the next morning at rehearsal. I had never read the play before—it was the English premiere of a little known English flop called Gents Will Always, the script as elusive as the name. George approached me from behind and asked "What happened to your boyfriend?"

I hardly turned around. "That wasn't my boyfriend," I answered, "that was Manny. He drove me here and it was too late last night for him to drive on to Raleigh."

"Huh."

George's *Huh* was based on the knowledge that Manny spent the night in my room.

"He's just a friend," I said. "Men and women can be friends, you know."

"Of course," George said and moved around so I could see him. He was wearing chinos and a KISSING ROCK THEATRE sweatshirt, both so new and starched and clean that he glistened like the dew. "Of course," he repeated.

"I go to school with him," I explained, "at the Hollywood Gayhouse. Playhouse."

George flinched. "Well," he said, "I'm glad to hear he isn't your boyfriend. You don't look good together. You need a big man to balance you visually." He continued, a scoff in his voice, "I don't believe in acting schools, they strangle natural talent."

George had no theatrical schooling and, apart from religious pageants and one community theatre appearance, he had no experience, but at ten a.m., I didn't know this and I went onstage with George, leading woman to his leading man, convinced that I was about to embark on my first assignment with a real-live working actor.

As George delivered each of his lines, he kept edging closer and closer to the footlights.

"George," I whispered in the middle of our scene, "you're upstaging yourself.'

"Huh?"

"You're turning your back to the audience."

"Well, of course I am. I can't see you if I don't."

"That won't happen if you stay up here on a level with me," I instructed but George was never one to accept instructions from a woman. It was the third or fourth show of the season before he got the hang of moving on a stage. He had such a magnificent presence, though, he could get away with poor manuevers. Even when he turned his back to them, audiences believed him.

I never encountered anyone who hated George—not even me, not even when he was passing in and out of my life like it was a revolving door. George was hale fellow well met to all men and dependable big brother to all women. It was difficult to tell when George was having an affair with a woman, he was so friendly to all of them. I had been married to him several months before I finally realized that George was a closet Lothario. I was never able to pin down which of his many woman friends were relating to him vertically and which horizontally.

Jason says there is no such thing as truth, only reality.

To my credit, I did not behave with undue jealousy at any time during our courtship or our marriage. Even George admitted I was not a possessive wife. I knew that he and I had something special and unique between us. He could have fornicated with half of Actors' Equity and it would not have severed the bond between us. We had to do that ourselves.

I read somewhere that everyone has a soulmate—the

other side of our personal coin. That's how it was with George and me. We were the male and female gender of the same soul. Our love should have been eternal, surpassing earthly conflicts. In a sense, I suppose it was—I love George as I always have. Our marriage didn't end, it kind of pittered off. There was no loud explosion, just the soft sound of a front door closing again and again and again until we both ceased to notice it. Our marriage drifted down a hallway.

At lunch break that first day of rehearsal, George suggested that we take our sandwiches to Kissing Rock, a granite slab that overhung the valley. It was picturesque and cool there. A constant breeze floated across the mountains and smelled of pine. It was romantic, too, just the two of us and the majesty of nature. I hadn't eaten one half of my tuna salad sandwich when George began to tickle the nape of my neck with his tongue. Before lunch hour was over, I lost my status as technical virgin. It was natural, effortless, painless and somehow expected, as though I'd done it before and with George. Our entire relationship, in fact, seemed as though we'd done it before and although George admitted that, he was reluctant to discuss it. He said it spooked him. At any rate, my deflowering was as swift and without substance as deja vu. George had a hard time believing I was a virgin. To console him, I exhibited a tiny spot of blood that might have come from my hymen or might have come from the abrasions on my fanny caused by sliding around on the rough surface of Kissing Rock. George then grew solicitous with guilt, insisting that he'd hurt me terribly. I think he rather enjoyed the vision of himself as a despoiler of virgins although, so far as I know, I was the only virgin he ever despoiled. His other women friends were of a more sophisticated nature than I'd been.

George wasn't an actor at all, he admitted to me that noon on Kissing Rock. That didn't come as a complete surprise to me. I had been working with him all morning. He was twenty-five, had completed three years of college and two

years at Divinity; he was a fledgling minister awaiting his final
year of schooling and his ordination. George was a seeker,
too. God, who would not allow me to lift a staff and herd His
sheep, had provided me with a shepherd.

Fantasies immediately flashed through my mind: George,
black-frocked behind the pulpit of a tiny wooden chapel set
in the grain fields of rural Kansas, serving up spiritual
sustenance to weary farmers; in the church yard, plump farm
wives shook checkered cloths across picnic tables and
children in overalls and pinafores played tag around the
great oak trees, their tiny New Testaments peeking from their
pockets; and I, the preacher's wife, planned and supervised
all the activity.

George, gleaming in white robes behind the massive altar
of a wealthy city church, its steeples spiraling into the
heavens; behind him, the great brass pipes of a mighty organ
played with soul-shaking fervor by a professional musician; a
fifty-person choir, robed in blue, voices rising in three
perfect parts to please the ear of the Almighty; George's
voice booming through the vast cathedral, soothing the
anxiety-ridden brows of the very rich, deftly diminishing
them so they might pass easily through the proverbial eye of
the needle.

I would write his sermons for him, edit the church
newsletter, hire and fire the music personnel, supervise the
Sunday Schools, promote the church activities, oversee the
Board of Directors, dun the stingy for their tithes. Like a
faithful, well-trained sheepdog, I would snap at the heels of
the parishioners and keep the flock within the safe perimeter.
I would leave my shepherd free to wander among the flock,
his pale hair glowing golden in the sun, beloved inspiration
to all.

In short, George would be the star and I the producer,
playwright, and stage manager, the basic trinity without
which no show gets on the boards.

It was a fluke that George was leading man at Kissing Rock

that summer. He'd been employed by the city of Boston, under the auspices of a federal grant, to serve as lay minister and basketball coach for the Parks Department. Divinity had recommended him for the job. George was a fair-to-middling athlete and enjoyed sports. He'd bought a new pair of hightop basketball shoes for the occasion. George and his sister, Susie, four years younger than he, were tight as ticks. Susie's best girlfriend's boyfriend was an acting student at Harvard. He had been employed by Kissing Rock but two days before he was scheduled to arrive, he received an offer to appear in a revue in New York City. The revue paid real money so the actor accepted this job. Mr. Harris, who had in his possession a signed contract from this actor, threatened to sue.

Meanwhile, George had had a falling out with the Dean of Divinity and the federal government hadn't sent as much funding to the city of Boston as expected. These events combined to render George jobless for the summer at the exact time that this actor was frantically looking for a sucker who'd go to Kissing Rock for twenty dollars a week. The actor sent George's photograph Special Delivery to Mr. Harris. Before Mr. Harris could reply, George was on his way to Kissing Rock.

George had never thought about wanting to be an actor and it certainly wasn't the twenty dollars a week that enticed him to Kissing Rock. George had a difficult relationship with his father, a self-made millionaire whose parents had fled Ireland during the potato famine. George's father pulled himself up by the bootstraps and owned a fleet of trucks which cornered the market on transportation of produce along the east coast. He'd been raised a Catholic but had married a strong-willed and socially prominent Presbyterian girl and had suffered the indignity of being excommunicated when he allowed his children to be baptized outside the Catholic Church. He was shattered when George expressed ambition to be a Protestant minister. He was further shaken that George had grown to be twenty-five years old and had never earned an annual living wage. George would have preferred a firing squad to spending that summer at his father's home in Boston.

George had always felt a calling to the cloth. He confessed he sometimes wept when he heard an entire congregation singing Beulah Land. He harbored a thousand questions in his bosom, just as I did. He, however, had done considerable research on these questions and advanced theories of his own.

He felt he had strong evidence to support the conclusion that Christ and Mohammed were the same man, despite the time gap between their births, a fact which he believed could be explained by calendar changes during the fifth, sixth and eleventh centuries. He expounded this theory in a letter to the Religious Editor at the *Boston herald* and this resulted in a two-page spread, the week before Christmas, in the Sunday edition of the paper. The Editor took a tongue-in-cheek attitude toward George's theory and the article made both George and the Divinity School look silly. George responded by writing an article for the *Boston Globe* which explained the resurrection as the spontaneous recovery of a heat-stroke victim. Nobody ever died, George claimed, from nail wounds. They might die from a resulting infection but that would take several weeks.

George's therory further expounded that vinegar was not the bitter substance we use to season salads, it was the common man's wine; that no less than 53 fellows had claimed to be the Son of God and risen from the dead during that century and that when a prisoner was to be crucified until death, they drove the spikes through the wrist bones, severing the main arteries. This brought George to these conclusions: (1) neither the Romans or the Jews intended Christ to die; (2) he was not entombed for burial but for recovery; and (3) consequently, there was no physical resurrection from a state of death to a state of life; and (4)

Jesus headed south where he was known as Mohammed.

The *Globe* published this article, complete with a photograph of George standing in front of the filigreed gates of Divinity. NEW MINISTERS: PROGRESS OR BLASPHEMY? was the headline.

Bishops berated George and Divinity from their pulpits on Easter Sunday. Telegrams revoking large endowments to Divinity appeared on the President's desk. The Dean had to take his home phone off the hook. He hustled George down to the public television station. George explained to those watching public TV that he didn't feel it blasphemous to explore and question religious doctrine; that religion, after all, was conceived by man and religious experience documented by human scribes. He was not challenging God, he stated, but questioning man's perception of God. The Dean said unequivocally that Divinity did not support or underwrite George's explorations and/or theories.

This was the situation between George and Divinity during that summer at Kissing Rock. George didn't know until late August that he would not be accepted for his final year of training. When he received the letter, he wept. We sat up half the night on Kissing Rock, watching the moon play hopscotch through the pines.

"I don't want to be a trucker."

"You're a fine actor, George, and, after all, the theatre is the pulpit of the people."

"I don't want to be an actor unless I can be a star."

I wasn't crazy about the prospect of starving in a garret, either, but I recognized George's ambition as the harbinger of unhappiness.

I'm very hungry and my stomach is making sounds that are disturbing to Solomon's sleep. He is lying on the first pew and he rolls his head toward me and stares with irritation. If we were lying side by side in a double bed, Solomon would probably be shaking my shoulder the same way I used to shake George's when he snored.

They say exercise reduces one's appetite although I've never found this to be so. I took up jogging because *Family Circle* told me that a well-run mile each morning reduces the jogger's appetite by half. I came back from a three-block run out of breath and ravenous. All the same, I'm going to take a walk around this sanctuary. It may not reduce my appetite but perhaps it will stop the rumbling in my stomach.

The moon is odd tonight. An hour ago she seemed so close and now she looks so far away. She has receded billions of miles into space, speeding away from earth, running away from me. I wonder if she glances back as she runs? Is someone in pursuit? Perhaps she forgot something and is hurrying home to get it, hoping I'll wait for her. Or, like the joggers, does she run because it makes her high with freedom and overcomes her pain?

I should like to run tonight. Run and run until my feet and legs lose feeling and my soul takes flight and scatters.

I adjust this blanket around me so I can walk without tripping on it. Solomon sees the tassels moving and he crouches, gives a shrill mew of warning and attacks them. I expect he'll chase them and me around the periphery of this church.

Oh, Solomon. Are you so young that you abound with energy or so old that you give every action everything you've got? I never had that kind of energy, not even in my childhood. I never in my life leapt from my bed to greet the day. I lifted the edge of my covers, perhaps, and peeked at it, considered it, assessed it and rose by force of will to endure it. Grandma used to pull me out of bed by my big toes. Once, in desperation, she unloaded an ice cube tray on my pillow. I have slept soundly through fire alarms, parades, wake-up services; clock radios are simply background music for my dreams.

Jason slept soundly, too, and he could nod off anywhere at any time. I used to drink half a pot of coffee after dinner. "How can you drink that and sleep?" friends asked. "If I don't drink it," I replied, "I can't stay awake past eight." Jason never liked the taste of coffee but papaya juice had the same effect on him. He drank it all day long and kept a jug of it beside his bed at night. I envisioned the interior of Jason's stomach looking like a honeycomb, thick and dripping with papaya juice.

I have never chortled at the beauty of a sunset or come near to fainting at the scent of newmown grass. Very sweet is too sweet for my tastes and perhaps too beautiful is more than I can comprehend.

As a child, when I proposed a new idea, Grandma said, "If you're so smart why ain't you rich?" Mother said, "Who told you that?" as though all knowledge had to be acquired from others, none from observation. And when we sat on the front porch singing on a summer afternoon, Grandma said, "Just move your lips." Mother said, "Stay on the tune," as though I knew or could help that I was born with a tin ear. It is to the above experiences that I attribute my hesitancy to advance new ideas or sing. Motherhood is a deadly weapon.

Just ask the Jasonites.

TEN

I AM looking at the heavens. I've never seen so many stars before; it seems they've multiplied themselves to please me. The walk around the room worked. I stumbled on a loose board behind the last row of pews and fell. I must have twisted my ankle because it's swelling now and tender to the touch. It has certainly taken my mind off the complaining of my stomach.

At Advent Christian College there were several courses considered "crip"—that is, easy credits requiring not much work. One of these was golf; another fencing; another basket weaving. The most popular of the "crip" courses, however, was star-gazing, listed officially in the college catalogue as Astronomy 101. It was held at eight p.m., after supper, on a dock which jutted into Advent Lake. There, as the professor droned in unison with the mosquitoes, students lay on their backs and stared up at the sky. Some brought flasks and quietly imbibed Seven and Seven, some necked rather heavily. On a number of occasions, it became necessary for the professor to ask who was shaking the dock.

I took Astronomy 101, 102 and Advanced Astronomy 102A and slept quite peacefully through all of them. Docks and boats are the best places for sleeping as they emulate the natural watery motion of the womb.

In Biblical times, the world was believed to be flat and the heavens enclosed it as much as one might cover an ant hill by placing a pyrex mixing bowl upside down over it so one could watch the action underneath and yet imprison and to that extent control the colony. It was thought that if you could walk far enough, you'd reach the place where heaven met the earth.

I hope that God does not regard us like ants. My Grandma had a method of dealing with ants. Every Sunday noon, after she fried chicken, she took the spitting frying pan out to the back yard and poured the boiling grease down anthills. If, from the ant's point of view, Grandma was God, she was as thundering, as terrifying and as vindictive as the God of Abraham.

As Jason described God, I don't think He'd intentionally pour hot fat on us but He might accidentally step on us; Jason's God is so engrossed in thoughts of magnitude that He has no memory of His smaller accomplishments.

I can recognize the dippers because Grandma used to point them out to me. She liked to sit on the front porch of an evening and note whose shades were up and whose were down and whose cars were out and whose were in. When Sputnik blinked its way across the sky above Advent, Georgia, Grandma regarded it with proper awe. Her cousin Ollie had travelled north to see the Wright Brothers' first take-off and had related the experience in detail to all the family. And Grandma had known a boy named Willie Sopers who'd constructed a body kite and flown to his death off Kolawalo Ridge. "But he went a good hundred feet first," Grandma always added, "he flew a hundred feet or more, he did."

"One of these days," Grandma said as she stared up at Sputnik, "we're going to travel to every one of those specks of light." Grandma revered the possibility of space flight as she did the thought of test-tube babies. "Scientists," she'd sigh and cluck her tongue, "can do just anything, I reckon."

Grandma had a gentleman named Mr. Abe. Mr. Abe was ninety but he still had an eye for the ladies. He visited every afternoon unless the weather was too bad to walk two miles to our house and two miles home. Mr. Abe was displeased with the space program. "We got no business up there," he said, "that's God's land, not ours, and we're trespassing. Can't nothing come of it but trouble. God meant us to be up there He'd of built a stairway."

Mr. Abe blamed every summer storm on the space program and when the hurricane of 1959 swept over Georgia, he wrote letters to Washington warning the President and Congress that we were courting doom. Mr. Abe's protests fell on deaf ears, both in Washington and in our house. Grandma had no patience with those who would impede progress. The Good Old Days, she said, weren't good a bit. She hoped to live to see the day that she could take a vacation to the moon instead of going to visit her sister Louellen in Mississippi. Grandma lived a good long time but not quite long enough.

I mentioned to Jason once that there was a man on Krypton who sent his son to earth in a capsule for the purpose of showing mankind the path to righteousness and brotherhood. Jason responded with a blank stare. He had no idea who Superman was. Jason didn't read and didn't like to look at pictures, either.

Grandma lived long enough to see my marriage to George begin and end. She had no use for play-acting and never attended moving pictures because the situations and the characters caused her to laugh or cry or care about them and she said this was immoral and dishonest because it wasn't real. She didn't have tears to waste on made-up people. She was a faithful fan, however, of Liberace and Gary Moore and talked back to their images on the TV. They were just folks being themselves; they weren't trying to put one over on her.

Grandma looked askance at George and he sensed it. I spoke to her about it. "Well," she said without looking up from the fritters she was frying, "everybody to their own tastes said the man when he kissed the pig. Ain't no skin off my nose."

Grandmothers, unlike mothers, know when to wash their hands of you.

My mother didn't approve of George, either, but she never would admit it. The one time that we visited Advent, George and I, Mother took him by the hand down to Advent Bank & Trust and introduced him to the personnel director. "Just in case," she said to me as though we were conspirators, "he matures and wants a real job. Oh, I wish the two of you would move down here. A fine boy like that with a college education could get to be the President of that bank. You all could qualify for membership at Greenlawn Country Club."

Grandma lived long enough to see Jason, too. When he was small, I took him down there several times to visit. Grandma'd look and him and shake her head. "If there is a heaven, you'll have a place in it for taking this little chinaman into your home." Jason, of course, was Korean and I reiterated this many times to Grandma, pointing out articles in the papers about the thousands of children made homeless by the Korean conflict. Grandma nodded and never stopped referring to him as the little chinaman.

My mother was dismayed and disoriented by Jason. Pudgy and definitely oriental in appearance, he did not fit her expectations of a grandbaby. he was not cute, rarely did an amusing thing and didn't speak. She made two or three attempts to bounce him on her knee but he fixed her with that ebony stare and she quickly put him back into the playpen. "I hate to say this, Josie," she whispered to me, "but

I don't think that child is all there." She tapped her forehead with one finger. "As if," she sighed and regarded Jason with pained eyes, "life isn't hard enough."

Since the postal service has been discontinued and the cross-country phone wires have fallen into disrepair, I haven't heard from Mother. In my last correspondence with her, I confessed that Jason, the professed Son of God, was her grandchild. She responded with a plea that I deny that to the news media. "I've got to live in this town."

Her attitude may have changed by now. Jasonites are everywhere, including Advent, Georgia. My mother generally allies herself with the winning side.

Solomon has found a plaything. It appears to be the top of a cut glass decanter and is shaped like a teardrop. He is batting it from side to side and the noise is shattering.

"Solomon, enough!"

He says he needs the exercise.

"Go catch a mouse."

"There are none," he answers. "I ate all the potential mommies."

"That was a stupid thing to do."

"I wasn't thinking," Solomon shrugs and swats the teardrop down the center aisle. It clatters as though a crate of bottles are being shaken. Before he chases it, he looks at me and admits wistfully, "They were all over the place— sometimes I ate so many that I threw up—who knew there'd ever be an end to them?—Oh, well." He sighs and sprints toward the back of the church.

Now he hits the teardrop with such force that it ricochets from pew to pew.

"Solomon, dammit! I'm starving, my ankle is swelling and you're giving me a headache."

I just stood up and tried to navigate the aisle. My intention was to seize that teardrop and place it out of Solomon's playful reach. My ankle will barely support my weight and throbs terribly. I can flex it, though, so I don't think that it's broken. When Solomon saw me get up, he swatted the teardrop with a hard right and it flew about the pews and hit the Judas window. There was a sudden sound of broken glass and I cringed and closed my eyes, fearing that the stained glass had shattered on the sleeping Jasonites outside. But there was silence. When I opened my eyes, I saw that the window hadn't broken but Solomon's plaything had. It now looks like a pile of uncut diamonds under Judas' feet. Solomon leapt to the sill, inspected the debris and turned his nose up at it. He is sitting at my feet now, carefully cleaning the splinters from his paws.

"Just sit still," I order him. "You have too much energy."

"It's in my nature," he replies. "I'm male."

"That," I snap back, "is a chauvinistic thing to say."

There may, however, be some truth in it. George got up every day at dawn and took a run around the park. He liked to work out at the gym, he played softball every day, weather permitting, with the Actors' League. Late afternoons, he'd drop by Prince Street for a game of bocce with the elderly Italian men and after supper he liked to go to the corner bar to throw darts with the fellows. He usually stayed up to watch the Late, Late Show and slept no more than four or five hours a night. Living with him was exhausting.

I didn't exactly lie around all day myself. In the mornings, both George and I "made the rounds", leaving our pictures and resumes with agents and standing in long lines at "open calls" where actors are called onto the stage to state their names and a voice from the dark auditorium says "Sorry, wrong type, next."

Actors gamble on a blue moon. The stakes are high and actors are by nature mystical beings who want to believe in good luck charms. You'd think they'd have been among the first to follow Jason but, in fact, Equity and SAG, the actors' unions, fought Jason in the battle of 44th Street. The actors held Restaurant Row and Shubert Alley for 72 hours, singing George M. Cohan songs and tap-dancing on the curbs. "Our talent will protect us from serenity," they said. The Theatre District fell to Jason when, near the close of the third day, a dance captain stationed beneath the canopy at Joe Allen's, leading his ensemble in a chorus of She's A Grand Old Flag, broke suddenly into Jesus Loves Me in three quarter time. Serenity is insidious.

George and I had to struggle for a living. George was handy and picked up some part-time work as an assistant carpenter. I worked two or three days every week as a typist through an agency called Skeeter's Girls. Skeeter's Girls never met Skeeter—our assignments were telephoned to us on Monday mornings and our checks arrived by mail at the end of every week.

As a Skeeter's Girl, I had many assignments. I typed shooting scripts for porno movies in the days when leading men wore black socks. I typed the transcripts of psychiatric sessions with a man who subsequently became known as the Manhattan Bomber.

Temporary typing is not the worst way in the world to earn a living. It only has two bad points: (1) it pays poorly; and (2) employers treat their typists with irreverence. Typists are the most underrated professionals in the work world. A good typist, like a surgeon, has a natural talent, superior manual dexterity, a faultless sense of rhythm. a rare ability to split her attention in five different directions. She must have a comprehensive knowledge of the language, its use and structure. A good typist knows her machine the way a racer knows his car.

Typists are generally shes because males have not discovered yet that typing is an art form. If all the typists in the world stopped typing and men had to confront the machinery themselves, typing would quickly become a highly-paid profession and every corporate board would include a Vice President in charge of Typing.

We consider machinery inanimate, although we know that cars, refrigerators, coffee pots, toasters and typewriters have distinct and individual personalities. Jason said all things are living and when we reorder natural substances such as reducing fossil fuel with additives and adding hardeners and coming out with plastic, we are only fusing several different life forms, much in the same way that the mating of a man and woman produces a third form of life.

I've typed too many years to question whether a sulky Smith-Corona, a giggly Royal or a pompous and bullheaded IBM Selectric is a figment of my imagination.

George and I spent two years living in a fourth floor walkup railroad flat in Greenwich Village. It was a wonderful apartment, the rooms were tall as they were wide. The doors and windows were charmingly cocked at opposing angles and the floor slanted to the north. It was rent-controlled and partly furnished; it came with bed, chairs and table—we scavenged the rest, lugging a battered sofa from the gutter beside the garbage cans and covering it with a bedspread and pillows from the Salvation Army; painting orange crates white enamel and using them for bookshelves and end tables; rescuing a chest of drawers with broken legs from an abandoned lot, painting it lavender—and propping it up on bricks.

In the bedroom and living room of the apartment, there were fireplaces which hadn't been used for a decade. George, coming from New England, knew something about fireplaces and took a curtain rod and poked fifty pounds of soot out of the chimney. When we lit our first fire, all the lights went out in the apartment. Upon investiation with a flashlight, we discovered that some previous tenant had installed an extra wall outlet in the living room and had run the wire through the fireplace in order to do so. He'd then fastidiously covered the wire with mortar so it would blend invisibly into the bricks. We sat in the dark until the fire burned itself out, then George put the ashes in a coffee can and proceeded to chip away the mortar and remove the wiring. We ended up with one less wall outlet but we had a working fireplace that was the envy of our friends.

From the bedroom, we had a view of an air shaft and the bottom part of Dorothy Londerman's kitchen window. Dorothy was a ballerina currently employed as a stripper. From our living room, we viewed Mrs. Leonetti's laundry fluttering on the line beyond the fire escape. I loved the apartment passionately. It was everything I dreamed a starving actor's pad should be. George was embarrassed by it. He avoided inviting his sister to visit us.

At ten p.m. every night, the Village streets began to rattle like a hot teakettle. The air turned sweet with pot and sharp with the aroma of espresso. Traffic circled slowly looking for parking places and mellow music drifted out of windows. Musicians played their compositions on fire escapes, their new notes wallowing in the cherry wood of their guitars before sifting through the cat gut strings. Snatches of drama came from radios sitting near apartment windows. The Village air at night was blue and smoky, thick with car exhausts, marijuana, Pall Malls and the simmering of our social revolution which seemed to emanate a soft aura of its own.

There were coffee houses, two or three to every block, dark, lit by candles and the glow of cigarettes, tiny flames mirrored and flickering in the chrome coffee urns, fertile as a womb. Poets and playwrights, singers and comedians called the coffee houses home.

I produced two of my one-act plays at the Cafe Expresso and after each performance I passed a hat among the audience. George picked up extra money reading poetry Saturday nights in a coffee house called Boo! which had been rigged to look like a haunted castle. When you stepped on certain floorboards, a spring released a stuffed bat that swooped wildly across the room, flogging customers and sending cappucino cups crashing to the floor. It was part of the atmosphere but the tourists coming in protested that the bat was spilling coffee on their suits. The menu was woven into macrame cobwebs around the corners of the room and the stage was a trucker's skid, set off in a corner, illuminated by a single worklight. Poets were encouraged to drop in and let George read their work aloud. George's voice was large and powerful. He read so beautifully that even badly written stuff sent a chill up your spine.

George and I had dreams.

"Everybody had dreams," Solomon interrupts. "I dreamed I'd catch a snake. I knew just how I'd catch it, too, and what I'd do with it. I practiced creeping up on it and pouncing until I could make the movements in my sleep. I would have been a good snake catcher. The best."

"But?"

Solomon moans and rolls onto his back as though holding an aching tummy. After I've rubbed his stomach with sufficient sympathy, he says, "But I never saw a snake."

"You never saw one?"

"Nope," Solomon sighs. "A snake never came my way."

ELEVEN

WOULD the Jasonites execute a woman with a broken ankle? I hope they don't ask me to stand before a firing squad because I can't. If they hang me, at least it will take the load off my feet.

"Just a touch of gallows humor, Solomon. I'm in a lot of trouble if I can't see the funny side.

"You're in a lot of trouble, anyway."

I sit here hour after hour watching the stars tiptoe across the sky and I scribble page after page in this old book. What if someone finds this and can't make out my writing? They could mistranslate something like "Jason's willing" to "Jason's killing" or "sex is irrelevent" to "sex is irreverent." I'll be more cautious, dot my i's, cross my t's and print words which might be mistaken. Goodness, writing takes a lot of concentration.

"Huh," scoffs Solomon, "I had a cousin travelled cross-country once, the people that tomcat didn't meet, what a bunch of weirdos, and the experiences—talk about interesting. I could write a book."

"It isn't easy, Solomon."

"It's easier than catching a mouse." He turns his nose up at me.

I fling the pen to the page. Solomon sniffs grandly and raises his tail.

I wag my finger at him. "You're illiterate."

"I have found more sophisticated means of communicating."

"You sound like a Jasonite."

He smiles a secret little smile.

"Solomon, are you a Jasonite?"

He turns his head and moves away from me.

"Solomon, are you one of them? Oh, no, Solomon, you can't be. You're the only friend I have left."

He turns suddenly, an impish look in his eyes, and springs into my lap. He strokes the underside of my chin with his head. I think he loves me but he's not one to talk about it. Solomon's a macho man. So was George. He never told me that he loved me, even when he notified me that we were getting married.

"No fuss now," he grumbled, "I don't want a big thing made out of this." He'd just been kicked out of Divinity and he wasn't in any mood for a church wedding. We were married in Advent by a Justice of the Peace, the same fellow who joined my mother and father in holy matrimony. The service was held in the same room. It was still painted industrial green with wilted white netting tacked around the edges of an altar to provide a festive touch.

George's father stated firmly that unless George returned to Boston and set his mind to making money, the family was washing their hands of him. George's mother wrote secret notes to him and sent him a twenty dollar bill on his birthday. George's sister maintained an active correspondence with him in direct defiance of her father. George didn't invite any of them to our wedding. He didn't tell them that he'd married me until his sister came to visit, uninvited, and saw me for herself. She thought George deserved better and I overheard her tell him so. To George's credit, he told her that he loved me. He just never told me.

I've been married to George for twenty-five years although we only lived together two of them and apart from glimpsing him on commercials on TV, I haven't seen him in twenty. I never met my in-laws. Boston hardly exists anymore. Fenway Park was one of the first Jasonite strongholds. They took it peaceably during the third game of the World Series. The Sox were losing, the fans were glum, slumping apathetically in the stands as the fourth inning got underway. The Jasonites slipped quietly through the parking lot and locker rooms onto the field, circled the diamond and lifted their hands and eyes in the classic gesture of surrender. The pitcher ceased winding up his fast ball and the batter sank slowly to his knees. Within seconds, serenity descended over Fenway Park.

Even though George never said he loved me, he was possessive and protective. When we went to a bar, he insisted that I sit next to a vacant stool. When I was working in a play, he called for me every night and escorted me home on the subway. We gave a reunion party for the Kissing Rock company in our New York apartment and, under the influence of cheap red wine, I flirted outrageously with Joey Thrasher. Joey had been the prop man at Kissing Rock but when he came to New York, he went to an open call and got a part on Broadway. It was a blue moon kind of thing, attributable to beginner's luck or to the Peter Principle, but it had a strong effect on George who had also stood in line at that same open call and hadn't even been asked to read. Joey had no talent and winning ways, a combination that enabled him to slide from Broadway part to Broadway part for a number of years until his boyish beauty began to fade.

"I can accept," George said, "that God doesn't like me but damned if I can believe that Joey Thrasher is His favorite."

My flirtation with Joey Thrasher was especially hurtful to George. He snatched me out of Joey's arms and, in front of all the guests, slapped me across the face with such force that it resounded the length of the apartment. Then George bellowed and ran into the bathroom and slammed the door. The guests cowered nervously. A whisper ran like the crinkling of paper and they began to nudge each other toward the door in an effort to effect an inconspicuous exit. My left cheek turned brilliant red and pulsed so strongly that I felt it blinking at the guests as I let them out the door. I could hear snorting in the bathroom and while it may have sounded like the ranting of an enraged bull to others, I knew it was the noise George made when he wept.

He was sitting on the floor beside the toilet, his forehead resting on the seat. His shoulders heaved so violently that his torso flailed between the bathtub and the bowl. I sat on the lid and pulled his head against my belly. He cried until his sideburns and the collar of his shirt were soaking wet. He locked his arms so tightly around my hips that I began to lose feeling in my legs.

"I never hurt a fly," he said when he could speak. "Never. Not in my whole life."

"I know." I blotted his face with a towel.

"Did I break anything?" He peeked quickly at my cheek and winced. "Oh Great God Almighty."

"It's just a bruise."

"Your jaw's not broken?"

"I don't think so."

"Wiggle it."

I did and it made a funny little crack.

"It's broken! I fucking broke your jaw!" George wailed again, rose to his knees between my legs and seized my face with both hands.

"Ow!"

George dropped his hands and tears rolled down his cheeks. "See? I broke it! I broke it, didn't I?"

I wiggled it again. "It's bruised, that's all."

"I better take you to the hospital."

"No!" I became dead weight when George tried to pull me up.

"Will they put me in jail?"

"I don't want to go to the hospital," I screamed. "People die in New York hospitals!"

George sighed and squatted in front of me. "Okay,' he said, "we can put some iodine on it."

"The skin's not broken."

"Some kind of salve, we must have some kind of salve." He rose and hunched over me, rummaging in the medicine cabinet above the toilet. A bottle of rubbing alcohol toppled out and grazed my shoulder before it skidded to the floor.

"Oh my God, what did I do now?"

"It's all right, George," I assured him. "The bottle didn't even break."

"I broke your shoulder!"

"No, you didn't!" I wrenched away from his fingers which were probing at my collarbone.

"You sure?"

"George! Stop pummeling my shoulder blades!"

"I want to make sure nothing broke," he said lurching toward the bathtub. "Cold packs, that's it. We'll put cold backs on that cheek." He turned the bathtub faucet on full force. "I'll soak a bathcloth and you hold it on your face, how's that?

"I never hurt a fly, you know."

"I know, honey." ·

"I'll kill that little son of a bitch if he comes sniffing around you again." George squeezed out the bathcloth with a vengeance.

"We won't invite him."

"I hope I see him at that open call tomorrow. I'll kick his ass between his ears."

"I don't even like him, George."

"How would you feel if Beverly got a leading role on Broadway?"

"Pretty pissed off." I could see George approaching my face with the compress and I flinched.

"Hold still." He pressed it to my cheek.

"Aiiiyah! Not so hard, George, it's sore."

"And what if I was kissing Beverly on the neck?"

"I wasn't kissing Joey on the neck!"

"Well, rubbing crotches with her, then. That's what you were doing. How would you like it if Beverly had a part on Broadway and you didn't and I rubbed crotches with her in our living room?"

"You're pressing too hard, George!" I peeled his fingers from my face.

"Wouldn't like me rubbing crotches with Beverly, would you?"

"No, I wouldn't! Karen wouldn't like it, either."

George knelt on the floor and giggled. "Remember how I set Beverly up with that salesman?" This memory struck George as outrageously funny and he hung his head over the bathtub, laughing. It caused an eerie echo in the room, like a pack of teenage boys goosing one another in the ribs.

"You stuck your nose in where it didn't belong, George," I snapped. "What God has joined together, let no man set asunder."

"God," George boomed into the bathtub, "didn't join you and Joey Thrasher!"

"I was talking about Beverly and Karen."

"God joined us," George bellowed, "You and me!"

"George, take your head out of the bathtub. It makes everything you say sound like the Final Judgment."

"Let's have a baby," he shouted to the porcelain.

"Are you kidding, George?"

"Why not?" *not, not, not* bounced off the walls.

"We can't support ourselves!"

"God dammit," George screamed, lifting his head at last.

"I suppose you're thinking that Joey Thrasher could support a wife and baby. Is that what you're thinking?"

"It never crossed my mind."

"Well, he could support a wife and baby, couldn't he? Couldn't he?" George came nose to nose with me as though I had some secret information and he was going to bully it out of me.

"I suppose so."

"Well, then," George yelled and smashed his fist against the door jamb, "get the hell out of my apartment and go live with Joey Thrasher!"

"George, stop beating your fist on the door, you'll break a finger."

"Go on," he groaned, "leave me. Joey Thrasher can affort to support you."

"George." I grabbed his fist and stopped him from making the swing. "George, are you listening to me? I love you."

"You're a fucking nymphomaniac."

"That's redundant."

George sniffed. "You never think about anything else. Groping Joey Thrasher!"

"I never groped Joey Thrasher," I replied defensively. "I thighed him. George, let go of my foot please. You're crushing my toes."

"Every night!" George stood and pressed his pants legs with the palms of his hands. "You want it every night."

"Ha! Ha, ha. Once a week is more like it."

"Well, once a week ought to be sufficient. I'm trying to build a career."

"You play softball every day," I nagged.

"That's relaxing." George creased his pants between his thumb and index finger.

"So is sex." This subject was a sensitive topic of discussion.

"That's easy enough for you to say. All you have to do is lie there." George attempted to exit the bathroom but I gripped his hip pocket and held onto it.

"I wouldn't just lie there, George, if you'd let me do anything else. You're addicted to the goddam missionary position."

"It was good enough for my father."

"How do you know?"

"Well, it's the only one he told me about. Let go of my pants. You're going to rip my pocket. Money doesn't grow on trees, you know."

"Your father expected you to show some initiative. Be creative."

"Creative? Creative!" George spun and flattened himself against the door, wild-eyed. "I am creative. I'm an actor! You think I'm not creative because I can't get work. You think I can't get work because I'm not good enough. You think because you've gotten a couple of acting jobs and I haven't gotten any, you're more talented than I am. Well, it's not true and don't you ever say it again!"

"I never said it, George."

"You don't believe I can make any money!" George wailed.

I tried to calm him. "You make more as a carpenter than I do as typist."

"I don't want to be carpenter! I want to be a preacher."

"The theatre, George, is the pulpit of the people."

George lifted his lip and snarled. "If you ever say that to me again, Josie, I swear to God I'll belt you."

"You already belted me, George." I pointed at my cheek which had turned from bright red to pale blue. George moaned. He took the wet washcloth from me and freshened it with cold water. "Here," he said, and placed it tenderly against my cheek, "does it feel any better?"

"A little," I lied.

"I never hurt a fly, you know."

"I know."

"Josie?" He looked into my eyes. We saw directly into one

another's souls. You might think that the inside of someone's soul would be a dark place but George's was as brightly lit as a bathroom in the middle of the night. I squinted against the glare of it. I could hear a helpless cry, too, as though something small and innocent was struggling for life against a mighty force. It put me in mind of the time Grandma flushed a baby bird down the toilet because, once touched by human hands, the mother wouldn't take it back. George's soul was swirling in the water.

Before Jason pulled the plug on the power companies, when electricity was abundant, there was a movement to freeze human beings and to defrost them at some future time. This was a particularly exciting concept to writers and artists.

Even if freezing people had come to pass, I don't think it would have resolved George's pain or mine. We needed to go back in time, not forward; to somersault backward like children do in the dry brown grass of mid-summer when they are bursting with good spirits and their grandmother has told them if they run in and out the kitchen and slam the screen door one more time they're going to get the licking of their lives. Perhaps if George and I had lived during the 16th Century, we might have been the scholars who researched and rewrote the Bible, sitting year after year at trestle tables, translating myths from Greek, Roman and Hebrew, tapping our toes against the lower rungs of our stools with the excitement of new possibilities. We might have changed the future of the world.

I would have, for instance, steadfastly maintained that Lillith be retained in the text—headstrong, defiant Lillith, God's first woman, created of the same clay as Adam (and not from any rib) and given life at the same moment. She had no patience with Adam's insecurities and bumblings; she stamped her foot and demanded that God provide answers to her questions and when He begged for silence she stomped out of the garden and went about the business of living on her own. If I'd been a writer of the Bible, I would have given Lillith the leading role.

The King James version of the Bible was produced by a handful of scribes in the employ of the Church of England. If the Bible had been due for rewrite in the 20th Century, it probably would have been done by students from Divinity employed under CETA grants. George might have even had a hand in it. He could have changed the course of history.

"No," Jason said, "you cannot alter the course of the world. You can only alter you. That is the only assignment God has given you: to find Her in yourself." Jason frequently confused his pronouns, gender being a human designation, not a divine division.

That night in the bathroom, after George had slapped me and we'd argued and I'd looked directly into George's soul, I put my arms around him tightly.

He nibbled at my ear lobe. "You know, Josie," he said, "I really think we ought to have a baby."

When he breathed directly into my ear like that, it gave me goosebumps.

"Something's missing from our lives," he whispered, "and I bet that's it."

I inserted my diaphragm carefully that night, checking the circumference with my finger and lathering the edges with jelly so George's sperm couldn't slither underneath the piping.

Solomon says that I'm unnatural. Everybody wants a baby. He would like to have a squirming pile of kittens himself so long as he had a mate with strong maternal instincts who would feed them, discipline them and clean them up. He would like to roll them over on their backs and play with them. When they grew big enough, he'd take them to the basement and teach them to hunt mice.

"That would," says Solomon, "make me feel as though I'd accomplished something in this life."

"Solomon," I remind him, "this church is damp and

cold—and you said yourself there are no mice left. A female cat, giving birth under these conditions, would probably devour the litter."

"It's been my observation," Solomon snapped sarcastically, "that females are sadly lacking in a sense of the romantic. There was a female who lived down the road always but I clawed her so passionately during our last encounter that she fled into the woods and has never returned. If emotions can be compared to a full half circle, a male swings from one extreme to the other. Females are limited to the middle of the curve."

With this staetment, Solomon turned up his nose at me and stalked haughtily into the vestry. He has turned his back to me but he knows full well I'm watching him.

"Solomon, if it were you who carried and gave birth to little lives you couldn't feed, would you think it romantic to watch them struggling to survive, to see them grow up deformed or die in their sleep?"

"It wouldn't be like that," Solomon growls, still not looking at me.

If I'd had a child, I certainly would have wanted George to be the father. But with his soul locked in the bathroom screaming and mine as yet unidentified, it seemed to me a poor time. George, however, became obsessed with the thought that motherhood would be the making of me and that the one great gift that he could give me was a baby of my own. Our sex life picked up considerably and I carried the diaphragm in its royal blue cardboard box from room to room in the apartment as though it were a pack of cigarettes.

Ultimately, George had his way. It was George who was responsible for foisting Jason on me. That's how I saw it at the beginning: a homeless infant had been foisted on me and blew my future plans out of the water. George and I had been living apart for some time then.

Solomon is curled up like a fetus against my belly.

A group of men cannot survive for any time at all without

women. Armies have their whores, Monks their cooks and cleaning girls, even faggots have to have their fag-hags. Whereas communities of women can and have lived quite self-sufficiently—Amazons and nunneries and the Isle of Lesbos.

"Bullshit," says Solomon. "You told me Jason said we were once one gender but God busted us in half so we'd need each other."

Well, I think haughtily, females got the best half.

"Ut-uh," Solomon argues, "males did. We're bigger, tougher and we're logical."

I've outwitted him. "But Solomon," I croon, "you know what Jason said about logic. It's a barrier between ourselves and God."

"Shut up, woman." Solomon presses his cold nose against my belly button. "Shut up and pet me."

I love to pet him. It comforts me as much as it does him. But it doesn't free either of our souls.

If the jagged edge of me had interlocked with the jagged edge of George and we'd fitted perfectly into a single piece, what a grand force we two might have become. But the qualities George revered most in himself were the very ones I found disgusting and George perceived my native talents as defects of character.

"In other words," asks Solomon, "you loved him despite his maleness."

"Yes," I reply, although the thought has not occurred to me before, not exactly that way. "And," I add, "he loved me despite, too."

"Weird," Solomon states. "Very weird. No wonder human marriages don't work."

Jason never took a stand in the battle of the sexes. "It's irrelevant to God," he said.

At one time, equality was an important issue to me. I was battling for equal pay in the Newsroom of Channel 3. Lucy Dobdaughter had organized the female employees in a stationwide job action. I could scarcely support myself and Jason on my salary and David Ledbetter who did the same work I did, in less quantity and with less quality, was taking home a third again what I made. I gritted my teeth, swallowed my personal grievances and joined forces with Lucy for the first and last time.

Every woman in the station slowed down, unanswered correspondence and untyped scripts were piled on, beside and under desks, on chairs and in the hallways. The Station Manager became wild-eyed and called Lucy into his office to negotiate.

Lucy emerged with her fist raised in the air, declaring victory. From that day on, she said, each of us would find an additional $10 in our pay. What Lucy didn't tell us but Martha, the chief gossip in Accounting, did was that as part and parcel of her negotiation, she'd doubled her own salary. Lucy was not defensive when confronted about this. She hoisted herself up on the nearest two drawer filing cabinet and sneered down on us.

At one point, when being gay was chic and being a lesbian was the *in* feminist thing to do, Lucy announced to one and all that she was a dyke and wore a lavender lapel pin that said PROUD DAUGHTER OF SAPPHO. Lucy was a political lesbian, a term describing someone who couldn't bear to make it with a man because her feminist ire was so intense she had an uncontrollable desire to chew testicles. It had nothing whatsoever to do with sexual orientation; something like being white and middle class while writing letters in support of civil rights for blacks, or a WASP who marches in Zionist rallies. The danger is vicarious and no personal commitment is required.

Lucy is fond of saying that if she'd been born a man, she would have been elected President. I expect that's true and that fact alone should suffice to illustrate what a devious flesh-eater Lucy Dobdaughter is.

Even in his sleep, Solomon smiles smugly.

"Don't get cocky." I shake him and he lifts his lip at me, half in threat and half in yawn. "There are more flesheaters among men than women. This may be a learned condition, however, not a congenital defect."

"He who gets a head start in the race is generally the winner," Solomon advises me.

I consider this a moment. "But Solomon, what are we racing for?"

"We're racing to see who's going to win. It's the thrill of the sport, the flush of winning. Winner is singular."

"Then it must be very lonely."

"Yes," Solomon admits, "it is."

Jason always said a Seeker has to come alone. "God isn't into groups."

Maybe that's what went wrong with George and me. We were both Seekers and of all the things we were competitive about, we were most competitive about making personal contact with Whatever's Out There.

"I think I had a religious experience today," he'd say when he returned from a full day of standing in line at open calls. "I was standing under a neon sign that said HAPPY'S RESTAURANT. The apostrophe and S were out in HAPPY'S and everything was out in RESTAURANT except the first R and the U. A workman was up on a ladder trying to fix it and he yelled, "Hey, Mister, watch your head!" A styrofoam cup of coffee landed by my feet and splattered on my saddle shoes. I looked up furious, and couldn't see the workman; he was obliterated by the glare of sun. What I saw was the neon sign flashing at me, double-time, HAPPY R U, HAPPY R U, HAPPY R U? Josie, what do you think that means?"

"You want spaghetti or a TV dinner?"

"God was asking me a question."

"There's one beer left in the bottom of the fridge."

"Do you suppose it's true that God helps him who helps himself? Why'd you buy this Cornish Hen?" He took out the frozen bird and shook it at me. "You could have bought ten macaroni dinners for what this cost."

"I found five dollars on the subway."

"What?"

"I wanted to stuff a hen for Sunday dinner. I've been tasting it all week. I sat down on the subway and the train lurched forward. Everybody piled on top of one another. And when the train started up again, there was five dollars lying by my foot."

"That wasn't God's doing," George growled, "it was just a dumb piece of luck."

"You don't know that for sure, George."

"Why would God speak to you and not to me? I'm the one who's trained to be a minister."

George got an acting job off-Broadway in a show that lasted seven weeks but, even working, he was not happy as an actor. I encouraged him to apply to other schools and finish his religious training.

"Divinity's the best," he said, "my reputation will have preceded me."

"Hogwash," I answered, and sent off letters requesting applications. I did convince him to fill them out although it took a full Monday night to do so.

"I can't stand it if they turn me down," he cried, "Josie, it'll kill me. Don't mail them, please!"

But I did. I watched the mail every day and intercepted the responses before George saw them. Whether it was because George's reputation had indeed preceded him or whether because the schools were truly overcrowded or because George, no longer a full-time student, had been reclassified by the Selective Service as 1-A, I don't know. Every one of them said No. I told Geroge that I'd never mailed the letters.

George got good notices when he opened in the play. "A sterling performance by a newcomer"—"a handsome Irish lad who's making his debut off-Broadway"—"a real comer, this boy may become a star."

"Oh, boy," George chortled when the papers came out, flailing them above his head and whacking the tin ceiling in our kitchen, "I wish to hell you had mailed those applications, Josie. I'd just write the bastards back and tell them they can shove their schools. I'm going to be Marlon Brando by next year."

George got an agent and a number of auditions on the basis of those reviews. Two months without getting work and the agent who'd been submitting him stopped calling. When George called her, she was always out to lunch.

He'd sent out forty-two pictures and resumes with covering letters and xeroxed reviews to summer stock theatres. Two replied. Kissing Rock. And Mountain Pass Theatre in Arizona. Mountain Pass was rated Z by Actors' Equity, the bottom of the barrel. Kissing Rock wasn't rated at all. Mountain Pass paid a salary of $125.00 a week, out of which the actor had to pay for his own room and board. That was $105.00 more than Kissing Rock was paying and George accepted.

I was, by then, in an off-Broadway play myself. It promised to run through the summer and so I'd be staying in the city. I had a small part in this play and it didn't stretch me creatively but it was a regular paycheck.

George answered an ad which appeared in Small Businesses You Can Start At Home, a bi-monthly newsletter to which we subscribed in hopes of uncovering some method of supplementing our income, but stuffing teddy bears or casting plastic flowers didn't turn us on and required capital investment.

The ad that George answered didn't have to do with business, however. It was a small block ad in the very back part of the book and it said BE A MINISTER, START YOUR OWN CHURCH, BE TAX EXEMPT. It claimed they could ordain you for $25.00 George sent the money and received a certificate in the mail which stated he was an ordained Minister of _____ Church (an accompanying note told him to fill in the blank with the name he'd chosen for his church) and the certificate, suitable for framing.

George was disgusted by the certificate and at the same time, wistful. He stroked it and cursed it and petted it and hurled it finally into the fireplace although he didn't light the fire. I later found it under his underwear in the top bureau drawer and when George left, the certificate went with him.

Things weren't going well with us. We were like two people on an airplane, mid-flight, each of whom has the distinct sensation that something has gone awry in the right engine but, without proof and having no faith in our instincts, we don't speak of it for fear we'll frighten the other one and/or be regarded as hysterical.

We were impassively miserable, capriciously dissatisfied, yet as dependent on one another as Siamese Twins. I began to thunder when I walked, just like my mother. George blustered like his father.

"If I hadn't married you," he said, "I could have gone to work for Daddy and inherited a multi-million dollar trucking company."

"If I hadn't married you," I retorted, "I could have returned to Hollywood and been an agent or a gossip columnist."

"If we had a baby, I could justify this marriage."

"A baby of ours would grow up crazy as a loon."

"Only if he inherited your father's genes."

"We can't afford for you to see a dentist. You go through life sucking on a clove."

"The baby won't have teeth the first year."

"You can get scurvy from eating nothing but Popeye Noodles. We may have it ourselves right now."

George smiled broadly. "I poked holes in your diaphragm."

"You what?" Panic seized me in its sweaty fist.

"Yep. With a fork."

"Oh God. Oh George. Oh no."

My period was late that month. I didn't tell George.

George's sister Susie was graduating from Vassar and invited George to attend the ceremony despite the fact that their father had declared if George came, he wouldn't. While George was gone, I made strenuous efforts to bring on my period. I ran up and down the four flights of our apartment building until Dorothy, the ballet dancer on the fifth floor, peered out her door.

"I thought there was a robbery," she said.

"I think I'm pregnant," I replied.

"Oh, that's nothing to worry about," Dorothy shrugged. "Happens all the time to the belly dancers where I work nights. I've got a jar of douche made up and sitting in the fridge."

It smelled like grapefruit juice and honey. I had to use soapsuds and a loofa sponge to get it off the inside of my thighs.

"Now go downstairs," she ordered, "and take a bath so hot it burns your fanny."

I did but nothing happened. I reported this to Dorothy.

"Oh dear," she sighed. "We'll have to progress to something stronger."

From the back of her closet, behind the shoes, she retrieved a ceramic crock.

"Jesus," I cried, "it smells like rotten apples."

"Lemons. And some herbs and spices. That's why I keep it in the closet."

"Is it going to kill me?"

"It would if you drank it," she assured me. "You can't get food poisoning of the vagina. Believe me, honey, if there's anything trying to live in your womb, this'll drive it right out."

Then I took another hot bath, this time with the juice of ten limes in the water.

Still no results.

Next Dorothy prescribed a massive dose of castor oil. And after that had done its work, she made me drink a glass of something which appeared to be milk but tasted like chalk and caused me to vomit violently for fifteen minutes.

"That's a stubborn little bugger you got in there," she yawned. "I'm going to make an appointment for you to see Helpful Hopkins. He's an orderly at St. Vincent's and he's got real medical instruments. There's a girl I work with, Uppin Adam, her mother does it, too, but she uses a coat hanger."

"How much," I wept, "is Helpful Hopkins?"

"Two hundred dollars."

George and I had $54.30 in our joint checking and the rent was coming due next week.

I wailed.

"Oh, do what I do," Dorothy advised casually, "go to Actors' Equity and tell them your father died. They make emergency loans without collateral. I've killed off nearly every member of my family since I came to New York."

I slept in a hot bathtub that night and practiced a hundred different versions of the speech I was going to make to George.

"This is my body," I was going to say, "and I have a right to do with it as I wish." And/or

"And what if this marriage doesn't work out, who's going to get stuck with the baby?" And/or

"The world is on the brink of self-destruction and I can't justify bringing a new life into it." And/or

"I have no maternal instincts."

"It's going to hurt."

"It'll stretch my stomach."

"My breasts will sag."

"Suppose it's deformed?"

"The crying will drive you crazy, you can't sleep if a faucet's dripping."

"Who's going to change the diapers?"

"I'm not ready, George. I'm not grown up myself yet."

"George, don't do this to me!"

By dawn, I'd decided not to mention it to George at all.

Dorothy made the appointment with Helpful Hopkins and I went across the street to St. Anthony's Church.

"I don't want a baby, God, I'd be a terrible mother. I haven't made my dreams come true and I'd resent the baby or expect too much of it just the way my mother did with me. George will end up sharpening knives in a hot pepper patch the way my father did and I'll thunder through my life with sadness in my eyes. God, if you love this baby, don't give it to George and me. I hope I've made my case clear. Thy will be done."

The night before I was to go to Helpful's office, located in a warehouse by South Ferry, I took another massive dose of castor oil and woke up in the middle of the night with severe cramps.

George, who was home by then, rolled over and watched me clutching my abdomen.

"Must have been that pizza pie I brought home," he said. "Take some Alka-Seltzer or neither one of us is going to get to sleep all night."

In the bathroom, I discovered I was hemorrhaging. Big bloody clots slid out of me into the bowl. I looked at them, seemingly as alive as little jellyfish, and wept with relief. I'd flushed them by the time George padded in, eyes swollen with sleep, and put his arm around me.

"You okay, Josie?"

"Just my period," I said. "Some months it's worse than others."

"Come back to bed and put your belly up against my rump," he counseled.

In bed, I snuggled to his back and cried until his pillowcase became wet.

"For Christ's sakes, you trying to drown me? You girls get so emotional this time of the month. No wonder a woman can't get elected President."

I cancelled my appointment with Helpful but put the $200 from Equity in a savings account under my own name. I hid the passbook in a Kotex box in case such an occasion arose again.

George was scheduled to report to the Mountain Pass Theatre in Arizona on June 10th. Given our financial status and the small amount of money George would be making doing summer stock, we knew we wouldn't see each other 'til the summer's end. We had no budget to cover bus fares back and forth for connubial visits. The evening of June 9th, which also happened to be the second anniversary of our first meeting at Kissing Rock, George took me out to dinner and to the theatre. He borrowed money from Dorothy for the dinner and he had gotten tickets to a Broadway show free through Equity. The show, an English import called 'Look Back in Anger,' was just about to close and they were papering the house.

At Romeo's restaurant, George surprised me by ordering a bottle of chianti. This made the evening special from the start. Since we'd been so broke, he'd taken to carrying a flask when we went out; we'd drain our water glasses and he'd fill them with the cheap wine we brought from home. He figured we saved 75¢ a glass that way. George suggested we order Romeo's spaghetti because the menu stated that it came with a full loaf of garlic bread. We wrapped the garlic bread in our napkins and slipped it into my purse so that George could take it with him on the long bus ride to Arizona.

No creative artist will be surprised by that. At the Playhouse, five of us would chip in one dollar each and one of us would go into Lou's Steak & Chicken (ALL YOU CAN EAT FOR FIVE BUCKS) carrying a flight bag.

'Look Back In Anger' was about a young man of our beat generation whose dreams seemed doomed to fail and who was damned mad about it. He had a wife who appeared to be a sop but turned out to have more backbone than we'd thought. They had several things in common with us. She'd aborted their unborn child, they both expected more out of life than God had allotted them and they were gnawing on each other's bones. In the final scene, they reconcile and recognize that one another is all that they can count on in this world.

I thought that God might have been trying to tell us something but George was made of tougher fiber.

"What a lot of hog wash," George bellowed when we exited the theatre. "A man gets what he works for in this world. If he fails it's because he's just not good enough."

It was with that whip that George ultimately beat his spirit to death.

We didn't make love that night even though we knew we wouldn't see each other for months. George was angry at the play and my diaphragm was full of fork holes. The next morning, George woke me when he leaned across the bed to kiss me goodbye. His college suitcase with the Divinity sticker on it was gripped firmly in his right hand. He brushed my forehead with his lips and sighed.

"Well," he said, clearing his throat, "see you, babe."

"Break a leg."

"Yeah. You, too."

Sitting up in bed, I could see him clearly at the front door of the apartment. He adjusted the police lock carefully so it would snap behind him. He was wearing the khaki pants he'd ironed the day before. The creases were knife sharp and the seat was shiny. He had polished his saddle shoes so often and meticulously that the white, although very white, was caked across the toes. His pants were baggy, George always bought his pants a size too large, but his black jersey fit him very tightly and was becoming. George had broad shoulders and a narrow chest. His hair was scraggly and curled over the tops of his ears and the back of his turtleneck. It occurred to me that George was the handsomest man I'd ever seen. He pursed those sexy pouty lips and the dimples deepened in his cheeks—he was surveying the living room one last time to make certain that he hadn't forgotten something.

"Me," I started to cry out, "you forgot me."

But he'd opened the door by then and set his suitcase in the hall. He pulled the door shut behind him and I heard the police lock clunk into place.

He sent me Playbills every week. On the front cover there was a photo of the Mountain Pass Theatre. It appeared to be high in the hills and clouds were floating just above the theatre marquee. One night I dreamed that I was there to see a show but George, though he was listed in the program, never appeared on stage.

Then I got a letter. It read: "Hey Josie, Road Company of *Mame* was playing in Phoenix so hitched over to see it on my night off. Guy who's playing Beau is leaving and set it up for me to audition for the replacement. Think I'm going to get it. Means real money. Kisses."

The next correspondence I received from George was postmarked Los Angeles, California.

"*Mame* is boffo here, we're SRO. They're holding us over for a month. Send me some clothes, please, esp. raincoat. Auditioned for a TV pilot but won't know til next week. We have a break between L.A. and Chicago so will come home for a couple days. Am bringing a buddy from the cast who's never seen New York."

They arrived without notice in mid-October. My off-Broadway show had closed and I was working as a Skeeter's Girl again. When I got home from work at seven, I found George and his buddy in the kitchen cooking supper. Her name was Sally and she had, she said, a special talent for meatloaf. She was blonde and tan, a California girl who'd joined the chorus of *Mame* while it was in L.A.

"Sally's teaching me the ropes out there," George bubbled. He was operating at peak energy and it seemed to bounce off the walls of our apartment and rumble around the corners of the room. It made me very nervous. I thought I heard a constant high-pitched sound but after checking all the electrical appliances, I decided I was hearing George's zeal.

There was no door on our bedroom, so, with Sally in a sleeping bag in the middle of our kitchen, we did nothing more than kiss good-night. George looked even better than he had the day he left. I never wanted him so much.

The next morning, I called in sick to Skeeter and dropped by the Sanger Clinic for a new diaphragm. When I got home, George and Sally were gone. The note, scribbled on a paper towel and left beside the sink, said: "I got callback on TV pilot. Be in L.A. til Thursday then on to Chicago. Left-over meatloaf in fridge."

In February, *Mame* closed in Washington, D.C. and George came home on Valentine's Day. He brought a box of chocolates for me but he'd put it on the floor of the bus where the heater blew on it and melted it into a glob.

"Well, it's the thought that counts," George said.

"That depends," I said, leading him toward the bedroom, "on what you're thinking about." But George was worn out.

The next morning, another buddy from the *Mame* company, her name was Irene, called to tell George that the fellow who was set to play Freddy in a bus and truck of *My Fair Lady* had just come down with hepatitis. The show was ready to roll at noon and they needed an immediate replacement. She knew that George had played Freddy in summer stock at Mountain Pass and figured that he would still recall the lines and lyrics. Could he be packed and at the Port Authority by one p.m.?

It was during this tour that his draft notice arrived in our New York mailbox. I forwarded it to him Special Delivery and a week later came home from a long day's typing to find this note on the kitchen table.

"Flew in this a.m. for my physical and packed some stuff. If anything is missing, I probably took it so don't worry. Got to make an eight p.m. curtain in Cleveland tonight so can't stick around. Hugs."

Two weeks later, I received a letter postmarked Ft. Benning, Ga.

"I don't have to die to go to hell," George wrote. "I'm there. They tell me I can pull an easy tour of duty if I sign up for Special Services. Two years in Korea entertaining the occupation troops."

George came back once more after that. Jason was an infant and we hadn't yet moved out of that village apartment to the upper West Side. Dorothy was baby-sitting while I worked addressing envelopes for the Adamant Collection Agency. She said George opened the door with his old key and she screamed because she thought he was a burglar. He said he couldn't stick around because he had a reading for a TV pilot in Hollywood the next day and packed up his few remaining clothes and personal effects. He left a large stuffed tiger in Jason's crib, along with a note which he tucked in the edge of Jason's diaper. It said, "See, I told you motherhood was what you needed. Be happy, both of you. God bless. Squeezes."

Once or twice, while watching the monitor in the Channel 3 Newsroom, I saw George on a soft drink commercial. There were palm trees in the background so I assumed that it was filmed in California. Another time, I saw someone who looked like George crossing at 43rd and Madison but before I could get to him, he boarded an uptown bus. George never asked for a divorce and I never really considered myself unmarried. It was as though George were out of town on just another tour; if he'd walked into my new apartment on the upper West Side, five or ten yeras later, a bag of groceries in one arm, a six-pack of cold beer in his hand, I would have looked up happily and said, "Well, it's about time, what'd you buy for supper?" Every now and then, I'd wake up in the night and be surprised George wasn't there.

"Why does it take us so long to accept things, Solomon?"

"Dreams die hard," Solomon replies, a tear in his eye. "I'm just a sucker for romance. I believe my mama must have felt that way about my daddy. Can you die," inquires

Solomon, "of a broken heart?"

"Oh, I don't think so," I reply.

Jason used to say "Everything is exactly as it should be, as you intended it to be. Regrets reflect a lack of faith and insight."

I sigh. George and I were on a juggernaut.

Even now, I sometimes get a sudden image of George's fingers. It floods my mind and blots out everything for just a second. And I know, without proof but with absolute certainty, that wherever George is at that moment, he's picking at his nose and hearing my voice as clearly as if I were beside him saying "Cut that out, George. That's disgusting!"

In some very basic ways, George and I are still dependent on each other.

The moon is heading down now. She seems to be drifting toward the windowsill as though she were going to settle there for a long day's snooze. Dawn will be breaking much too soon.

I'm going to speak to Solomon in whispers from now on. I don't want my voice to serve as an alarm clock for my executioners.

God, hold the moon high for another day or two. I'm not ready to give up life yet. I'm just starting to put the pieces of it into some kind of order.

I need more time.

Jason says that time is timeless but that's too simple for my complex mind. I'm accustomed to living in minutes, hours and days, to months and years which progress as I expect them to, one following the other.

I can actually see the movement of the moon. So can Solomon. He leaps to the sill below the Judas window and bats a paw at the silver ball beyond the glass.

"That's it, Solomon. Catch the moon and bring it here."

Solomon looks at me, disgusted, and bounds down to the floor. "You fool," he says, "that ball is out of reach."

TWELVE

WAR BABIES was the name of the agency which actually strong-armed me into taking Jason although the official papers were signed by Save A Child, Inc. Everyone over ten years of age must know that Save A Child has been the largest and most reputable of all placement agencies for over a century and receives funding from twelve nations as well as from Ford and Rockefeller. In war or peace, wherever Americans spilled their seed, Save A Child, like the Red Cross, could be counted on to be there. They had a waiting list of thousands of approved adoptive parents.

War Babies, on the other hand, was a little known small outfit located in downtown Seoul. It had been established by a Rev. Turner Harris who was a missionary by trade and had a heart of gold but no head for business. War Babies tried to place the handicapped and crippled infants which Save A Child couldn't or wouldn't touch.

Actually, Jason was not officially a war baby. The Korean conflict had been settled by the time of his birth and although American troops remained in Seoul, the fighting had ceased, and both Save A Child, Inc. and War Babies were winding down their efforts. War Babies, in fact, had closed its nursery altogether and dismissed its few employees with the exception of a receptionist and the Executive Director (Rev. Harris) who were in the process of packaging and storing all their files. Not three weeks after I adopted Jason War Babies' irate landlord in Seoul claimed the rent was past due and confiscated all their files and furnishings, trucked them to the dump and had them combusted with the city garbage. I was assured War Babies had very little information about Jason, anyway, and their former Executive Director had since returned to his missionary post in Africa where he was inaccessible by phone or mail.

I had no reason to investigate Jason's origins until he was four years old and claimed to be the Son of God. Although the manner in which Jason came to me was unusual, the papers were in order and clearly stated PLACE OF BIRTH: SEOUL, KOREA; DATE OF BIRTH: MARCH 27, 1959; PARENTS NAMES: MOTHER AND FATHER UNKNOWN; NO. OF PLACEMENT: 6336. I became alarmed at Jason's insistence that he was divine and at that time called Save A Child, Inc. at their New York headquarters.

I was working as a Skeeter's Girl at Rockefeller Center, filling in for a vacationing typist who was employed to cut the stencils. While this was more interesting than typing an endless stream of envelopes, it strained my eyes to stare all day long at a navy blue master into which my typewriter keys were cutting virtually invisible letters. I had a throbbing headache by noontime every day. There were no day-care centers for working mothers in those days and if I hadn't had the good luck to have Mrs. Leonetti for a neighbor, who'd raised eight children and felt great emptiness without a baby in the house, I don't know how Jason and I would have gotten by.

Rockefeller Center was just two blocks away from the

Save A Child, Inc. building so on my coffee break one morning, I used the pay phone by the elevator (Skeeter's Girls were not allowed to use the office telephones) to make an appointment.

"Oh," said the young woman who answered the phone, "You don't need an appointment, we have computers. Just drop by and bring the baby's placement number. Ask for Mr. Quitman in Records. He'll punch the information up for you."

With high heart and hopes, I trotted over to Save A Child, Inc. on my lunch hour that very same day. I knew Jason's number by heart and I convinced myself that the read-out sheet would say FOUND IN HUT WITH UNIDENTIFIED MOTHER AND FATHER SLAIN PROTECTING NEWBORN SON. I knew full well the war was over at Jason's birth but I was clutching at straws and praying that the straws weren't in a manger.

"6336," I announced to Mr. Quitman, a wiry old gentleman who sat strapped in a desk chair which was equipped with large wheels. The computers were banked behind and on the sides of him as though they were a stage set and he was the one man show.

"6336," Mr. Quitman repeated and spun in his chair. With one hard push of his left foot, he rolled to the right bank and began to punch its buttons. There was a whirr of machinery and then three red lights lit up. Mr. Quitman looked puzzled, then pushed off again to the left bank where he repeated the same procedure and the same three lights came on again. Mr. Quitman whirled and stared at me. "6336," he said, "you sure of that?"

I'm never sure of anything so I closed my eyes and pictured the document in my head. The purple ink said 6336.

"I'm pretty sure," I said to Mr. Quitman.

"Well," he sighed, "I'll see if Sadie knows anything about it, then." Sadie was the third computer and he rolled over to it. "You say the kid's Korean?"

"Yes."

"You sure of that?"

"I'm not sure of anything," I answered. "That's why I'm asking you. But the papers say Korean." I rubbed my temples. I already had a tiny tender ache above my eyebrows from squinting at the stencils and I could feel it just about to blossom into a full-fledged lulu.

Sadie lit up with red lights.

"Sorry, lady," Mr. Quitman shrugged, "you didn't get that kid from us."

"The papers," I snapped, "are signed by Save A Child, Inc."

"Well," he sighed, "What can I tell you?" And he turned his back to me and busied himself doing something that I soon began to realize had nothing to do with me.

I'm not a demanding person. I avoid conflict. But that very morning Jason had told me that Mrs. Leonetti, a staunch Catholic, would never meet God because of that altar she had erected in her living room which was adorned with religious statuary and surrounded by vases of silk roses.

"False idols," Jason squeaked, quite angry.

"But honey," I argued, "those are just statues of Mary and Jesus and the Saints."

Jason sucked viciously on a graham cracker and the brown mush coated his fingers. "It's a waste of adoration. Mrs. Leonetti's doomed."

I was leery of leaving Jason with Mrs. Leonetti that morning but I had to go to work and had no choice.

"Don't you say a word to Mrs. Leonetti," I ordered Jason. "She loves those statues. They are her life."

"That," Jason retorted, "is precisely the problem."

And so, because I was worried about what might be happening at that very moment between Jason and Mrs. Leonetti, I went to the front desk of Save A Child, Inc. and pounded my fist on the reception counter.

"I want to see the Executive Director."

"She's out to lunch," the young woman replied, startled. "I can let you speak to her secretary on the inter-com."

The secretary's voice crackled. "May I ask what this is in reference to?"

"The Korean baby you gave me in 1959," I yelled at the box.

"Well, we don't take them back," the secretary laughed snidely.

"I don't want to give him back, I want some information on him."

"See Mr. Quitman in Records," she ordered and clicked off.

"Ring her again," I snapped at the receptionist who did so.

"For Christ's sakes," the secretary bellowed, "I'm trying to eat my lunch, what there is of it."

"Mr. Quitman has no record of my baby," I insisted. "I want to speak to the executive Director."

The secretary growled. "What's your name?"

When I told her, she made a little cry as though someone had hit her on a sore spot. "Oh what the hell," she said, "come on back."

The door marked Executive Director in bold gold letters was closed. Through the murky glass, I could see a woman sitting at a desk in the anteroom, feet up. I tapped on the door.

"Come in."

She was middle-aged, drinking what appeared to be a cup of hot broth. She had a sour look on her face and she sat in the secretary's chair, feet propped on the typewriter, one high heel dangling in the well. Beyond the secretary's desk, a door stood ajar. It was labeled Mrs. Marguerite Wilkes, Executive Director. I turned my nose up at the insensitive secretary and stomped into the private office beyond.

"Where're you going?" The woman at the secretary's desk patted her blue hair into shape and sat up straight.

"I want to see Mrs. Wilkes!" The private office looked as though it had been recently looted. On the floor were the contents of files. On the desk, unopened mail and un-answered correspondence was piled so high that I couldn't see if anyone was sitting at the desk.

"Well," I said out loud to the cluttered room, "no wonder this place can't find Jason's records! I've never seen such disorganization."

The blue-haired woman leaned through the doorway and beckoned me back to the outer office. Red-faced, she admitted with a sigh, "I'm Mrs. Wilkes."

"You're not Mrs. Wilkes. You're her secretary."

"Alas," said Mrs. Wilkes, "I have no secretary. She broke her leg skiing and while recuperating fell in love and married the orthopedic intern. I myself have been suffering from diverticulitis and my doctor has put me on a liquid diet. We're opening three new sites in Viet Nam and I've lost six temporary typists who walked out when they saw this mess. To boot, my trusted friend down the hall has proved to be a Judas and is reporting every moment of this chaos to the Ford and Rockefeller Foundations in the hopes that I'll be discharged and he will get my job. I served twenty years overseas for Save A Child. Listen girl, and learn a lesson. When you give your all to someone, they'll kick you in the ass. And now you."

"I just want some information about the baby you gave me." I was overwhelmed by Mrs. Wilkes' fury at the world.

"Can't help you, honey."

"The adoption papers are signed by this agency," I argued, "and your computer has no record of the child." Mrs. Wilkes didn't respond so I sidled closer to her and asked seriously, "Are you sure you're Mrs. Wilkes?"

Mrs. Wilkes moaned and collapsed into the secretary's chair. "I don't even know how to make this damned thing backspace." She wailed and hit the typewriter with her fist. It shuddered and made a tingling noise which I recognized immediately as a broken spring on the ribbon reverse.

"Oh dear," I said.

"I say that I'm my secretary," explained Mrs. Wilkes, "because one has to maintain appearances. Suppose you'd been a spy from Ford."

"I'm just one of your adoptive mothers looking for information about my child," I reassured her.

"I know who you are," Mrs. Wilkes sighed, "I recognize your name. As if I didn't have enough woes as it is." Mrs. Wilkes looked up at the heavens.

"I know his number," I said, "it's 6336."

"Yes, I remember." Mrs. Wilkes put her head in her hand. Her stomach grumbled. "That's a number we never use officially."

"What do you mean?" My heart was picking up cadence and my palms began to sweat. "What do you mean it's not an official number?"

"Oh, no, dear, not in this agency. Our dear departed founder, a Mexican-American oilman from Texas, was deeply superstitious. We use no numbers which can add up to 666. We do not, for instance, use 3366, 6633, 3636, 33336 and so on. The number 666 has great religious significance to our founder and he forbade our ever assigning it, in any combination whatsoever, to any of our children. I have no idea why, dear, you know how those hot-blooded Catholics are. I do hope you're not one. I haven't the energy to apologize for offending you."

"No, I'm not," I assured her. "So why did you give that number to Jason?"

"Jason?" Mrs. Wilkes smiled. "What a nice name for him. So you named him Jason."

"Why did you give him that number?"

"I had to give him some number, didn't I? The document wouldn't look official without a purple number."

"Why aren't Jason's records in your damned computer?" I was shouting rather loudly by that time.

Mrs. Wilkes put her finger to her lips. "Not another word," she vowed aloud to herself, "I'm in quite enough trouble as it is."

"Please," I begged.

Mrs. Wilkes turned her face away so she wouldn't see my tears. "It has been my experience," she said firmly, "that every time I put myself out to do someone a good deed, I pay a heavy price. It's a dog eat dog world," she concluded.

"I swear I'll never tell a soul."

Mrs. Wilkes pursed her lips tightly and shook her head.

"I'll go to the authorities."

She smiled weakly. "Well, dear, that will probably get me fired for sure but it won't secure a bit of information about Jason. I'm the only one who knows and I'm certainly not going to tell you if you put my job on the line. One hand," she added, "washes the other. What are you going to do for me? Nothing." She answered herself, "nothing at all."

"Aha, Mrs. Wilkes." I was thinking fast as mothers do when they are protecting their young. "But I can do something for you. I can save your job."

Mrs. Wilkes raised her eyebrows, surprised.

I leaned toward her and whispered. "I can type one hundred words a minute, Mrs. Wilkes, and compose letters on my own and use a dictaphone. That, Mrs. Wilkes, is what I can do. Six foot executives have been known to pound their foreheads on their deseks begging me not to leave them."

Mrs. Wilkes' jaw had dropped open.

"And," I continued, tantalizing Mrs. Wilkes with my tone of voice, "I can file and put up with growling bosses and I'll go out at lunch time and smuggle you a chicken salad sandwich."

Mrs. Wilkes moaned orgasmically.

"And all this, Mrs. Wilkes, for $2.50 an hour and every piece of information you have about my son, Jason."

Mrs. Wilkes stuck out her trembling hand. "I generally pay $1.95 to Temporaries," she said, her voice shaking.

"$2.25," I countered.

"Bargain," she said and gripped my hand.

It took me three weeks, working overtime, to get Mrs. Wilkes in shape to defend her job successfully against the assault of her ambitious Public Relations man. And during those three weeks, the story of Jason's beginnings took shape. Mrs. Wilkes, day by day, remembered more. A fragment here, a fragment there. "Oh by the by," she'd say depositing another half dozen dictaphone tapes on my desk early in the morning, "I remembered something last night, not important perhaps, but it might interest you..."

The final story went like this:

In March of 1959, Save A Child, Inc. was occupying a large building at the main intersection of downtown Seoul. War Babies was located one block east, off an alley, in a dingy string of small first-floor rooms which had, prior to the Conflict, been used as a house of prostitution. War Babies placed all their infants in homes. This feat required great effort and a certain amount of luck because it is difficult to place handicapped children without sizeable support from foundations and a healthy advertising budget.

The War Babies nursery was empty and the help had been let go except for Rev. Harris and one receptionist who were putting the place in order so they could close up shop for good.

"Now," said Mrs. Wilkes as she told this part of the story to me, "I was stationed at Seoul Save A Child, Inc. and I was quite friendly with Rev. Harris who was a regular saint. When the babies were all placed, Rev. Harris was so run-down and nervous that I advised him to take a day off and play golf. His receptionist, a young Korean woman whose name I forget if, in fact, I ever knew it, had taken off for an assignation with a U.S. soldier whom she'd seen sing "The Street Where You Live" during a Special Services benefit to raise money for Save A Child. I know this for a fact because I was present at the entertainment, of course, and saw Rev. Harris' new receptionist making a horse's ass out of herself ogling that soldier. I told Rev. Harris about it, but he shrugged. He paid his help so little, he had to take what he could get. Well, this receptionist had just lit off with her lover and left the office door wide open—right in downtown Seoul, there was the poor Rev. Harris' filing cabinets and battered typewriter just sitting there for anyone to steal. The lord was with him and nobody stole a thing but when the receptionist returned from her romantic interlude, her young soldier at her side, in order to lock up for the night, she found a newly born male infant, wrapped in a U.S. Army jacket, in her *In* basket."

I could picture Jason, curled up in the top deck of the wire basket, like a jaundiced Didee doll, his thick black cap of hair and his mesmerizing ebony eyes peering over the wrinkled collar of a khaki jacket. He wouldn't have cried, not Jason, but he would have stared at them with such depth and insight that their spines shriveled.

"The soldier," Mrs. Wilkes continued, "was an actor/singer assigned to Special Services and he had access to a jeep. At the receptionist's request, he drove hurriedly to the Officer's Club outside Seoul and tracked down Rev. Harris on the 16th hole. Rev. Harris moaned at the bad news, dropped his clubs and accompanied the soldier back to the War Babies office where he unwrapped the infant, examined it perfunctorily and, still wearing his golf shoes, ran down the block to my office. 'It's a healthy child,' he assured me, placing the infant on my desk, 'and it seems to have all its parts.' Unfortunately," Mrs. Wilkes sighed, "I had received orders from New York that very day instructing me to accept no more children who required investigation. When a young mother voluntarily gives us her child to place up for adoption, she signs a paper and all is well and legal and easy as sliding down the storm door. But in the case of an unknown infant, an abandoned child about whom nothing whatsoever is known, well that's a horse of a different color. The authorities must be advised, a thorough investigative search must be made for the next of kin and if none are found, the child must be held one year before adoption can be finalized. It's costly and time-consuming—both those requirements were unacceptable to Save A Child at that time. We were in the process of phasing out our Seoul operation so we could focus all our energies on Viet Nam. I could not accept an unknown infant. Rev. Harris had no idea where to begin to search for the child's family; he had no prospective parents left on his list; furthermore, he was emotionally exhausted and he believed if he had to remain in Seoul the length of time such an investigation would require, he would not be able to return to his beloved Africa but would spend the remaining few years of his life in an insane asylum. 'Please,' he begged, 'this is only one small baby, slip him through, lie a little, Marguerite,' he pleaded, 'it's for a good friend and a worthy cause.'

"Aha, you see," Mrs. Wilkes said softly, "now you can tell how much trouble my soft heart gets me into. I said to Rev. Harris, 'Save A Child just happens to have a planeload of infants leaving at seven this very evening for New York City. They have been examined, inoculated and passed by American Customs so they can be deplaned and taxied immediately to their new homes. Rev. Harris, if you can find some sucker in New York City who'll take this child and keep their mouth shut, I'll forge the papers and a certificate of birth, I'll assign a Save A Child Inc. number to him and we'll squeeze his crate onto the aircraft just before takeoff. No one will be the wiser.' Rev. Harris raced from the office into the street, the baby underneath his arm. No more than twenty minutes later, he was back with the same soldier who'd been with the receptionist when she discovered the baby. The soldier recommended you, my dear. He said you were a fine Christian woman who needed a baby for your salvation. He guaranteed that you'd accept the child if we mentioned his name—which was, John Something?" Mrs. Wilkes screwed up her face, trying to recall.

"George," I said. "It was George."

"George. Are you sure?"

"Well, that's the name your messenger mentioned when he delivered Jason to my door."

"Well, then, it must have been George," agreed Mrs. Wilkes. "I was only concerned that we didn't have time to test the child for venereal disease. He didn't have one, did he?"

I knew George had recommended me. That was the only reason I opened my apartment door at seven-thirty a.m. to a complete stranger, bearing an infant and stating he was from Save A Child, Inc.

"This is a present from George," said the stranger, "he wants you to watch over this baby for him."

I thought it was a temporary arrangement although I later noted that the papers I signed stated clearly that this child was my responsibility for keeps. At seven-thirty in the morning I wasn't thinking clearly, and by the time the messenger handed me the papers to sign, a newborn infant was clinging to my neck smelling sour and helpless. It awoke in me a maternal instinct. I also thought that if George sent me a baby, he must be coming home.

For many months, I assumed that George was the father of the infant. But as I grew to know Jason, I changed my mind. Jason and George hadn't a single quality in common.

When Jason first took to the street and got international attention, George wrote a letter, postmarked Butte, Montana, to Jason, claiming to be his father.

Jason, who could not read and did not wish to learn, asked me to read it to him.

It said:

"Dear Son of mine: I guess it is about time that I tell you I am your father before you make any more of an ass out of yourself. I was stationed in Korea during 1959-60. I am also married to your adoptive mother although she may not have spoken to you of me recently. I don't know who your real mother is for sure, however, but I think I can pin it down to three or four first names. I found you in my makeup kit just before I went onstage to do a show at the Seoul Officer's Club. I had gone into the bathroom for a minute and when I came out, there you were, naked as a jaybird with a note scotchtaped to your belly which read, 'Thanks a lot, Soldier.' I didn't recognize the writing. My entrance music was playing so I left you in the arms of the elderly Korean cleaning woman who, when I came offstage after singing a medly of old-time hits, had disappeared and taken you with her. The very next afternoon, I saw you again in the *In* box at the office of War Babies. I recognized you right away and saw to it that you got a good home with my wife who needed a baby to take care of. I am currently in no position to offer you financial aid but I feel it my responsibility to give you some fatherly advice. It is difficult enough for a racially mixed, foreign born adopted boy to get a foothold in this country without dressing like a hippie. Go on a diet and take that weight off, too. It'll hurt your heart and you'll have a hard time with the girls. Find a sensible job and apply yourself to it. With spunk and ambition, you can attain your dreams and if you don't, it's your own fault. I hope I've given you food for thought. Don't go out in the streets again. You look silly and it's embarrassing to me. Hugs. Your Father."

When I finished reading the letter, Jason placed both hands on his belly and squeezed the flesh as though assuring himself it was still there. Then he raised his eyebrows in what appeared to be complete bewilderment.

"God," he said finally, "is my father."

I felt badly reading George's letter. The handwriting was sloped and depressed. He sounded more conservative than ever. Had George ended up the same man as his father, after all?

Scarcely a year later, when the Jasonites were everywhere and Jason's new order of things had disrupted the world as we knew it, George appeared on TV, claiming to be Jason's father. It was just before the networks collapsed and we received it on the network feed in the Channel 3 booth. It was the topic of conversation for several days in the employee's coffee room. At that time, no one knew my relationship to George and Jason so their comments were completely without bias. Sam Dowdy said George looked to him to be a first class heel who'd deserted his wife, fooled around with foreign women, knocked some poor illiterate girl up and then farmed his son out for adoption. Sam Dowdy thought that George was doing it to make a buck. "He'll start endorsing soft drinks, you wait and see," Sam said. But the Jasonites moved much too quickly for that to ever happen. Soft drink companies were going under by the dozens and even though Coca-Cola carbonated and bottled papaya juice and advertised it as 'a little taste of heaven'—they still went out of business. On the black market, the remaining supply of Cokes skyrocketed in price.

George never made a nickel claiming to be Jason's father. I don't think he did it for the money. I think Jason's divinity offended George's sense of logic.

"This makes George sound like a heel, doesn't it, Solomon?"

Solomon shrugs, thinks a moment, then agrees.

"George was the kindest, gentlest, and warmest man I ever knew."

Solomon yawns. "Just another tale," he says, "of the Great God Anglo-Saxon Male."

"I can't think of anything harder in this world than to be born an Anglo-Saxon Male."

"And have the whole world handed to you on a platter?"

"The world weighs too damn much," I reply.

"The master is the slave," Solomon spits as he says it. "Oh, how profound, Josie."

"Jason used to say that it is easier for a rich man to pass through the eye of a needle than it is for an Anglo-Saxon Male to contact God."

"Your dear sweet George," Solomon comments sarcastically, "was nothing but a self-serving roue."

"When the messenger brought Jason to me, he also brought a bank draft for $2500.00 signed by George. I expect it represented all of George's savings while he was in the service."

"And you spent every penny of it on the little bugger, didn't you?"

I clung to the thought that George was coming home to join us. I didn't even name the baby until he was six months old. Then, I went back to work as a Skeeter's Girl and on a lunch hour I bought a little book in Whelan's drugstore. It was pocket-sized and it listed hundreds of names. WHAT TO CALL HIM was the title. It was pin-striped blue. I read the names at lunchtimes and coffee breaks and late at night after I'd put the baby to sleep.

Gregory, Luther, Ralph, Roger, Bert, Fred, Jeffery, Harold, Bryan, James, Henry, Marcus.

Then one night I dreamed that I was on the waterfront, standing on a pier that jutted out into the Hudson. Garbage floated idly by. George was standing in a canoe beside the pier, just below me. The canoe was rocking in the water. "Where do you think you're going, George?" I hollered down to him, "You'll never make it out there in a small canoe." George, who was wearing a silver helmet and carrying a giant spear, shouted back at me, "I must sail on, I must find the golden fleece." He pushed off, scattering the garbage with the nose of his canoe, and I stood a long time watching him paddle with his spear toward the shoreline of New Jersey.

When I awoke, I knew the baby's name was Jason.

It was Marguerite Wilkes at Save A Child, Inc. who got me to Dr. Binbaum. During the three hellish weeks I worked for her, I shared some of my fears regarding Jason.

"He honestly believes that he's the Son of God," I said.

"Well," Mrs. Wilkes replied, "you must have put that in his little head. Where would a four-year-old get that kind of notion?"

"But he does things."

"Like what?"

"Things." I knew if I explained them, Mrs. Wilkes would think I'd lost my mind.

"I can't help you, dear, unless I know what kind of things. They may be perfectly explainable, you know. You never had a child before. You're inexperienced."

"Well," I relented, "he disappears."

"He what?"

"Disappears." I snapped my fingers. "One minute he's there and the next minute he's gone."

"Oh, dear," Mrs. Wilkes moaned and reached for her address book. She began paging through it nervously.

"Just as I'm about to call for help, he reappears. He never stays gone long. Mrs. Leonetti has noticed it, too, but she thinks that his movement is simply quicker than her eye and that he's hiding in the closet or something. She has cataracts and her vision's fuzzy. Sometimes," I continued, "when I'm at work and Jason is with Mrs. Leonetti, I can hear his voice in my head. I can't understand the words but I can hear the sound of his voice very clearly. He knows what I've been doing even when I don't tell him. I'll come home from a day's work and he'll say I'm glad you didn't buy that stuffed elephant for me, it would have been a waste of money."

Mrs. Wilkes had found what she was looking for in her address book; she held the page open, her finger pointed at a name but I kept talking anyway since it was the first chance I'd had to say any of these things out loud.

"Once in the middle of the night, I woke up and saw Jason standing in his crib, his arms lifted above his head. His eyes were open wide and, in the dark, they seemed to glow. I could hear music everywhere but not real music, not music made with woodwinds, brass or strings. It was like the music of the universe, the sounds of nature come together. I screamed and held my ears. Jason looked surprised but when he saw that I was actually in pain from the sound, he lowered his hands quickly and the music stopped."

"Dr. Binbaum," Mrs. Wilkes interjected quickly, pushing a pencil and a note pad at me. "Write it down, Josie, Dr. Hubert Binbaum, 12 Central Park West, EN2-7345. I've been going to him for years and he's wonderful."

"Mrs. Wilkes, Jason and I can hardly get by. I can't afford a shrink."

"Oh, Dr. Binbaum works through the Horatio Clinic," Mrs. Wilkes assured me, "where you pay what you can. I believe all the severe cases are treated at the clinic, at any rate. I, of course, see him privately."

I called Dr. Binbaum that very day.

I spent many years with Dr. Binbaum and I wonder if I could have survived Jason's boyhood without psychiatric support. On the other hand, Jason always claimed that Dr. Binbaum, along with books and thought and logic, stood directly between me and God.

"Josie," cries Solomon suddenly, "look!"

Outside the Judas window, the golden glow of a beginning sunrise. Still the moon, paper white now, remains stoically in the pale blue sky as though she is my faithful guardian angel.

"Don't leave me," I whisper to her but I can see the sunlight growing brighter. This moment reminds me of Dr. Binbaum who, invariably, just as I was getting to something good, would slap his hands on his desk and smile apologetically. "Time's up, Josie." Then he'd advise me to "Hold the thought until next time."

THIRTEEN

JUST walked to the Judas window to stretch my legs. My
ankle has stopped swelling; I think it's even gone down;
or, perhaps, my mind is just in such a whirl that I can no
longer feel the soreness. I promised myself I wouldn't peek
out at the Jasonites but I did. They are curled like embryonic
creatures not yet developed or ready to be born, scattered
on the sand, each a different size and shape; some reach out
with one arm or a foot, some are completely concealed
within their polyvinyl bedrolls and have no human definition
whatsoever. Nothing stirs out there. From where I stood it
was hard to believe that they were even breathing. The sun is
rising much too quickly but the moon stands stalwart. She
won't run off and leave me to the Jasonites' devices. She is my
friend, my mother, my daughter, myself. She offended man
with her serenity and he built a craft and skidded onto her
soft surface, conquered her, jabbed his flags into her virgin
flesh. She is wiser now, my moon, but no less constant.

Dr. Binbaum was a lamenter of the first order. He

sometimes fancied himself to be the reincarnation of the prophet Isaiah. He didn't show this side of himself to every patient. Dr. Binbaum and I had a very close and unique relationship. Sometimes, Dr. Binbaum told me, a session with me put him in mind of shaving, speaking to himself in the mirror.

I first saw Dr. Binbaum at his private office, located on the mezzanine of what had once been a mansion on Central Park West. There were marble columns and steps like great half circles. The carpeting was ruby red and plush. The ceiling in the lobby arched upward like a great cathedral and from its peak a chandelier with 20,001 crystals hung ominously. I know it had 20,001 crystals because there was a small bronze plaque to that effect mounted near the teak handrail that curved beside the marble stairs. Everyone ducked when they entered the lobby and saw that chandelier; reflex action.

Dr. Binbaum's office was composed of three large rooms each with vaulted ceilings held up by a band of rococo plaster some three or four feet wide. The windows were arched and some ten feet high or so themselves. It was a suite for giants and Dr. Binbaum, who was six feet tall, was dwarfed by his surroundings. The first room had a bronze plaque on its double doors: HUBERT H.H.R. BINBAUM, III, M.D., Ph.D. and above that, a 3x5 index card pinned to the door with a thumbtack which read Dentist Office Next Door. It was the reception area. It could have been a ballroom or a state dining room but, as Dr. Binbaum scheduled his patients a full hour apart, there was one overstuffed chair near the door and, on the far side of the room, his secretary's desk and four ebony black filing cabinets.

Beyond the reception room was Dr. Binbaum's office. It was the largest of the rooms and Dr. Binbaum used very little of it. He had placed his desk so he could see out the window and watch the comings and goings at the bus stop across the street. In the middle of the room, there was a sofa, covered with a gay floral print, which faced Dr. Binbaum's back. The third room, which I could see through the gaping door, was absolutely empty though carpeted richly in royal blue. Dr. Binbaum explained that he'd expected to use that room for his group therapy sessions but since he had affiliated himself with the Horatio Clinic, his groups met there and he had no use at all for a third room. He considered buying a sofabed and sleeping there. That seemed to him to be a logical use for the space as it connected directly to the bath and a small kitchenette. But, he said, he had inherited a ten room townhouse just off Gramercy Park and if he took to sleeping in his office, he didn't know what to do about the town-house. It had been in his family for five generations and he could hardly bring himself to sell it or rent it to a stranger.

I expected Dr. Binbaum to be small and wizened, scrawny, serious, needlenosed. He was rangy, built more like a cowboy than my preconception of a New York shrink. He had hands like hamhocks and feet so large that when his shoes got worn in, his big toenail made an impression in the tip end of the leather. All his life, he admitted, his feet had hurt him. He'd spent thousands having special shoes made until he realized they hurt him just about the same as did the largest size (carried by Thom McCann so he returned to wearing cheap shoes and sometimes cut slits in the sides and toes with his pen knife).

Dr. Binbaum had long shaggy hair before it was the fashion. His haircut (or lack of one) had nothing to do with style. He just never could make the time to get to the barber. As I grew to know Dr. Binbaum, I offered to bring in my E-Z-Cut, a device I'd ordered from Sunrise House by mail and which did an excellent job of trimming Jason's thick hair. From that time on, whatever haircuts Dr. Binbaum got, he got from me during our sessions. He was extremely farsighted and couldn't read at all without his glasses. He wore them night and day and sometimes, forgetting that he had them on, slept in them. Consequently, he'd broken off the ear pieces on both sides and ingeniously replaced them with pieces snipped from a coat hanger and bent at one end to fit around his ears. At the other end, he'd made a tight little hook which enabled him to wire the pieces onto the eyeframe by using paper clips. This arrangement, he said, was most comfortable. He tied a piece of string from one ear piece to the other so that when he wearied of wearing the glasses, he could let them hang down like a necklace. I never knew if Dr. Binbaum had a wife although he and I became close friends. I never went to Dr. Binbaum's home; he never came to mine. I never shared a meal with him, a drink with him, and certainly not a bed. Dr. Binbaum cherished his professional ethics. I never even called him Hubert though I asked him to address me as Josie. I never knew his age. I'd estimate he was a man of forty but at the time, he seemed ageless and without gender. For many years, he was my best friend. And, he later admitted, I was his.

I am the sort who looks perfectly calm at the very moment I am stumbling over a precipice into the abyss of madness. I look radiantly healthy when I am running a fever of 104 degrees. My body denies its imperfections. But Mrs. Wilkes had intimated that I was nutty as a fruitcake; it had suddenly occurred to me that I might be wholly responsible for my son's believing he was the Second Coming; I was awed by the magnificence of Dr. Binbaum's building, and I'd never had occasion to visit the office of a psychiatrist before.

Dr. Binbaum was engrossed in watching the activity at the bus stop when I entered the room. He was leaning across his desk, holding his eyeglasses in place, squinting fervently and smiling.

I pointed at the sofa. "Am I supposed to lie down on that?"

"What?" asked Dr. Binbaum. With his back to me, he couldn't see where I was pointing.

"Am I supposed to lie down on that couch?"

"Are you tired?"

"Not really."

"Well." That was his answer.

After a minute or two, I sat cautiously on the cushion nearest the door.

"I think the bulldog's going to bite that man." Dr. Binbaum put his hand across his mouth and giggled. "He probably deserves it."

Just then, a bell went off in a clock on Dr. Binbaum's desk. He spun in his chair and faced me.

"Why are you here?" Dr. Binbaum removed a Lucky Strike from behind one ear and lit it.

"Marguerite Wilkes sent me."

"Who?" Dr. Binbaum fumbled on his desk for an ashtray and finally settled on a styrofoam cup half filled with cold coffee. It sizzled every time he flicked an ash.

"Marguerite Wilkes. She's a patient of yours."

"Oh?" Dr. Binbaum smiled blankly.

"She said that I should talk to you about my problem."

"Yes?" From the smile on Dr. Binbaum's face, I could have sworn he was smoking grass.

"And that I should tell you first off, I have no money."

"Clinic card!" Dr. Binbaum screamed at the top of his lungs. The secretary flew into the office and dropped an application and a little green card in my lap.

"You fill this out," she whispered, "and bring this card with you every time you report to the Horatio Clinic." She scurried out of the room, clearly terrified of Dr. Binbaum.

"Is that all?" I held up the card and application. "Should I go now?"

"Hell, no," Dr. Binbaum replied, "you're already here. Talk to me."

"You're going to think I'm crazy."

"Everybody is," he smiled.

"Not as crazy as I am."

"They all say that. The whole damn world is competing for the Crazy Title."

"My son Jason is the Son of God." I dropped it, then sat

back and waited for the explosion.

"Hmmm," replied Dr. Binbaum. "Does that make you the Virgin Mary?"

"He says that he's the Son of God, the Second Coming. Only he says it's actually not the Second Coming, that he's been here many times before and every time we do him in, one way or the other."

"Sounds like he's the one who should be seeing me." Dr. Binbaum daubed his cigarette in the cold coffee with a hisssss, then dropped the butt in the cup. I could picture it, brown and soggy, floating and unwrapping.

"Ugh," I said.

"Ugh, what?" Dr. binbaum leaned toward me with interest.

I stuck my tongue out. "That cup," I gagged, "that cigarette butt."

"Oh." Dr. Binbaum peered into the styrofoam. "Just a natural process of decomposition," he explained and tilted the cup so I could get a better view.

"Do you find yourself unduly sensitive," he asked, "do things affect you more than they do others?"

"My son," I continued, "who thinks he's the Son of God is four years old."

"No kidding." Dr. Binbaum grinned. "Precocious little dickens, is he?"

"Did I do this to him?"

"I don't know," Dr. Binbaum shrugged.

"I don't think so." And then I told, in some detail, the story of Jason's advent to Dr. Binbaum. About halfway through, Dr. Binbaum snored. I stopped and asked if he was listening or sleeping.

"Both," he replied. "I listen when I sleep. In the alpha state, I have some of my best perceptions. Continue please."

I'd told him the story of my parents, of wanting to be a minister, of wanting to be a writer, of my marriage to George and was just beginning to embark on Jason's weird activities when the clock went off on Dr. Binbaum's desk.

He slapped the desk with the flat of his hand and his eyes opened.

"Time's up," he said. "Hold the thought until next week."

And I left my first session with Dr. Binbaum feeling as though absolutely nothing had been accomplished.

Perhaps, I told myself, Dr. Binbaum was only qualified to treat light to medium crazies. Maybe he couldn't handle a heavy-duty case like mine. I never would have gone to my second session, scheduled two days later at the Horatio Clinic, if Jason hadn't flown.

I came home from work bone-tired and instead of stopping at Mrs. Leonetti's on the third floor to pick up Jason, I went directly to our apartment and put a can of Campbell's Minestrone in a pot on the stove to heat up for supper. I ran a quick tub, thinking I'd soak my aching body five or ten minutes, then I'd leap out refreshed and retrieve Jason. I would be sparkling, good-humored and have renewed energy to face the evening. Our supper would be steaming on the stove, ready to eat. I must have fallen asleep the moment that I sat down in the bathtub. My chin was bobbing in the lukewarm water when I smelled smoke and woke suddenly. Just as I opened my eyes, Jason flew in through the open window of the living room. He hovered above the tub—not flapping his arms like they were wings, just kind of bobbing in the air while flexing his toes and fingers. He wasn't filmy like a ghost or even blurred at the edges. He was chunky, solid Jason looking exactly like himself except that he was flying.

"Thank goodness," he said, "you woke up. I was afraid you were going to burn the house down. Better do something about the soup quick. I'm hungry as a bear."

With that, he twirled and flew back out the window. I saw him spiraling down toward Mrs. Leonetti's like a leaf dropping on a windless day.

The pot on the stove was red-hot. There was no soup left

at all, just a thick layer of black crust which seemed to be welded to the bottom. I scraped at it for several minutes with a wooden spoon, then screamed in fury and hurled the pot into the garbage can where it instantly ignited several discarded paper towels. I seized the flaming can and heaved it into the bathtub. Smoke rose like Hiroshima and seeped through the apartment. The smell of wet ashes permeated every room. I dashed about, stark naked and still soaking wet, opening all the windows. I dug the oscillating fan out of the closet. An hour later, after I'd aired the apartment, scrubbed the garbage can, bathtub, bathroom floor, kitchen floor, stove and sink, I got dressed and stumbled down the stairs to collect Jason.

He met me at the door.

"Everything OK up there?" he asked. "I would have helped but Mrs. Leonetti might have missed me."

I ruffled his hair lovingly. "Yeah, honey, everything's okay now."

"Swell," Jason sighed. "I'm starved."

The next day I kept my appointment with Dr. Binbaum.

The Horatio Clinic was located in Greenwich Village. The building had, at one time, been a fire station and one entered through giant arches, crossed an oil-stained concrete floor, climbed a narrow set of metal stairs and emerged suddenly beside the receptionist's desk. I had completed filling out the financial form which Dr. Binbaum's secretary had given me. I handed it to the receptionist at the Horatio Street Clinic and she punched the figures up on an adding machine. She perused the total and shook her head.

"Must have entered something wrong," she said and checked the tape against my statement. "Nope," she assured herself, "I'm right. Lady," she said to me, "you're living at a deficit."

Every inch that Jason grew, I got another couple of thousand dollars in debt.

"We have a policy here at Horatio Clinic," said the

receptionist, "that every patient has to pay something. Something. Even when, like you, they have no means left." She glanced down at my application once again and winced. "Something," she repeated. She tapped her pencil on the desk for a moment, then asked, "How about a dollar a session?"

"I can do better than that," I huffed. My pride had been hurt. I hailed, after all, from the struggling American middle class where being poor connotes laziness and sloth; where working your butt off and still being poor connotes total and absolute failure as a human being. I hated myself enough for that and I despised admitting I couldn't afford anything.

I don't know if Dr. Binbaum ever knew I only paid a dollar for a session (his private rates were $40.00 an hour) but I expect it pleased him if he did. He often said I did as much for him as he for me if, in fact, either of us did anything at all for one another. Dr. Binbaum had some doubts about the value of therapy but none at all about the necessity for good chats between Seekers. Oh yes, Dr. Binbaum was a Seeker, too.

Binbaum had attended a Yeshiva for one year before his intellectual parents, shuddering over the stories of ancient bloodshed and suffering he learned at school and wept all night about, removed him and enrolled him at Trinity. That one year had its effect on Dr. Binbaum, though. He often dreamed of lions and human slaughter, of mass carnage and a God who stoically turned His back when He was sought; he dreamed of locusts and boils and death by thirst, starvation, cannibalism. Dr. Binbaum was as traumatized by the Old Testament as I was by the New.

And like me, he called out. And listened. And heard nothing.

In our session, for instance, I spoke of Jason's flying and mentioned that his placement number from Save A Child, Inc. had been 6336.

Dr. Binbaum continued snoring.

"6336," I repeated, "the three sixes!"

Dr. Binbaum's head rolled toward his shoulder and he mumbled, "Yes, uh-huh."

"*Let him who has understanding reckon the number of the beast, for it is a human number, its number is six hundred and sixty-six.*"

He knew from the tone of my voice that I was quoting from the Bible and he shook himself and sat up straight. "What," he said with interest, "does that mean?"

"Six hundred and sixty-six is the number of the Anti-Christ," I explained. "Revelation 13:18."

"I never read the Revelation," Dr. Binbaum admitted.

I told Dr. Binbaum the story as Mrs. Williams had explained it to us in her Bible Class: "Just before the end of the world, a wise man will rise to power. He will seem to be a humanitarian and he will bring peace everywhere. He will give everybody numbers instead of names. He is, however, the devil's advocate and the beginning of the end. Wars, destruction, pestilence. Out of the holocaust, only one hundred forty-four thousand male virgins will remain alive and will be redeemed by the Son of God who will arrive just as the action quiets down. And the number of the Anti-Christ is six hundred sixty-six."

Dr. Binbaum sat up in his excitement. "Part of that corresponds to Daniel's prophecies. But I never heard about the male virgins."

"That's in Revelation," I explained.

"One hundred and forty-four thousand of them? And they're the only ones going to heaven?"

"Yep," I sighed.

Dr. Binbaum leaned forward thoughtfully. "Do you suppose," he asked, "there are that many? Perhaps," he said, answering himself, "if you include very young boys. I wonder, if being exclusively homosexual counts."

"Chaste of women is the exact phrase," I added. "Chaste in Greek is the same word as virgin."

Dr. Binbaum seemed to be rummaging in his memory.

Squinting his eyes, moving his lips. "Ah yes," he shouted, "The King of the North, that's it! *He shall give no heed to the gods of his father or to the one beloved by women; he shall not give to any other god for he shall magnify himself above all.* And then," continued Dr. Binbaum, excitement rising in his voice, "The King of the South will attack him like a whirlwind but the King of the North will prevail and take over Egypt. Then comes Michael, Prince of my people, who will deliver us." Dr. Binbaum coughed from talking so loudly and then he smiled. "The prophecy of Daniel," he explained. "It has lots of phrases in it like *shame* and *everlasting contempt* and *the abomination that makes desolate.*"

"Mrs. Williams said that the end is already on us."

"Yes?" Dr. Binbaum leaned across his desk, fingers out as though reaching to seize whatever information I could give him.

"She said that the first thing has already happened. The beginning of the end is when the Jews reclaim their land and occupy the Holy City. And then they have to fight with Egypt over it." I went on, "The King of the North, whom Mrs. Williams took to be Soviet Russia, will side with the Egyptians against Israel."

Dr. Binbaum licked his lips as though I'd whetted his appetite with a vision of delicious food.

"And ten nations are supposed to come together and aid Israel. And from their midst a leader will arise and he will bring peace and prosperity. Then he'll be struck a mortal blow and we'll think he's dead but he will rise and he'll assign us all numbers. And he'll rule about four years before everything goes kaput."

"What happens?" Dr. Binbaum was hanging on my every word.

"A great explosion."

"Ah," said Dr. Binbaum, "Daniel thought so, too!"

"And most of us are dying and angels come down singing a song but nobody knows the words to it except the one hundred and forty-four thousand male virgins. And the Son of God redeems them."

"Holy moly," breathed Dr. Binbaum. "And I thought the Yeshiva was scary. You got all this from Mrs. Williams?"

"Every bit of it."

"Do they charge your parents to teach you that?"

"Nope. They do it free."

"Well," said Dr. Binbaum, "at least Malachi promises to send us Elijah to warn us that the end is coming so we'll have a chance to shape up."

Dr. Binbaum and I were so engrossed at that point, we were nearly nose to nose. "Well," I whispered, "that's why I don't think Jason is the Anti-Christ. He doesn't head ten nations..."

"Give him time," Dr. Binbaum whispered back, "he's only four..."

"...and another thing is that nobody is supposed to recognize the Anti-Christ. The way Jason goes around doing weird things, he'll give himself away."

Dr. Binbaum spoke softly into my ear. "Do you think he could really be the Son of God?"

"Who knows?" I shrugged. "Why not, it's time and he has all the qualities—but I can't be the mother of the Son of God. God doesn't even speak to me."

Dr. Binbaum shivered. He was talking so closely to my eardrum that his words popped. "We may be onto something big here," he said.

"But how," I asked very softly, "can we know for sure?"

Dr. Binbaum rocked thoughtfully in his chair for a moment, then leaned back triumphantly. "I know," he cried, "ask him if he's the Anti-Christ. Confront him with the 6336. That ought to get his dander up."

"He's just a child," I argued.

"If he nows he's the Son of God, he also knows if he's the Anti-Christ." Dr. Binbaum was very satisfied with this approach.

"But Dr. Binbaum, you have to keep in mind that it may be me."

"You're the Son of God?" That seemed to interest Dr. Binbaum even more.

"No, but I may have made Jason think he is. Maybe I'm so crazy that he caught it."

"Can't hurt to ask, can it?" Dr. Binbaum was excited by the prospect and he danced his fanny all over his leather cushion. "Go home right now," he chortled. "Ask him. Call me up and tell me what he says!"

Solomon is clinging to my shoulder now, nearly upside down trying to read every word I'm writing. "Don't stop," he pants. "What happened?"

I did just like Dr. Binbaum told me. I asked Jason.

"6336," I said to him. "That was the number assigned to you by the adoption agency."

"So?" Jason was eating marshmallow fluff out of the jar with his fingers.

"6336. That adds up to three sixes, Jason, and it says in the Bible..."

Jason groaned. "How many times do I have to tell you about the Bible?" His mouth was full and when he opened his lips to speak, the fluff formed a picket fence.

"Six hundred sixty-six signifies the Anti-Christ." I screamed the words at him. "Jason, are you the Anti-Christ?"

Jason's nostrils flared. He fixed me with that ebony stare. An intense golden aura grew around his head and pulsed as though it were a living thing with a heartbeat of its own. "First off," he replied sharply, "many early scholars interpreted that number as six hundred sixteen. Some of the 17th Century group thought it might be nine hundred ninety-nine. I don't know what it's supposed to be. I wasn't paying attention. God nor I proofread the Bible. We were grappling with important issues. I can tell you, though, that I knew John and he was a superstitious fellow. Ran from black cats, never walked beneath a ladder. Maybe he thought six hundred sixty-six was his unlucky number. Who knows? Who cares?"

Jason's aura grew as vivid as a sunburst and I had to look away. When I dared to turn to him again, he was stuffing marshmallow fluff into his mouth as though nothing had occurred.

The pulsing aura ought to have convinced me, I suppose, but, as I said to Dr. Binbaum, who answered his phone at the beginning of the first ring, "the devil is a powerful critter. Surely he could make an aura pulse."

"Then how are we going to find out," Dr. Binbaum lamented. "How can we know for sure?"

"Maybe," I suggested, "I could bring Jason in to see you."

"No," Dr. Binbaum snapped, "don't do that!"

"He's just a little boy," I reminded him.

"He might be the Son of God," Dr. Binbaum responded, his voice quivering, "and if he is, I'm not ready."

"Neither am I, Dr. Binbaum."

"But you don't have a choice, Josie, I do. I need some time to get my shit together before I come face to face with Elijah. If indeed," and Dr. Binbaum seemed to have recovered his composure, "that's who Jason is."

So I continued loving Jason, doubting Jason, fearing Jason, doubting myself and fearing sometimes for the both of us. Jason, who knew everything I thought, said this grieved him mightily.

And I continued seeing Dr. Binbaum because, like me, he wasn't sure. We shared a hope that Jason was who he claimed to be, and a simultaneous terror that, if so, we were somehow responsible for doing something about it—warning the world, maybe, alerting everyone that the Second Coming was underway, that the final countdown had begun.

But we weren't sure. We couldn't be certain.

If Jason was, why would God have selected Me? We worked for several years on that one. And if he wasn't, what had I done to cause this incredible hallucination? We stayed with that one year and a half. And if he was, and we went through a period of being pretty sure he was, what was incumbent upon us?

"Solomon, I suppose if there are Seekers left in the world now and any of them can read this book, they might speculate that I'm a witch, an Anti-Christ, sitting in this abandoned sanctuary questioning the Bible, crying to the moon, speaking to a familiar."

"A who?" asks Solomon.

"A familiar. An envoy of the devil. According to myth, familiars are usually black cats."

"I'm not black," retorts Solomon. "Under all this dust, I'm mostly white. I have some grey spots and they're nicely placed, too. You have no idea how much I clean and clean and clean myself but my environment makes it impossible for me to reach my full potential."

"Am I a witch, Solomon? Can I be a witch and not know it?"

"I met a witch once," Solomon tells me. "She used to come here to perform circumcisions."

I played a make-believe witch for one year on Panda Playhouse, live every morning at seven a.m. But Happy Witch was a jolly sort in her polka-dot moo-moo with her turned up pigtails and bells on her shoes. She sang songs and introduced cartoons and read off the names of the little viewers who were celebrating birthdays that day—and kept smiling even though she was being tormented by Peter Panda and Silly Goose (puppets whose dialogue was improvised by Ginger Grosswoman and Lucy Dobdaughter) from their perch atop the Magic Castle.

Playing Happy Witch was a trauma in my life. When I was in the newsroom and Ginger snapped at me or Lucy sneered, I could get up and walk away—but Happy Witch was On The Air Live and had to stand there in front of God and everybody, smiling bravely as Peter Panda and Silly Goose vented their hostilities on her. If Happy Witch had been a real witch and possessed of demonic power, she would have smote them.

Happy Witch was one of my first assignments at Channel 3. Dr. Binbaum convinced me that I was getting nowhere as a Skeeter's Girl and that there must be somewhere I could make a decent wage while using my writing and performing talents. Bouyed by his enthusiasm, I made up a resume and sent it to every television station in the greater New York area.

I took the job at Channel 3 and expected to stay there until death or retirement. Channel 3 was like a family. I recall those years with warmth and love, but I had terrible, traumatic times there, too.

"What have you gotten me into?" I screamed as I stormed into Dr. Binbaum's office. "A goddam Panda and a fucking Goose are chewing me up and spitting me out every morning at seven."

"I noticed," Dr. Binbaum snickered. "That goose has a quick wit, hasn't she?"

The goose, of course, was played by Lucy Dobdaughter. At Channel 3, everyone wore several hats. Lucy was officially Assistant Station Manager but she also wrote promotion copy, covered occasional news events and played Silly Goose on Panda Playhouse. Ginger Grosswoman, less facile than Lucy, and less highly paid, wrote news copy, held up cue cards for the newscast and played Peter Panda.

No one had time to write scripts for Panda Playhouse. There was no incentive to do so. The Channel 3 management had no interest in the quality or ratings of the kiddie show— they were simply, and at as little cost as possible, meeting the FCC requirement that they provide an hour of children's broadcasting every day. Spot sponsors like Mattel and Chocks bought time on kiddie shoes across the board, regardless of the quality or the ratings. I doubt that anyone from Mattel or Chocks ever saw Panda Playhouse on the air. The format of the show was this:

7:00 a.m.	LIVE OPEN	Happy Witch rides broom equipped with Mattel Vroom Motor over Manhattan singing Up In The Air Junior Birdmen and improvises opening material "Welcome kiddies, etc." (1:30) which leads into
7:01:30	MATTEL (LIVE)	Mattel Commercial/Talking Gorilla/ Product Demonstration by Happy Witch (Copy on cue card)
7:02:30	LIVE INTRO	Happy Witch intros OUR GANG AT THE CIRCUS (:30)
	OUR GANG CARTOON	
7:03:00	FILM	OUR GANG FILM AT THE CIRCUS (running time 4:02)
7:07:02	LIVE	Chocks Vitamins Commercial/ Charlie Chocks pillow
	CHOCKS	Product Demonstration by Happy Witch (Copy on cue card)
7:08:02	FILM MATTEL	Mattel Commercial/Space Flight Battery Operated Flying Missile (running time :60)
7:09:02	LIVE CASTLE	Happy Witch, Peter Panda, Silly Goose at Castle. Read Birthday Babies' names, sing Birthday song, improvise (5:02)
7:14:00	LIVE CHOCKS	Chocks Breakfast Drink Commercial. Product Demonstration by Happy Witch/copy by Peter Panda and Silly Goose (on cue card) (:60)
7:15:00	LIVE INTRO	Happy Witch, Peter Panda, Silly Goose intro
	LITTLE IOD.	LITTLE IODINE'S TONSILS (:30)
7:15:30	FILM	LITTLE IODINE'S TONSILS (running time 3:36)

On the average, Happy Witch spent about twelve minutes every morning at the castle with Peter Panda and Silly Goose. It seemed like twelve years. There were no scripts so I have nothing except my memory to support the charge that every weekday morning for a full year I was verbally molested by two hand puppets.

HAPPY WITCH: (Flying to the castle on her Vroom Broom) Well, boys and girls, look where we are! Isn't that Peter Panda's castle just below us? Let's swoop down for a better look! (SPECIAL EFFECTS SWOOPS AND TWIRLS HAPPY WITCH) Well, goodness, I believe there's Peter Panda now—and his good friend, Silly Goose. Look there, they're waving. Let's visit them, shall we? It's always such fun to visit Peter Panda and Silly Goose. Good morning, Peter Panda. Good morning, Silly.
SILLY GOOSE: Well, look what just fell out of the sky. And I was hoping for good weather.
HAPPY WITCH: Why, it's beautiful weather outside today. The boys and girls will have a good time in the park today.
SILLY GOOSE: Why, Happy Witch, I'm ashamed of you, telling boys and girls to go to the park. Don't you know there are muggers and perverts in the park? Peter Panda, why does Happy Witch want the boys and girls to get killed?
PETER PANDA: It certainly sounds like it.
SILLY GOOSE: And where are your manners, Happy Witch?
PETER PANDA: Yes, why didn't you bring your manners?
SILLY GOOSE: Did you invite her to the castle, Peter Panda?
PETER PANDA: Not me.
SILLY GOOSE: You should never drop in uninvited, Happy Witch. It's very rude to come barging into someone's castle the way you do.
HAPPY WITCH: But Peter Panda waved at me.

PETER PANDA: I was waving you *on*.

SILLY GOOSE: You're teaching the boys and girls bad manners, Happy Witch, and if I were their mothers, I'd be angry at you. Furthermore, it's dangerous to go flying in the air. Do you want the boys and girls to think they can go flying in the air? Peter Panda, what would happen to the boys and girls if they went flying in the air?

PETER PANDA: They'd fall down and break their necks.

SILLY GOOSE: Is that what you want to happen to the boys and girls, Happy Witch? If you were really a witch, you wouldn't need a motor.

PETER PANDA: You're a phony, Happy Witch. Boys and girls, all of you who think Happy Witch is a phony, write to me in care of the Castle.

SILLY GOOSE: Peter Panda, I think that Happy Witch doesn't even like the boys and girls.

PETER PANDA: Boys and girls, if you think Happy Witch doesn't even like you, write to me in care of the Castle.

HAPPY WITCH: I love the boys and girls. I do! I love them so much that I'm going to show them a wonderful new cartoon about their good friend, Little Iodine.

SILLY GOOSE: That's not a new cartoon. You showed it to them last month.

PETER PANDA: Happy Witch is lying to you again, boys and girls. If you think Happy Witch is lying to you again, write to me...

I consoled myself by believing no one watched Panda Playhouse except Dr. Binbaum. I knew Jason didn't. He said TV scrambled his vision. I suspect that whatever internal electronic system prevented Jason from being photographed also short-circuited the images on a television screen. But when Fober, the hip young director who came to Channel 3 many years later, first saw me, he cried, "Oh my God, you're Happy Witch!"

Reluctantly, I admitted that I had once been that hapless

creature.

"I watched you every morning," he said gleefully, "every single day. The whole frat house did. We thought you guys were better than Laugh-In."

At a later point in my Channel 3 career, I had to hostess a teenage dance show at 4 p.m. weekdays. It was Ginger's job to scout up high school groups to participate and she failed miserably to do so. Often, we had to squeeze four or five young couples into a corner and shoot them from three angles to make them look like more.

The first time I had to hostess A WOMAN'S WORLD, Channel 3's live noon interview program, my guest was a housewife from Rego Park who carved the heads of Presidents in bars of Ivory Soap. Ginger had read about her in the *Daily News* and secured her for the show. The woman had never been on TV and had no wish to be but Ginger wept when she called her on the phone and pleaded that we couldn't find another guest on such short notice. Once in the studio, the woman shook so violently that the table rattled. On the air, I asked her if she'd been doing these sculptures long. She shook her head. I asked if she had any formal training. She shook her head again. I inquired what her family thought of her hobby. She said nothing but became wild-eyed. She began to breathe rapidly and her shaking increased. I asked her if she'd ever carved the faces of her own children in Ivory Soap. With that, she scooped her sculptures off the table, stood and cried, "I told that girl I couldn't do this, I just hope nobody on my block is watching!" She ran out of the studio.

I looked up at the clock and hoped no one was watching, too. Thirteen minutes to go. Me and the little red light.

"Solomon, has anybody in the world made a public fool of themselves as frequently as I have?" I was in an off-Broadway play in 1958 where I was required to wear a backless, strapless dress with stays inserted in the bosom to hold the top up. On opening night, with a full house and critics on the aisle, I bent over as I'd been directed to do and when I straightened up, the stays didn't. I was the first topless actress in America. I blushed all the way to my bare nipples and got a resounding round of applause.

I long for dignity and respect. When I looked out the window of our upper West Side apartment and saw Jason walking on the Hudson River, I didn't worry that he'd sink and drown. I cringed for fear someone would see him and know that he belonged to me.

I have a chronic case of Foot in Mouth disease. It's partly because of this that I turned into a near-recluse during the years I was raising Jason. What with Jason saying he's the Son of God at home, and my making daily faux pas in front of a live camera, I just couldn't bear going to dinner at someone's home and saying something that would bring the conversation to a gasping red-faced halt. Apart from speaking what I had to speak on the job in order to earn my salary and talking to Dr. Binbaum in my early evening sessions, I opened my mouth as infrequently as possible. Jason didn't like conversation anyway.

Jason, Jason. I loved you.

It took Dr. Binbaum to help me know how much.

I will not turn and look at the Judas window, Solomon. I can see the light intensifying in this room. The sun is up. I feel its heat. I see its light. But I'm not going to turn around and look again. If the moon is gone, I don't want to know.

FOURTEEN

JASON was not a normal little boy. That is, he didn't roller skate in the hallway, snitch apples from carts on the street, deal in Acapulco Gold at recess or engage in bloody fistfights. He never mugged a little girl or old lady after school and he wasn't disruptive in the classroom. He was a welcome enigma to his harried teachers. His report cards bore gold stars in Deportment and Personal Hygiene. In Reading and Spelling he received Cs. Perhaps if he'd been enrolled in public school in Advent, Georgia, instead of the upper West Side of Manhattan, someone might have noticed that he couldn't read or write.

I knew he didn't like to read and that he regarded words as a barrier between humankind and God. I'd seen him recoil at the sight of a bound volume and shut his eyes against signs and billboards. But it somehow did not come clear to me that he *couldn't* read. His seventh grade home room teacher, Mrs. Homer, noticed it immediately. She was of the old school and required her students to sit during classes, hands visible above their desks. Talking out of turn brought a hearty smack from Mrs. Homer's ruler and it was rumored that on more than one occasion, she'd connected a right jab to a stubborn student's jaw. She did not consider spray-painting the classroom with graffiti to be an acceptable form of self-expression nor would she tolerate being addressed as Mother-Fucker, a fact which rendered many of her students speechless. Although Mrs. Homer was white haired and nearing sixty-five. she weighed a solid two hundred pounds and could lift any seventh grader off the floor with one hand. She was Black as a moonless midnight and when she bared her teeth, they flashed like the sharp edge of a mighty sword. The School Board was, at that time, deeply engrossed in progressive education and Mrs. Homer was a painful thorn in their sides. The year Jason was her student, she failed the entire seventh grade and defended herself by stating that she had given them exactly the same test she'd given students ten years previous when the average grade was B-. The School Board overruled Mrs. Homer and stated publicly that Longfellow, Thoreau, Emerson and A.E. Housman were irrelevant.

On the first day of school that year, Mrs. Homer discovered that Jason was illiterate. She required each student to stand beside their desk and read a stanza from *The Village Blacksmith*. Every student in the room got at least one word right— a *the, an* or *a*—though none of them knew *spreading* or *chestnut* and only seven recognized *tree*. Jason, however, stood wordlessly beside his desk, ebony eyes empty of discernible expression. After Mrs. Homer ascertained he was not being a smart-ass, deducing this from the fact that the other students laughed at him instead of cheering his silence, she alerted the Principal who suggested that perhaps Jason had a learning dysfunction. "How then," she demanded to know, "did this child progress to the seventh grade?" Given no satisfactory explanation, she telephoned me at home that night.

"If I were you," Mrs. Homer suggested, "I'd hie myself over to that grade school and ask some questions. You want me to, I'll come along."

I'm glad Mrs. Homer accompanied me. She knew just what to ask.

"You gave this boy Cs," Mrs. Homer challenged Jason's sixth grade teacher. "You gave him a C in reading and he can't read a word. You gave him C in writing and he can't print the alphabet. You gave him C in penmanship and he can't sign his name."

"I give them all Cs," the teacher admitted under Mrs. Homer's assault. He was a young man, long-haired and intense. He emitted an aura of despair. "If they don't attack each other or me, they get a C," he sighed. "And Jason drew well with crayons and made remarkable human likenesses in Play Dough."

When Mrs. Homer recovered from her palpitations, she advised me that, regardless, she was going to have to flunk Jason in the seventh grade. As it turned out, she flunked the entire class and when she was overruled, Jason slipped into the eighth grade with the others.

No one but Mrs. Homer ever noticed Jason's inability to read. His eighth grade teacher, however, was concerned about his lack of sociability and referred him to the school psychologist. I feared that Jason would announce he was the Son of God and the school would ship him off to an institution, but that didn't happen. Jason sat quietly through three sessions without announcing anything at all. "I'm not ready to come out yet," Jason told me, "the time must be just right." So the school psychologist's report read, "A shy and mannerly oriental child whose behavioral characteristics are attributable to his ethnic traditions."

At the time Jason was in the seventh grade, I was no longer seeing Dr. Binbaum. Dr. Binbaum had moved to Southern California to establish the National Naked Confrontation Center; when that was raided and closed down in

1978, Dr. Binbaum returned to New York City but by that time Jason had taken to the streets.

The sun is up now. The heat of it, filtered through the stained glass, burns the back of my neck. I shift my chair to avoid it. My stomach feels as though someone has seized it in his fist. It's definitely past daybreak now but I refuse to look out that window again.

Solomon nudges my hand with his nose. "Get the lead out."

Dr. Binbaum and I met at least three times a week for over four years. The first year (and during crises), we met five times a week. One such crisis, I recall, occurred when I discovered the leg from our Thanksgiving turkey had disappeared during the time it took me to set the table. Jason denied eating it. I made him breathe into my face but there was no smell of turkey. In regard to food, I had reason to distrust Jason. It was not that he intentionally lied about what he ate—it was that he ate so frequently and to such excess that he often could not remember what he had or hadn't consumed. I knew I hadn't devoured the turkey leg and since we had no dinner guests, I remained puzzled until after we had eaten and I opened the doors beneath the sink to scrape the plates into the garbage. There, jutting from the open flap of an empty Giant Size box of Borax, was the missing leg. Gnawed to the bone. When I reached to retrieve it, there was a scuffling inside the box. I withdrew my hand quickly and slammed the doors. Dragging Jason by the hand, I stomped furiously to the Super's apartment and found a note pinned to the door. "Gone to New Jersey for the holiday. Happy Thanksgiving!" We walked Broadway from 96th down to 74th before we found a hardware store open. The rat trap cost three dollars and the proprietor admonished me to keep Jason's fingers away from it. "Anything big enough to carry off a turkey leg," said the hardware man, "is the size of a half-grown cat."

I loaded the trap with turkey skin and giblet gravy. I set it carefully and slipped it under the sink between the garbage can and the Borax box. As I withdrew my hand, the trap released spontaneously and made such a thundering sound in the metal cabinet that I fell backward on the floor. The Borax box jumped with surprise. I closed the cabinet quickly and raced into the bedroom where I donned my knee high winter boots. I ordered Jason to stand on a chair. Again, I set the trap and slid it into place.

Late afternoon as Jason sat on the windowsill considering the sky and I had fallen sound asleep watching reruns, the trap went off. The thunderous snap was followed by a nearly human scream. I donned my boots and peeked behind the cabinet doors.

Not only was she the size of a small cat, she was long-haired and fluffy. Until I glimpsed her face, I thought maybe I'd killed somebody's kitten. She was gray and white, Solomon, and colored something like you.

"You're sure it was a rat?" Solomon inquired, wrinkling his nose with interest. "A rat that big would last me all week long."

"It was a rat, a wharf rat. Long-haired, quite pretty actually, and very pregnant."

"Oh dear," Solomon interjects, a note of envy in his voice. "You know they have litters of fifteen, sixteen." He sighs and smacks his lips.

"I know, Solomon. I know. You see, when I saw the rat—it had been struck across the head by the trap and was very, very dead—I began to weep copiously. Jason, who was always sensitive to my discomforts, knelt down beside me and released the creature from the trap. He held it in his hand and stroked it twice and then placed it on the floor."

"Put it in the garbage," I instructed him. "Wrap it in a paper towel and put it in the garbage."

But as I said it, the rat shook its head as though it had awakened from a nightmare, stared at me with bewilderment in its eyes and in a single bound, dove back into its nest inside the Borax box.

"See?" Jason touched my shoulder consolingly. "It's feeling just fine now. It's going to have babies soon." He smiled happily.

"Oh, Jason," I replied still weeping, "isn't that terrific."

We first caught sight of the babies about eighteen hours later. She was moving them one by one into a rat hole she'd chewed during the night. It was located in the molding of the bathroom, just beside the tub. I'd heard the gnawing sound but I'd closed my bedroom door and Jason's just in case she decided to take a midnight tour. At daybreak, when I ventured into the kitchen in my boots and Jason wandered out to join me, we watched in amazement as Mama Rat transported her seventeen newborn infants to their new quarters.

Three months and two exterminators later, we still had one rat loose in the apartment. I believe he was the eldest son and must have resembled his father for he was short-haired and jet black with a touch of white beneath his chin. Half the size of his deceased mother, he was snaggle-toothed and brazen. He moved about the apartment as though he were paying one third of the rent. Jason had no fear of him at all. In fact, they seemed to have some kind of understanding.

When I told Jason I would go raving mad if the rat ever came in the bathroom while I was dripping wet and vulnerable, the rat took to peeking first before he entered. If he saw me there, he gallantly retreated to the kitchen cupboard where he feasted on raw spaghetti or paper towels. Like Jason, he ate almost anything.

The Super, fed up with my complaints, employed a Mr. McNulty who hung out at the bar downstairs and had once won first prize in a rat-shooting contest in his native Ireland. He assured me when he arrived at my apartment with a bottle in one hand and a loaded pistol in the other, he was a marksman of some note. Our rat happened to be napping at the time of Mr. McNulty's arrival and when I pointed out the rat's lair in the bathroom molding, Mr. McNulty aimed his pistol at the opening, fired, took a healthy swig of whiskey and considered the deed done. A moment later, our rat peeked out inquisitively, then, spotting Mr. McNulty's weapon, darted across the toes of Mr. McNulty's spectator shoes and dove beneath the living room sofa.

Mr. McNulty seized the sofa by the arm and flung it away from the wall. He aimed and fired at a dustball. The rat, meanwhile, had taken cover behind the kitchen stove. He peered out at us from the ballcock on the gas line. Mr. McNulty aimed. I threw myself across Mr. McNulty's arm.

"No," I cried, "don't shoot the gas line!"

At that same moment, I caught a glimpse of my shishka-bob skewers dangling from their brass holder above the stove. I seized one and with it pinned the rat's head to the floor. I moaned, and averted my eyes from what I'd done. Jason removed the skewer from my hand.

"You bring it back to life," I warned, "and I'll break all ten of your fingers."

Mr. McNulty dropped the carcass in a brown paper bag and, after requesting ten dollars for his services, departed to dispose of the remains.

I threw the skewer in the trash. Then I sobbed.

"I never killed anything before," I cried. "And it's so easy!"

"It's just as easy to heal," Jason advised me. "But you trust Fear more than you trust Love."

"Oh, don't start with one of those parables, Jason, I just killed something for the first time in my life!"

"It was a creature living in God's world," Jason reminded me.

"I know that," I screamed in response, "why do you think I'm crying?"

Jason sighed. "And God had everything so nicely arranged to begin with."

"I can't believe God intended for rats and people to live

together in an apartment," I yelled in my defense.

"God," Jason replied, "didn't intend for you or the rat to live in an apartment."

"Well, we can't turn around now, Jason," I argued. "We're too far gone in this direction."

"Oh, I don't know," Jason smiled mysteriously. "Wonders and miracles still hover here and there, though I admit they've been somewhat dissipated by your automobile exhausts."

"Dr. Binbaum," I laid my head on his chest at my session that night. (Dr. Binbaum had taken to lying on the couch and I to kneeling at his side), "the kid is six years old and he's speaking like a Prophet."

Dr. Binbaum, half in slumber, responded quietly. "It's easy to kill, Josie. And easier the second time."

I gripped Dr. Binbaum's shoulders. "Have you ever killed something?" I shook his shirt impatiently, eager for the answer.

"Oh," he yawned, "flies and wasps. A couple of mice and two teenage muggers. I broke the first one's neck with a karate chop and knifed the second one with his own switchblade."

"Dr. Binbaum!" I stared closely into his face.

He opened his eyes halfway and peered over his glasses which were resting askew on the bridge of his nose.

"You killed two teenage muggers?"

"No," he admitted, "but I fantasize I did. They ripped off $134.00 cash, my silver money clip and all my credit cards. It took me three months to get my driver's license reinstated. Sometimes in my fantasy I pull a gun from somewhere and shoot them both in the balls."

"But you wouldn't really do it. You wouldn't really kill a person."

"Sometimes maybe I wouldn't, sometimes maybe I would," Dr. Binbaum shrugged. "So far I've only been mugged once and it was on a day I wouldn't." "They," said

Dr. Binbaum, "are not civilized enough to live in this world."

Dr. Binbaum talked a tough line but I watched him once spend half a session shooing a mosquito out the window with a Kleenex because he couldn't bring himself to slap it. The mosquito became so disconcerted by Dr. Binbaum's waving of the Kleenex that it veered into a pane of glass and killed itself.

"Death," reported Dr. Binbaum sadly, "is a difficult subject."

We discussed it often in our sessions. I explored the meaning of my father's death/or/suicide but was unable to summon the sense of rejection or make contact with the repressed fury which Dr. Binbaum assured me I had. I did discovered that I harbored a deep respect for my father because he tried it here, didn't like it and moved on quickly, undeterred by guilt, responsibility or fear of death. He left no maudlin suicide note to assuage his ego, no syrupy love letters to my mother or me designed to be folded and slipped inside the family Bible to preserve his memory, he made no requests or demands regarding the disposal of his remains.

As Jason often said, "It's no big deal, just another state of Being."

Dr. Binbaum and I both believed we'd been in this world before. Dr. Binbaum had recollections of being an African woman, heavy breasted, bearing a wooden jug of water on his head. He also thought he had invented ice skates in the 4th Century in Norway.

"Jason says all time is happening right now. You and the African woman and the Ice Skate Inventor are all living simultaneously."

Dr. Binbaum pressed the butt of his hand against his forehead signaling that one of his migraine headaches was about to get underway. "Is Jason happy?" he asked.

"He billows with bliss."

"I tell you what, Josie," Dr. Binbaum placed both his hands on my shoulders as though he were a King beknighting someone. "You get Jason to tell you a parable a week and we'll study it, you and I. We'll get it by and by. If we think on it enough, we'll get it."

I shook my head. "Jason says we mustn't think on it. That's exactly what's keeping us from getting it."

"Well," he sighed and made a little helpless squeaking noise as he did so, "get him to say something profound each week and we'll lie down here in the office and try not to think about it. We'll get it then, won't we?"

Jason was most uncooperative.

"You can't think about not thinking."

"We'll lie very still," I promised. "We'll hardly breathe."

"You'll talk about it and the words will foul you up."

"I swear we won't. You can write it on an index card and we won't speak a syllable to one another."

Jason shook his head vigorously. "It doesn't mean the same thing when it's written down. You have to Know it."

"How can I Know it, if I don't know what it is I'm supposed to Know?"

Jason sighed. "You may be hopeless."

"I'm trying, Jason," I screamed at the top of my lungs.

"All right, all right." He sat on the floor, legs spread wide open, arms raised. I watched him for several minutes. At last, he looked at me. "Okay," he said, "you get it?"

"I see you've split the crotch of your blue jeans again."

"You didn't get it."

"You're going to have to say it in words, Jason. I don't have ESP."

"Yes," Jason argued, "you do. It's in the clutter somewhere."

"Well, I can't locate it!"

"Okay," Jason stood, he was little more than waist-high then, and spoke these words: *"Death is not a horseman. Life is but a dream."*

Dr. Binbaum and I shared these words, whispering them hoarsely and mysteriously, then shouting them angrily at one another. Finally, we lay down (he on the sofa, I on the floor) for the purpose of basking in the aura which we hoped we had created when we yelled the words. Dr. Binbaum slept quite soundly until the alarm on his desk clock went off.

I reported to Jason that neither Dr. Binbaum nor I had experienced a revelation about *Death is not a horseman. Life is but a dream.*

"Stream," Jason corrected, "*Life is but a stream.* No wonder you didn't get It, you weren't listening."

Dr. Binbaum was bright-eyed and bushy-tailed when I arrived for the next night's session. "I got It," he chortled and clapped his hands. "I can't explain it, but I got It."

"How?" I was virtually panting for the answer.

"I repeated it a hundred times before I went to bed. *Death is not a horseman. Life is but a scream.* It's profound," he gasped admiringly.

"Stream," I interrupted. "*Life is but a stream.*"

"What?"

"I heard it wrong, too, Dr. Binbaum. I thought he said *dream.* But it's *stream.*"

"Not *scream*?"

I shook my head slowly.

"Oh dear," said Dr. Binbaum.

Jason made many proclamations and Dr. Binbaum and I grappled with them each in turn: *Life is not solid matter but solid matter is life; Godly is Singular; She who dances likely sings;* and *All are God but few are Godly.*

We tried writing down the proclamations and varying the punctuation, as *Life is not. Solid matter but solid. Matter is Life.* We sometimes worked on the assumption that we'd again misunderstood, as *God! This thing you are!*

By mutual agreement, Dr. Binbaum and I began to speak to others of these proclamations. Neither of us disclosed the source of the statement.

Sam Dowdy had just returned from a vacation in California where he'd attended an EST seminar. "*All are God but few are Godly,"* he repeated it several times in his resonant bass voice. He turned on his mike and listened to the words echo through the control room. "Yes," he agreed, "I like that, believe I'll use it as the tag on tonight's newscast." Then he shared the news he'd received at the EST seminar in California—that he was a little God come down from heaven himself.

Dr. Binbaum even reached out to strangers. He once seized the saffron robe of a Hare Krishna on 57th Street and, placing his palm over the goathide to silence the tambourine, said *"Life is not solid matter but solid matter is life."* The Hare Krishna stuck two fingers in his mouth and whistled. In seconds, Dr. Binbaum was surrounded by saffron robes, lifted from the ground by his elbows and ankles and dumped into a trash can.

Dr. Binbaum wrote Jason's words on the inside of public toilet stalls and returned daily to see if any comments or addendums had been scribbled in reply. *She who dances likely sings* was the most popular one. In the men's room at Grand Central, it eventually covered an entire wall. Likely screws, too, likely sucks, likely cums, etc.

Undaunted, Dr. Binbaum hired a plane to skywrite *Godly is Singular* above Manhattan but the wind was high that day and only God Sing was visible. He stood in Central Park all morning waiting to hear someone comment on it. Finally, an old lady in a wheelchair glanced up and saw the puffs of smoke spiraling across the sky. "What's it say?" she inquired of her nurse who answered, "It's an advertisement for a musical on Broadway."

For nearly two years, Dr. Binbaum and I were Jason's unofficial Apostles. We spread the word but encountered no one who understood it.

At last, Jason emitted a proclamation that Dr. Binbaum thought he understood. It seemed to hit him hard. It had some personal meaning which he didn't share with me. It changed his life for the time being, though, and certainly changed mine.

"*Man must disrobe to enter Paradise.*"

Dr. Binbaum's eyes lit up. He yanked his tie off and shouted, "Whoopee, Josie, I think I got It now!"

"Divest," he muttered, "that's the ticket, divest."

"Of earthly goods? Is that it?"

"Come naked unto God," he nodded, "and He will receive you." At that point he removed his shirt and flung it at his desk. "Damn, Josie," he said, "I got It."

The next morning at nine a.m. his secretary telephoned my office to cancel all future sessions. Dr. Binbaum, she reported with a puzzled and embarrassed tone in her voice, has packed up and gone to California on a religious mission.

Several months after that, the UP machine tippity-tapped out the information that the federal government had allocated two and one half million dollars to the National Naked Confrontation Center, an Experiment in Intrapersonal and Religious Process, under the direction of Hubert H.H.R. Binbaum, III, M.D., Ph.D. Through the years, we received film clips on the Center's progress though we couldn't use them on the air because the participants were naked. There were confirmed reports that Mescaline, Peyote and Cocaine were being used in controlled experiments at the Center and had proven effective in easing terminal patients into the dark and fearful voyage of death.

UP revealed that the Center was using LSD to explore the creative processes of visual and literary artists and the results, which appeared to be photographs of an explosion, were the closest humankind had come to revealing the true landscape of man's mind. Dr. Binbaum became very rich and famous. He received a Nobel Prize for religious research. Soon after that, it was rumored that Dr. Binbaum had purchased a mansion in Palm Springs with a mushroom shaped swimming pool larger than a football field. Next we heard that an Italian designer of some note had admitted creating silk shirts and trousers to Dr. Binbaum's order, the cuffs of both pieces embroidered with H.H.H.R.B., III, M.D., Ph.D. in gold thread. It was shattering news.

But even before this happened, I had ceased to be Jason's Apostle and had become an unbeliever. It didn't come over me in a sudden brilliant flash the way Dr. Binbaum's revelation attacked him. Day by day, after Dr. Binbaum fled to California and Jason eased into Junior High School devoid of reading and writing skills, I noticed a tiny flickering light in the back of my mind. It intensified slowly over a number of months and finally revealed this: Dr. Binbaum was crazier than I and Jason was the craziest of all. Jason might be, in fact, the craziest person in the whole world. This was not an easy revelation to accept. And with the inbred survival instinct of my kind, I vowed to shield him from harm unto my death.

So I ignored Jason's claim to divinity. When he spoke in parables, I changed the subject. I operated on the premise that if I refused to recognize Jason's affliction, it would disappear. After all, my Philosophy I professor at Advent Christian College had assured me that if a tree fell in the forest and no one was there to hear it, it couldn't make a sound.

My behavior seemed to have no discernable effect on Jason. He moved from house to school and back again each day and sometimes, after supper, he'd say "Excuse me, please," emit a resounding and appreciative belch, and disappear out of his chair. He somehow completed most of his high school before his calling came. It was Easter vacation of his Senior year, a time when all his classmates were busy planning proms and private parties and looking to a summer of unemployment and legal drinking. Jason woke up one morning and said, "Well, this is it."

I realize that I still have this blanket on my shoulders and I'm sweating. I push it to the floor. I notice that my ankle is slightly stiff but not sore.

"No wonder you're hot," Solomon notes. "It must be noon."

"No, Solomon, I don't think so. Mid-morning, maybe."
But I won't look out the Judas window to see for sure.

Solomon stretches and strides to the window. He leaps to
the sill and peers out the crack.

"Whew," he tells me, "the sun is blazing. It's going to be a
scorcher. How can the Jasonites sleep in this heat?"

"Don't look a gift-horse in the mouth," I warn. "Come
away from that window, Solomon. Don't call attention to
yourself."

Solomon springs and hits the floor with a thud. "Sorry,"
he shrugs. He examines his paws for damage. I realize my
palms are cold and sweaty.

Solomon bounds on the table, sits smack in the middle of
the written pages and meows.

"All right," he demands, "tell me how you killed Jason."

"I didn't kill him, Solomon," I retort.

"Well," Solomon advises, "you better gallop right along.
The heat may not wake the Jasonites but sooner or later
they'll have to pee. If I were you, I would regard this time
strictly as a short reprieve."

"I do, Solomon, I do."

He moves aside so I can put the pen to paper. He has left
hairs all across the page. I brush them off with the side of my
hand.

"Solomon," I chastise him, "you're shedding on my
book."

"Get on, Josie, with the death of Jason."

"I hate to write it down," I admit, "because it makes it
seem so final."

"I have to know," Solomon says.

Well, as my Grandma used to say, if it doesn't taste bad, it
can't be doing you any good.

FIFTEEN

NEVER learned to Be, Solomon. Jason once advised me to just keep repeating I Am, I Am, I Am and soon I would recognize that was the only piece of knowledge required. I could never stop with just I Am. I had to keep on going. I Am Taller and Smarter than Ginger Grosswoman, Fatter but Nicer than Lucy Dobdaughter, Saner but Weaker than Dr. Binbaum, Lonelier but Braver than George."

"Cats hardly ever compare themselves," Solomon boasts.

"Abstract thinking is what makes man superior to beast."

"If cats were foolhardy enough to have a spoken language, we certainly would have no room in it for comparative adjectives."

Jason loathed pronouns, personal, relative, demonstrative, indefinite and especially interrogative. On my first wedding anniversary, Geroge, in a sweet effort to encourage my writing, gave me a gilded paperweight inscribed WHO, WHICH, WHAT? Jason wrapped it up and presented it as a Christmas gift to Mrs. Leonetti who had already, so he said, travelled so far from Godliness that she'd likely never make the trip back. Poor old Mrs. Leonetti. She worked so hard to please. St. Anthony's regarded her as a regular saint, but Jason grieved her as a lost soul.

Jason had little compassion for Mrs. Leonetti. "There is no end and no beginning," he'd remind me.

That's why the Jasonites feel no guilt about executing me. They perceive there is no start or finish to life, just a continuous process of Being.

For me death is still a Headless Horseman.

When Jason took to the streets that Easter Sunday, he did nothing spectacular. He didn't fly or dematerialize. He didn't speak through a bullhorn or dress in a strange manner to attract attention. He'd been walking around the same neighborhood for years and had attracted no notice at all. That day he strolled onto the sidewalk, dressed in his khaki cut-offs, a pair of rubber thongs, a faded Adidas t-shirt and raised his hands. It was as though time wound down. For a radius of two hundred yards, everything slowed its motion. A circle of golden light appeared around the entire area, mesmerizing those inside of it and blinding those outside so they couldn't see within. Absolute peace, a quiet softness like the moment just before you fall asleep, descended on everyone within the circle. They say that many of the people just outside the circle clawed at the golden light, trying to break in. The people watched from high windows, looking down into the circle, reported that all eyes were riveted on Jason. And when the circle of gold flickered and went out, the first flock of Jasonites were kneeling with their arms around each other. Jason was kneeling, too, and touched the flesh of all those within his arm's reach.

I didn't see this for myself. When Jason said it was time for him to go, I was scrubbing scrambled egg out of a frying pan with a Brillo pad and too irritated to pick up the tone of finality in his voice.

I lived with Jason nearly eighteen years. I witnessed his

wonders and miracles and many times was blinded by his golden aura but I did not succumb. I agree the world is in a terrific mess and has been for God only knows how many hundred years and I don't have trouble believing that God (though He has never deigned to speak to me personally) might send someone to avert earthly disaster. I do, however, resist the thought it's Jason. Albert Einstein was no genius to his mother. A mother's heart says: This child is mine and therefore cannot possibly be more than I am.

While Jason's personal magnetism brought most of the world to its knees, I stood back, untouched, and watched the action carefully, prepared to step in quickly, if and when I had to, to protect my boy's life.

There must have been a thousand articles written by learned men and women attempting to explain Jason.

Jasonites don't appear to live in family units, neither do they move in clusters. Someone compared them to a flock of birds. They travel together for safety and companionship but each remains independent. The primary quality of the Jasonites is that they have absolutely no interest in things. Ownership is unwelcome, disgraceful and unholy. Acquisitions are an anathema to Jasonites.

They depend on no one yet, if they have excess, they give it to whomever asks. If they are without, they ask and receive. If they make a thing of beauty, a mobile of seashells, for instance, they hang it on a tree. If someone passing by admires it or despises it, it makes no difference to a Jasonite. They find joy in the doing, not in the effect. They seem devoid of ego as we think of it—yet, they stand erect and walk with dignity, as though they know they are God's creatures and expect nothing more but accept nothing less. They have no purpose except to Be.

Sam Dowdy once took a poll on the Channel 3 News, asking viewers to write in and state, in 25 words or less, their concept of paradise. These are some of the answers I remember:

"Just me and my family. Big piece of land. Modern house. Dishwasher. Swimming pool. No taxes. No neighbors. Color TV. Eternal youth."

"Everybody would like each other in Paradise. Hugging and kissing. A lot of parties. Good food. No fights."

"Plenty of booze. Plenty of broads."

"The animals would talk and everything we have to buy would be free."

"I wouldn't have to do anything I didn't want to and nobody could give me any orders because I'd be the boss."

We received over 200 responses and no one wanted to just Be.

Serenity is threatening. No one volunteers to be serene. It's an unknown quantity; we tremble at the thought of it, anticipating that a good dose of serenity will disable us, make us vulnerable, disqualify us from the rat-race. We don't want to lay back. We want to conquer.

About my frequent anxiety attacks, Jason asked, "How important is it?"

"Important!" I'd scream in reply. "I'm being overcharged, ripped-off, defrauded, harrassed, and taken advantage of. Somebody's got me by the short hairs!"

Jason shrugged. "How important is it?"

"A person just can't let people push her around. A person has to have backbone, be aggressive, stand up for their rights. I have to fight! Otherwise I'm a sucker, a pushover, a coward, a failure."

"But," Jason sighed, "how important is it?"

Like everybody else, I feared serenity. I associated serenity with surrender. Not me! I am the fearless captain of my soul and I intend to go down with the ship.

That's how the wars against the Jasonites began. The first six months of Jason's ministry, he was located on the upper West Side of Manhattan and the rest of the world considered him an amusing, harmless kook.

Some people admired him, the way one envies the wild

antics of a madman.

"Boy, I'd like to lay around all day like those Jasonites," they'd say, or "I wish my wife would become one so she'd shut up and stop nagging."

Then suddenly, because no one had taken Jason seriously, no one expected it, the economy of the West Side collapsed. Most Westsiders had become Jasonites and Jasonites don't work for wages, pay taxes, rent or purchase manmade items. It didn't happen slowly but so insidiously, one Jasonite casting a smile on an unbeliever who became a Jasonite and cast his smile on his wife and children and their smiles spread to supermarkets and the public schools and ... it didn't take long and it was scarcely noticeable as it happened. The shopkeepers, having become Jasonites, opened their doors and gave away their stock. The local police precinct, most of whom lived in Staten Island or in Queens, noticed that their telephones had ceased to ring and crime was almost non-existent but they attributed it to a harmless religious revival in the area. They spent their workdays with their feet up, playing poker.

Then, one morning at the A&P Regional Offices, an ambitious junior executive demanded to see the computer read-outs for the past quarter. He was startled, almost apoplectic, to discover that the twelve West Side A&P stores had reported no receipts in months. He called Grand Union who, on ordering a read-out of their own computers, discovered the same thing. They called McDonald's who called Burger King who called Kentucky Fried Chicken and so on. The very same week, Citibank computers kicked out foreclosure notices on 3,892 West Side apartment buildings on which the bank held unpaid mortgages. 7,451 repossessions were ordered on automobiles registered to West Side residents and at City Hall, the assistant to the tax collector found that 86% of West Side property taxes were in arrears.

The Mayor called an emergency meeting of the City Council. They theorized that the whole problem had been set in motion by the West Side Landlord's Committee to protest rent-control and that the private industries concerned were "striking", as it were, in sympathy. The City Council issued subpoenas for the West Side landlords. Some of these landlords were Jasonites so did not respond.

At the time the economy of the West Side collapsed, it occurred to New Yorkers in other neighborhoods that Jason might just jog through Central Park some evening, prance up the steps of the Guggenheim and fling serenity like confetti across the chic East Side, a terrifying prospect for boutique owners, not to mention the plethora of advertising agencies with offices located on Madison Avenue. Greenwich Villagers, who traditionally cherish anxiety, vowed to defend their neurosis with their lives and stationed volunteers from the Twelfth Street Block Association at all subway entrances. If the drunks and junkies on the subway stairs suddenly emitted auras of serenity, the volunteers were to blow their plastic whistles and the bells of St. Anthony's were prepared to ring twelve times warning all Villagers who held dear the ideals of psychopathology to grab their loved ones and make a run for Wall Street—the area, it was correctly assumed, that would be the last to fall.

The citizens of Manhattan buzzed with anxiety and brought pressure on the Mayor to remove the threat of Jasonism. The Mayor, in knee-jerk reflex, ordered the police, the city marshals and the National Guard to march on the West Side and drive out the Jasonites.

The attack occurred just after midnight, June 2nd. The Jasonites were sleeping in the streets, in the alleys, on fire escapes or in any of the open-doored apartments from 72nd Street to Cathedral Parkway. The National Guard rolled in from the 96th Street exit of the West Side Highway, devastating Riverside Drive and taking Broadway. The police entered through the park at 81st Street and seized Central Park West and Columbus Avenue. The Jasonites were driven onto Amsterdam Avenue where they stood, fifty and sixty deep across the street, sleepy-eyed and bewildered. The City Marshals marched toward them from the North and South, bayonets fiercely thrust forward. The bayonets, unearthed from storage at the east side Armory, were vintage World War I and rusty. Above the heads of the trapped Jasonites, the Mayor flew in the WNEW weather helicopter, shouting down his megaphone, "Give up now, Jason, and we won't hurt you. We'll," the Mayor promised, "we'll send you to Vermont."

And then all hell broke loose—or heaven broke loose, depending on your point of view. The battle was filmed from the air and when I screened it, I saw a blinding flash of light in the middle of the crowd between 95th and 96th just in front of Hanratty's. I knew that it was Jason. Instantly, the Jasonites seized garbage can lids, car radio antennas, hubcaps and broken bottles. Their ranks burst open and they scampered up fire escapes, bounded across rooftops, dashed in flanks down alleys and covered the West Side. They had no guns, no bombs, no tear gas. They used what they could find. They ripped parking meters from the sidewalk and, four Jasonites holding each meter, ramrodded approaching battalions. They fought like wild dogs unleashed. I never saw Religious Fervor until I watched the Jasonites fight.

10,000 Jasonites died in the battle of the West Side. Only 120 Police and Guardsmen were killed or wounded and rumor had it that those deaths were due to friendly fire. We know for sure a Lt. Ramon Gonzales shot Sgts. Peacher, Johnson and Rijos in the back, thinking they were Jasonites.

They say if you look directly into the eyes of a zealous Jasonite, your soul is lost to them forever. Within the week, thousands of the police and guardsmen who fought the battle of the West Side, returned to become Jasonites.

To the untrained eye, it would appear that the Jasonites fight savagely. Their intensity and zest is overwhelming. But to date, in fact, no one has been able to prove conclusively that any Jasonite has caused the death of any unbeliever. In each and every major battle, the number of wounded and dead unbelievers is minimal and corresponds statistically with expected losses due to friendly fire. The number of dead Jasonites, however, totals close to a million now—that body count is based on the number of corpses found after battles in the streets and includes the continents of North America, South America and parts of Europe. The body count was computed by the Pentagon while it was still in operation. The Pentagon went under in the battle of Washington, D.C. last week. I suppose one could call this World War III except the press, with its unerring ear for a catchy phrase, has named it Chasing Jason. And that has been the prime objective of the International Army of Unbelievers.

The Jasonites, compulsively neat, have picked up all the guns dropped in the streets during battles and they each carry one, neatly tucked into the waistband of their khaki shorts. Some people theorize that the guns are just for show, that Jasonites have no way of getting ammunition and it would be against their religion to fire a pistol. I'm not sure about that. The Jasonite guards who brought me into this Church wore pistols and looked to me as if they'd use them.

"There's no hope, Solomon. Not for me, not for anybody."

"Oh," Solomon nuzzles me, "there's always hope."

"Not for unbelievers. The day the Jasonites outnumbered us, our cause was lost. It's only a matter of time."

"Well," consoles Solomon, "perhaps they'll lose their fervor without Jason to lead them. Say," he grins, "I'll bet you're going to be a National hero. They'll erect a statue to you."

"For killing Jason?" I am horrified.

"Ah," Solomon winks, "fame at last." He purrs sheepishly. "Just a little gallows humor."

"It's not funny, Solomon."

The Army has been chasing Jason with stepped-up intensity the past few months, a virtually impossible task what with Jason's ability to appear and disappear and the fact that Jasonites don't talk. Even sending a spy into their ranks won't elicit any information. In fact, every spy the Army sent in became a Jasonite and never came out. Chasing Jason was like chasing moonglow.

So while they flew night missions in their Green Flies and bivouacked on the periphery of places their computers guessed Jason might show up, they were looking for a needle in a haystack.

No one knew I had any relationship to Jason.

Jason frequently donned his sunhat with tiny fishes dangling from the brim, and the CUNY jacket which he'd picked up on the street after the battle of Riverdale and came home to our apartment for a hot meal and a nap. That's what he said he came for, but I sometimes fantasized he came because he wanted to see me.

The press knew he was in the New York area because the oil refineries went silent in New Jersey, passengers drifted off to sleep while riding the Cyclone at Coney Island and, smack in the middle of the Daily Double at Aqueduct, the jockeys halted their steeds, dismounted and, smiling vaguely, wandered off the tracks. As I watched the reports tippity-tapping in on the wire services and read the International Army's speculations as to Jason's exact location, I smiled contentedly, knowing exactly where he was: curled in his youth bed, guard rail up, snuggling the bundle of his old Roy Rogers pajamas as though they were a teddy bear.

The street battles made Jason unhappy. A pallor of sadness settled on him and it made my heart heavy to see weariness in his dark eyes. He lost no weight during the skirmishes but he skinned his elbows, knees and stubbed his toes; his eyelids grew puffy and his face became drained of color. He was, of course, appearing and disappearing all over the globe and flashing his brilliant aura a dozen or more times every day. It took a lot out of him.

Jason was safe at home, snuggled in his bed, the day I

blew it. It was Good Friday, Channel 3 News was on the air live and Lucy Dobdaughter was filling in for Sam Dowdy who had twisted his ankle climbing the twenty-two flights down from his penthouse; since the Con Ed employees became Jasonites, there was no power for elevator service in most parts of the city. Just before the broadcast, Lucy told Ginger that she had a scoop and was going to drop a major bombshell on the newscast. Ginger immediately whispered this secret to everyone who'd listen and passed little notes about it to those who wouldn't. Lucy expected this. The entire news staff lined up at the monitor to watch the show.

"I have a guest with me tonight," Lucy sneered into the camera. "A guest who may shed light on the most perplexing mystery of our time, a guest who may resolve our present worldwide confrontation, who may be the secret weapon that will end this hideous nightmare known as Chasing Jason. Here she is, flown from Seoul, Korea, courtesy of United Airline's one remaining 707. America, meet Donellen Geitupeis, the mother of Jason."

She was hardly as big as Ginger Grosswoman. A bird of a thing and made to look even smaller sitting next to Lucy's sneer. Donellen had spidery fingers that fluttered and flashed with rings of many colors; her earrings dangled to her narrow bony shoulders, her clog shoes clanged against the chair rung. She had blood red inch long fingernails reminiscent of the talons of a hawk fresh from the kill. Her eyes were shifty.

"Ah yes," she singsonged. "Ah yes, I have baby boy Jason when I was eleven years old. I do not know a man. I believe I get the baby from the whirlpool bath at the Haitsung Health Club. I so poor I gave baby to rich American."

I didn't think before I acted, of course. I just flew from the control booth and the next thing I knew I was live on camera, having flattened Donellen against the cyclorama with one hand. Lucy Dobdaughter leapt onto the anchorman's desk.

I had Donellen by both flimsy shoulders, slamming her

against the canvas flat.

"You're not Jason's mother," I screamed, "I am! I raised him. He's been mine for over twenty years and I know him better than anybody."

Camera three moved in tight to get a closeup. I could feel the lens extending near my shoulder. I spun and screamed into the camera, "I am the mother of the Son of God! Josephine Mary Caldwell, mother of Jason, producer of the Second Coming!"

Fober and Martha dragged me off the set and into the newsroom. The Station Manager was leaning over my desk signing my severance paycheck. Lucy Dobdaughter offered to ghost-write my life story. Ginger Grosswoman begged me to tell her what Jason was going to do next.

I cleaned out my desk as though I were in a trance.

Then it struck me. The authorities knew who I was now; they'd come to my apartment looking for Jason.

I ran crosstown like an Olympic contender. I saw a Jasoncycle leaning against a lamppost. The sidewalks were littered now with these devices which the Jasonites concocted from discarded bikes, motors, from old blenders or vacuum cleaners, and fueled with methane produced by solar heat in garbage cans. Both the fuel and the bikes are left on the streets for use by any Jasonites. I'd never ridden a Jasoncycle but I mounted it, flipped the the switch and prayed some Jasonite had already fueled it with excrement. It putt-putted me to our apartment building. I dropped it, at the entrance of the building, and raced up the stairs. My fingers shook so violently, I could scarcely open the lock. The chain was on from the inside and I screamed, "Open up, open up!" I didn't want to call out Jason's name in case someone should be listening in the hall. There was no response from inside the apartment and so sweating and trembling, I heaved my weight against the door the way cops do in movies. Pain seared my shoulder with each thrust but finally the door gave way with an ear-splitting tearing of the wooden frame. The door fell forward so quickly that I lost my balance and sprawled across it, ripping my velveteen slack suit on the splintered wood.

"Jason, Jason!"

He was not in his youth bed. I was terrified he'd disappeared and would, unknowingly, reappear as the troopers came through the door to kill him.

"Oh God," I cried, "help me!"

At that moment, the bathroom door opened and Jason padded out, barefooted, sleepy-eyed.

"I went crazy," I admitted to him. "I got in front of the TV cameras and told everyone that I'm your mother. They're going to come here looking for you."

Jason sighed as though he knew that this was coming.

"So disappear! Hurry!"

Jason spoke softly. "I can't."

"What do you mean you can't?" My voice was high with hysteria. I peeked out the broken doorframe.

"I can't disappear. I just tried to and I can't. This must be it."

"You're always disappearing, you've been doing it for years."

"I think I've lost my power," he replied sadly.

I saw him straining. The veins in his neck stood out, his cheeks bulged.

"See," he said. "Nothing."

"Then fly!"

"I can't. I can't disappear. I can't fly."

"You have to! They'll kill you, Jason!"

Jason sighed. "I guess it's Why Has Thou Forsaken Me time again."

"No!" I screamed to the heavens. "Don't do this, God!"

"Sooner or later, I have to die for your sins," Jason reminded me. "Nothing to get excited about. Really."

I threw my arms around him. "They won't get you this time, not over my dead body!" I grabbed his arm and dragged him through the demolished doorway, down the hallway, down the stairs. The Jasoncycle was still lying at the entrance of the building. "You drive," I ordered him.

Jason flicked the switch and started the cycle. I climbed on the back fender and wrapped my arms around his pudgy waist.

"Where are we going?" he inquired. He seemed to be in no hurry.

I slapped his flanks as though he were a horse. I pointed to the east. "We're going thataway."

I didn't know a thing about the roads surrounding New York City but I knew I had to get Jason out. They'd be looking for him on the West Side. "East," I kept pointing the direction to him. We putt-putted through Central Park. "Keep going east."

The streets were full of Jasoncycles. No one took special notice of us.

"There," I shouted in Jason's ear, "Take the Throgs Neck Bridge!"

"Now where?" he called back as we neared the end of it and passed the vacant toll booths.

Ahead a sign said 495 East and the road had a name I recognized from writing about traffic jams.

"There," I screamed, "take the Long Island Expressway!"

The road had been deserted for a year, since Jason took Detroit. The Auto Workers sauntered off their jobs and hopped onto Jasoncycles so there were no parts available. Within a few months cars were rendered useless.

At Exit 54, Jason had to eat and pee. The Howard Johnson's stood abandoned, all doors open. Jason said the men's room was spotlessly clean and he helped himself to several Hojo lollipops and a fudge candy bar. In the parking lot, in a Howard Johnson's plastic swing-top trash-can, some Jasonite who'd travelled this road previously had prepared a load of methane. Jason fueled the little motor. We circled back onto the LIE.

I felt safe, my arms wound around Jason's golden waist. There'd be no New York City cops out here, I thought. No one will recognize us. "We're free," I shouted to the abandoned two-family houses on the right. "Free," I hollered to the vacant ranch-style developments on the left. "From here on out, nobody's chasing Jason except me."

By midnight, we saw Exit 73 glittering in Day-Glo numbers. Last Exit, it warned. We veered to the right and to the left and were on a smaller road.

My heart leapt to my throat. Behind a clump of trees just past the desolate Shell Station, a patrol car sat hidden as though waiting all year long for the traffic to begin again. I could see two officers in the front seat, fiddling with their radar dials, hoping for a speeding Ford to set their world in motion.

"The State Police," I screamed in Jason's ear. "Burn rubber!"

The patrol car pulled out after us. Its exhaust billowed clouds of black smoke, its fenders rattled like a thunderstorm. Steam hissed from its grill and seeped out of the edges of the hood. It wore tires of three different sizes and staggered forward in jerks and leaps.

We took off up a hill. The road was narrow and black as pitch. Jason was squinting, trying to keep the cycle on the pavement. We could see the single headlight of the lurching patrol car moving at about the same speed we were but with far less grace. We passed a trailer camp and saw Jasonites camped out on the roofs. They sat up and watched us pass but did not wave. We curved to the right, then to the left and suddenly our road ended.

"Which way?" Jason didn't know right from left so I pointed to the right, knowing I was also giving directions to the patrol car. I only hoped I was heading us toward a state line. A fallen sign beside a deserted farm stand said To Orient. I knew enough geography to be sure that New York State was nowhere near China.

A large restaurant on our left stood open and a Jasonite was sitting on the stoop. He was eating something. In the parking lot, another Jasonite was adding fuel to a methane container. Jason's attention was drawn to the Jasonite who was eating. He swung the cycle toward the restaurant, his mouth watering. I grabbed his earlobe.

"Don't stop now," I ordered, "the cops are on our ass."

The engine of the cop car had begun to make a screaming noise. Even so, they were still in pursuit.

"Straight ahead, Jason," I demanded, "keep on going straight ahead!"

"I'm starving," Jason cried.

"Your stomach will lead you to your death," I protested, "you can survive without food for a month if you have to!"

Jason moaned. I squeezed his earlobe and he kept going. He whined regretfully, as the restaurant passed out of sight and whimpered when, almost immediately, a deserted diner rose into view.

"No," I commanded him. "Eyes on the road. Think about your life, Jason, not your belly. You fat lug, I love you!"

And then we saw the sign. It was ten feet tall and at least that wide. It was battered and in disrepair, shabby letters fluorescent in the moonlight.

MOSES CROSS-SOUND BRIDGE it said UNDER CONSTRUCTION. LINKING OUR LONG ISLAND VACATIONLAND WITH THE SUNNY CONNECTICUT SHORE! ANOTHER GREAT ACCOMPLISHMENT OF (and then it listed the Governors, Mayors, County Executives, Road Commissioners, etc., of both states) FOR THE GROWTH OF INDUSTRY AND TOURISM. GOOD BRIDGES MAKE GOOD NEIGHBORS!

I remembered reading news reports about it. The citizens had protested the construction of a Cross-Sound Bridge. Said it would erode their banks, foul their fishing, unload too much traffic on their narrow roads. Channel 3 had done five minutes on it; the film clip showed fishermen and farmers linking arms in a vain attempt to stop the bulldozers. Then the steelworkers walked off their jobs, the road crews joined Jason.

Beyond the MOSES CROSS-SOUND BRIDGE sign there was another sign, striped with honeysuckle. Something about Island's End. And at its feet, another sign: Orient Ferry. Good God, I realized, shocked. Long Island is an island and we've come to the other side! No ferry was going to be running. The maritime workers were Jasonites. I wondered whether Jason and I could figure out how to operate a boat if we could confiscate one. Jason was mechanically inclined but I had no idea how to read a nautical map and Jason couldn't read at all.

The patrol car was limping after us in long strides, its one eye casting a bouncing light ahead of it.

I knew I had to make a decision.

Straight ahead, I guessed, was the end of the road, the ocean and a ferry which we might or might not be able to operate. To our left was a bridge which might or might not be completed.

I screamed my order in Jason's ear, "Turn left!" and tapped his shoulder so he'd see my arm stretched in that direction.

The road was pitch black and slightly hilly. Each time we putted up a rise I saw the moon but only for a moment. To both sides were summer cottages, steps broken, trellises hanging, berry vines thick around the sills and creeping in the open windows. Automobiles were pushed into the ditches along the roadside, stripped of tires and parts, their grills dipping into the muddy trenches like hogs about to wallow.

Suddenly the road opened wide. An empty, half-roofed kiosk guarded the entrance to the bridge. It swung across the Sound like a cobweb, attached at both ends but swaying gently from the middle. Perhaps they had intended to hang sandbags or something to weigh it down but hadn't gotten to it before the workers walked off to become Jasonites.

"It's going to be like riding a bike on a giant swing," I warned Jason, "think you can do it?"

Jason shrugged but didn't stop.

"Well?" We were on the approach.

"Why not?" he asked and passed the kiosk. "I know the end of this, anyway."

Behind us, the patrol car seemed to pick up speed. A last gasp, perhaps, before death. It came charging toward us.

"Hit it, Jason, step on it!" I kicked his calves as though I was wearing spurs and jerked his earlobe like it was a bit.

The bridge did not rise into the air like the George Washington or pictures I've seen of the Golden Gate. It swung downwards from the high cliff like a jump robe held by Long Island and her girlfriend Connecticut. Once we began the descent, there was no stopping, even though I could see that the patrol car was slowing near the kiosk, giving up the chase.

Salt air lashed our faces. The Jasoncycle motor stopped chug-chugging and was running with the wind. We must have been going downhill thirty miles an hour.

"Listen," Jason called to me, then turned his head so he could look directly in my eyes. The wind whipped his hair from the back and it framed his face so he looked small again. "Listen," he said. His eyes were luminous and moist, "I care."

"What?" I thought I'd heard him correctly but what with the howling of the wind and the squealing of the cop car and the incessant swinging of the bridge while we were sailing downhill, I felt both deaf and nauseated. Jason had never emitted a sentimental sentence in his life.

"I care," he repeated loudly.

Then with a WHISSSHHH, the front wheel of the Jasoncycle dropped into space.

"Oh shucks," Jason hollered as he plunged through the open middle of the uncompleted bridge, "Here we go again, God, here I come!"

I felt Jason flying forward and I let go of him. Even now, that's what I feel most guilty about. Although I couldn't have held him back, and if I'd kept my arms wound tightly around his waist, I would have plummeted into the Sound along with him, letting go still seems to me to be a coward's choice. But I did and I grasped the seat of the Jasoncycle with both hands. A steel beam jutted several feet beyond the surface of the unfinished bridge and as the Jasoncycle toppled into the chasm, the beam speared the back wheel and held both the cycle and me dangling above the Sound. I saw Jason, dimly silhouetted against the sky, arc into space, then cannonball past the startled moon and SPLAT into the water fifty feet below. When he hit, the spot exploded like a geyser and the salt spray suddenly glowed gold. Then it flickered, faded and receded. I could see nothing below me then but ordinary waves undulating gently on the surface of the Sound. I was still staring down, my eyes searching that spot and the surrounding area, hoping Jason's head would bob to the surface. He couldn't swim a stroke. He'd flunked the free course at the Y that he took when he was seven.

"Jason, Jason," I was weeping when the two patrolmen tip-toed carefully to the edge of the abyss and pulled me up to safety.

"Don't cry, lady," the tall cop, who introduced himself as Scotty, consoled me. "That fellow won't be bothering you again."

The short cop, whose name was Luke, knelt at the edge of the precipice and peered at the black water. "Guess he'll wash up on somebody's beach sooner or later. We don't have enough men left these days to drag the Sound."

They had kept the patrol car running just in case it wouldn't start again. Its one eye seemed to me to be getting weaker.

"Don't want to get stuck this far out," Scotty explained as they loaded me into the back seat of the car. "I don't believe there's ten people left east of Riverhead who haven't got the virus."

"The virus?"

"You know, the virus. The Virus." Luke got into the car and leaned with one arm over the front seat. "Why, it's practically taken over the world."

"It's one of those new bugs," Scotty continued, sliding into the driver's seat, "probably brought on by shooting things into space. Might have come back on a moon-rock. Makes you feel all the time like you're fishing early on a summer Sunday morning. I guess they'll find a cure for it, sooner or later. Scientists can do just about anything these days."

"You may have got it," Luke grimaced sadly. "That fellow who kidnapped you was a carrier. It's highly contagious and carriers are everywhere. Scotty and me been hiding out the past year and a half in the Home Appliance Center in Riverhead. Once somebody gets the virus, they've got no use for stoves and freezers. It's the safest place around."

I suddenly realized that while New York and the national news media had identified Jason as a radical religious leader, many small towns all across the world had been cut off from communications for so long that they might well have devised their own interpretations as to who the Jasonites were and what had caused the international holocaust. It occurred to me that these patrolman didn't know Jason was wanted in all states, didn't even know they'd been chasing Jason.

"The reason we followed you," Luke said, "is that we figured you were being kidnapped. We could tell the way your eyebrows were all knotted up that you didn't have the virus yet."

"Myself," Scotty put in, "I think it's some form of that Legionnaire's Disease. They never did do enough research on that. I believe if they'd found a cure for that way back in '76, they could have nipped this thing in the bud."

"We were getting goddam bored just sitting in those

bushes. Been three months since a car passed by."

Scotty fiddled with the CB. It cracked and spit and hummed. "Some of the elements got busted," he explained. "Sometimes it works, sometimes it doesn't. We got access to a lot of radios and CBs in the stores but batteries are at a premium. Most of them have gone bad now. Even when we get something working, we don't get much reception."

A voice blasted suddenly over the CB. Luke and Scotty grinned at one another.

"Hot dog," Luke said.

The broadcast was an All Points Bulletin for Jason.

Luke and Scotty looked puzzled when the voice concluded and signed off.

"Are they telling us that if we catch this one fellow, Jason, everybody else will get well?"

"That's the theory," I replied.

We were lumbering past the restaurant and the two Jasonites were still there, sitting on the steps.

"Don't look at them," Scotty warned me, "You can get it even looking at them."

"He drowned," I wailed suddenly.

I had to tell someone and there was no one else. No one but Jasonites for miles and miles. I told Luke and Scotty everything. In the middle of my outpouring, a tire blew on the car. Luke cursed under his breath. Scotty veered to the shoulder of the road. But they were so fascinated by my story that they simply rolled up the windows, locked the door and kept listening. I wept as I related what had happened. I could see they didn't believe every word of it, especially the part about Jason's divinity.

"You mean to tell me that the fellow who just went off the bridge was Jason?" Scotty stared at me in the rear view mirror.

"My son." I began to sob again.

"And without him, this catastrophe is over?"

"That's what they say."

"Who says?"

"The unbelievers. The International Army."

"Army?" Scotty slapped the steering wheel. "You mean there's been a war going on?"

I nodded.

"Hell," Luke said, "this thing is a lot more serious than we thought, Scotty."

"We better get the word to somebody that we got the leader." Scotty panted with excitement as he continued. "They'll want to know that Jason's dead, won't they. Shit, we could get a medal. We could go down in history."

They must have fooled with the CB for twenty minutes before accepting that their mike was broken.

"Well, Luke, we're going to have to go in town and get a tire, that's all. Then we'll drive somewhere, find somebody, do something."

"Right," Luke answered and opened the car door for me. He scratched his head. "Tell you the truth, though, I don't know where to go."

I was heavy with Jason's death and it was all that I could do to walk behind them into the town. Victorian houses stood sedately along the road, doors and windows open, curtains flapping as though it were the middle of a tourist summer. Paint peeled on clapboard and roof shingles curled but, apart from the natural weather damage, there didn't seem to be much vandalism. Every old house had a porch which stretched across its front and was framed in gingerbread. On each porch were lumps which I took to be sleeping Jasonites. I wanted to run to them, shake them awake and scream, "I've killed Jason!" But though I appeared to be immune to Jason, Scotty and Luke might not be. I didn't want to be the only unbeliever on Long Island.

"Jason, Jason," I called silently, "why didn't you take me with you?"

"I you hadn't let go of my waist," I fantasized him replying, "I would have. If you're all alone now, it's your own fault. Anyway, I've told you, Seekers must come alone. Godliness is singular."

At the end of the street, by the harbor, I looked to my right and saw hundreds of cars. Three abreast across the street, parked bumper to bumper.

"Not one of them in working order," Luke commented. "They been sitting here since the day the ferry unloaded and during the two hours traffic was stalled, trying to get a hundred fifty cars down the prime shopping street in tourist season, some of those—what do you call them?—"

"Jasonites," I prompted.

"—came along. The drivers of these cars got out and followed them. I expect we got enough parts here to keep our old car running twenty years but neither Scotty or me is mechanically inclined."

"Here's a tire," said Scotty. "Looks like it would fit." He pointed to a spare in an open trunk.

"Well, while we're here, let's look around, see if we can find a match for it," Luke suggested. "We been running that car gimp-tired for too long. I expect we're ruining the axle."

It was a fatal move. Luke peered into another open trunk and there, curled up against the spare, was a Jasonite. Awake. He caught Luke's eyes with the serene look and I saw the brilliant gold flash that heralded the birth of one more Jasonite.

"Come on," Scotty hollered, "get the lead out, Luke. We got to get a move on!"

Luke turned, smiling like an angel, and looked directly into Scotty's face. Another golden flash.

I wondered if it would make a difference if the Jasonites knew Jason was dead. Maybe they weren't as adept at non-verbal communication as they pretended to be. Maybe they needed to be told. What could I lose? I was the only one left!

"Jason's dead," I screamed. "Jason's dead! I led him to his death!" I stood on the hood of a semi-trailer, its sides boldly labeled DANGER, CARRYING RADIOACTIVE WASTE and I screamed until my throat ached.

"Jason is dead!"

And then I collapsed against the fly-splattered windshield and, staring at a plastic figurine of Mary on the dashboard, I fell unconscious.

When I awoke, I was lying on the first pew here. It was mid-afternoon and the stained glass Judas checkered me with many colors. I heard a voice, reciting from Isaiah:

"For behold, I create new heavens
and a new earth;
and former things shall not be remembered
or come into mind.
But be glad and rejoice for ever
in that which I create"

I knew the voice was familiar but I couldn't place it. The voice continued.

"For behold, I create Jerusalem a rejoicing,
and her people a joy,
I will rejoice in Jerusalem,
and be glad in my people;
no more shall be heard in it the sound of weeping
and the cry of distress.
No more shall there be in it
an infant that lives but a few days
or an old man who does not fill out his days,
for the child shall die a hundred years old,
and the sinner a hundred years old shall be
accursed."

Who was it? I tried to lift my eyelids. It wasn't Jason's voice, I was sure of that.

"They shall build houses and inhabit them;
they shall plant vineyards and eat their fruit.
They shall not build and another inhabit;
They shall not plant and another eat;
for like the days of a tree shall the days of my

people be,
and my chosen shall long enjoy the work of their
hands."

I knew. I had to sit up and confront him. My feet were
dead weights, my arms immobile. I groaned.

"Before they call I will answer
while they are yet speaking I will hear,
The wolf and the lamb shall feed together,
the lion shall eat straw like the ox;
the dust shall be the serpent's food,
they shall not hurt or destroy
in all my holy mountain."

It took every bit of effort I had but I pushed myself
upright. I faced him head-on.

"So saith the Lord."

"Dr. Binbaum."

He smiled benignly when I called his name and reached
out one hand as if to bless me. He was dressed like a Jasonite,
cut-off khakis, pistol in his waistband, rubber thongs from
Woolco. He wore the same gerry-rigged glasses except that
now the lens was gone from the right side. That made it
appear that his left eye was larger than his right and that,
alone, gave him an unearthly look.

"You're no Jasonite!" I stood and pointed my finger
accusingly at him. "Jasonites don't recite the Bible. Jasonites
don't read books. Jasonites don't speak aloud except when
necessary. Jasonites don't cause their fellow men to kneel
around their feet." That's where the other Jasonites, perhaps
two dozen of them, were.

"You know too much, Josie," said Dr. Binbaum. "Knowledge is a barrier between you and God."

"Ha!" I countered. "My knowledge is a barrier between
you and your ambition."

"We have no ambitions," stated Dr. Binbaum. "Ambition
and Expectation give way to Serenity. She who dances also
sings."

"And life is but a *scream*," I taunted him.

"We came to this place because it's rich with natural bounty. The fields are fertile and the salt air cleanses the human soul. And," he whispered feverishly, "real estate out here is bound to go up. It's a buyer's market. Commuting distance to Manhattan, you know."

"Manhattan's dead," I cried. "And Jason hated real estate."

Dr. Binbaum lowered his eyes mournfully. "Yes, we have mourned his death all morning. Jason, betrayed by his own mother. Ah, Josie," Dr. Binbaum lamented, "how can a mother kill her child?"

"I was trying to save his life!"

"He was divine."

"If he was so divine, why couldn't he evaporate or fly or bounce off the waters of the Sound as if he were a rubber ball? Why didn't God save him?"

"Everything," said Dr. Binbaum, "is as it should be."

And the trial began.

It came clear to me, during the trial, that Dr. Binbaum had set himself up as the head of this colony of Jasonites, though Jasonites are not supposed to have a leader. Dr. Binbaum called them his sheep and this his church. I could see the resistance in their eyes. They recalled Jason saying God doesn't live in four walls. But winter gets cold and windy here and Dr. Binbaum is a persuasive man. When he pronounced judgment on me, he referred to himself as the Right Reverend Dr. Binbaum and I noticed the raw edges of his cut-offs were embroidered H.H.H.R.B., III, M.D., Ph.D., D.D.

"She shall be sentenced to the final and everlasting state of humankind, forevermore."

He didn't say another word. He departed with the Jasonites at his heels and left me in this church alone, one Jasonite guarding the door outside. "Final" echoed in my ears.

The girl who brought this blanket to me said Louie sent it.

Now that I think back on it, perhaps she said Huey sent it. Huey is what Dr. Binbaum's lady friends call him.

"It must be noon now, Solomon. It's hot in here. Why don't they come for me and get it over?"

"Beats me," shrugs Solomon. "Maybe they can't stand the sight of blood."

"It's hard to believe you're jesting when the end of my life might come within the hour."

"No point in postponing the inevitable," Solomon muses. "that's what my Mama said to me the first time that I flinched over a nest of baby mice."

"I can't wait any longer!" I shouted, not caring if my voice carried to the Jasonites outside. "I'm going crazy from waiting, Solomon." Resolutely, I limped toward the massive door. "I'm going to beat on that door until somebody opens it."

"If he opens the door," Solomon squeaks with excitement, "you could run."

"I couldn't run far. Where would I run to? There's water on three sides of this town."

"You could steal a Jasoncycle and take off," Solomon prompted. "Can I go with you? I could ride in the basket if there is one."

"And leave your home?" I'm surprised at Solomon's request.

"You have so many adventures, Josie, and I have none at all." It is difficult for Solomon to admit this and he looks away from me. "Besides," he adds greedily, "you say there're rats in New York City."

"Just like Jason." I am touched. "Always thinking about your belly."

"You get him to open up the door," Solomon plans, "and I'll claw his legs and we'll both make a run for it."

"I'm not much of a runner, Solomon," I remind him.

"You will be when you're running for your life."

SIXTEEN

I BEAT against the door, beat on it with my fists. There was abject terror in my voice.

"Hit it harder, Josie!" Solomon cheered me on from a safe distance. "Yell louder, so they'll hear you!"

I flailed at the door until my fists were tender and my voice hoarse from screaming. No one came.

"Try the doorknob," Solomon suggested, himself retreating further into the shadows.

"It's locked," I argued. "Why are you hiding?"

"So if something happens to you," he replied sensibly, "*I* can run for my life."

I tried the doorknob. The door swung open, groaning with its own weight.

"It wasn't locked?" Solomon giggled as he asked this.

"Of course it *was* locked," I snapped at him. "It was locked last night, you know that, there was a guard and everything."

Solomon shrugged and crept out of the shadows.

"They've gone," I whispered. Solomon crept closer to the door. I scanned the parking lot, the road, the treetops, I tiptoed to the corners of the building and peeked around them.

"They've gone," I cried joyously and broke into a run. My ankle hurt some but I was too relieved to care. I was halfway across the parking lot, heading for the deserted street beyond when I turned to see if Solomon was following. He was stretched out on the sunlit stone steps of the church, cleaning his paws and absorbing a blistering dose of afternoon sun. "Solomon!"

He looked up at me, squinting, a pleasant stoned expression on his face.

"Solomon, aren't you coming with me?"

"I prefer not to run in the afternoon," he purred and closed his eyelids against the golden light. "Extreme heat takes the wind out of me."

"But the Jasonites."

He lifted his head slightly. "I don't see any," he shrugged. "Besides, Josie, the Jasonites won't hurt me unless I'm with you. A mangy German Shepherd, now there's a danger."

"But I thought you were my friend."

"I am." He rolled onto his back and presented his belly to the sun. He wasn't gray, he was a white cat with gray markings, just as he'd claimed. "And a handsome sonofagun, too, don't you think?"

"The Jasonites could not have gone far," I argued. "Maybe they went to eat. Just because they're not here right now..."

"Don't ask for trouble," Solomon advised. "If you stay right here, you can see them coming and run then. As for me, I've been up all night and I'm tired and hungry. I intend to take a relaxing sunbath, an invigorating catnap and then, with my wits about me, I'll stroll into the woods there and hunt up a few mice."

And with that, my friend Solomon dozed into a peaceful-looking sleep.

I couldn't sleep. It would have been foolhardy to lie down. I didn't know where the Jasonites had gone—nor what their plans were to dispose of me. I walked carefully and slowly up the main street of the Village, keeping a watchful eye out for Jasonites curled up on porches or under spreading elms. Not a Jasonite in sight. The air hung hot and humid and smelled of salt. The Victorian houses lined the street, shoulder to shoulder, their magnificence humbled by neglect. There were no sounds. I couldn't hear a bird though I stopped and held my breath to listen. Except for the deserted man-made structures, it seemed as though I had stepped back to the beginning of all time. As though the heartbeat of the earth was muffled, as though no living creature had yet been born. I peered up through the leaves into the summer sky above me. It must have been the way the heavens looked to Lillith. I continued walking three blocks south, my footfalls making the only sounds, when suddenly I heard—

Dr. Binbaum's voice. Fierce and terrible, a singular sound cutting through the silence.

"You must seek no other God."

I walked softly and stayed close to the buildings. I stepped onto the narrow front porch of a yellow house and saw, across the street, on the oil-stained concrete slab of a deserted Shell station, Jasoncycles, dozens of them. Mounted on each, bare legs straddling the bikes, were Jasonites. In the dark interior of the garage bay, sitting six feet up on a hydraulic lift, was Dr. Binbaum. The one lens left in his spectacles caught sunlight and gleamed out at the crowd like the angry eye of Cyclops.

"You must seek no other God before me," he bellowed.

The Jasonites were clearly restless. I could hear the metallic clanging of their cycles bumping one another. Almost in unison, each Jasonite put his right foot on the pedal of his bike as though to take off.

"Don't go," Dr. Binbaum warned, his voice echoing within the mechanic's bay. *"Don't go."*

"But I've seen him," one of the cyclists called out, her voice ringing crystal in the still hot air. "He is risen."

"Tell us again!" It was the young girl who'd brought me the blanket. She sat on the shoulders of a young man so that she could better see across the crowd. "Tell us again about Jason!"

"It was on a beach in Jamesport," the woman cried. It had the sound of litany. "Early this morning. I had rested for the night under the shelter of the nuclear waste depository. I heard his voice. I heard him call out. And when I crawled on hands and knees out from my shelter, I saw him standing on the beach. His belly shone like burnished gold."

"And what did he say to you?" The Jasonites locked hands in excited anticipation.

"He said, 'I'm famished. Is there someplace around here I could get something to eat?'"

The Jasonites cheered and wept. "Take us to him," they begged, "Hurry!" And before Dr. Binbaum could slide off the hydraulic ramp to stop them, the cyclists had mounted their machines and were whirring out the drive.

"Stop," Dr. Binbaum wailed and lunged at the last of the cyclists, clinging to the saddle of a Jasoncycle until its rider picked up enough speed that Dr. Binbaum lost his grip and crumpled to the sidewalk.

When the procession of Jasonites had turned right and were proceeding westward, I cautiously crossed the street and approached poor Dr. Binbaum. His shoulders heaved with sobs.

"I could have saved them, Josie," he cried. "I was their leader, I could have shepherded them to God."

"No," I explained. "They're chasing Jason."

"But they need a man like me to organize them, to translate God. I can show them what is good and what is evil. I can translate the word of the Almighty into language that their minds can grasp." He mounted his own Jasoncycle with renewed vigor. "They are my sheep. I am their shepherd. I will reclaim them. Josie, Life is But A Scream."

I seized the handlebars of his cycle. "I don't understand. Yesterday you sentenced me to death!"

Dr. Binbaum snorted with irritation. He lifted one ham-hock hand to adjust his spindly glasses. "Goodness me," he sighed, "you have always had a tendency to make a drama out of everything. I never sentenced you to death."

"You don't want to kill me?" I could feel cold sweat breaking out across my body.

"You read so much into everything," Dr. Binbaum grumbled. "What I sentenced you to was:...."

I repeated it with him, out loud. There was intense anger in my voice. *To the final and everlasting state of humankind, forevermore.*

"Yes," he said and smiled as though pleased with himself.

"What does that mean?"

Dr. Binbaum pushed off on his Jasoncycle. "Time's up," he called back, "Hold your thought."

I ran after him for half a block, flailing my fist in the air.

I sat down on the curb, exonerated. I no longer had to fear for my life. I was God-knows-where out on Long Island and for all I knew, I was the only person left here. I could try to make my way to the place where Jason'd been seen, but if Jason were alive, he could come to me much faster than I could go to him. If I were to find a Jasoncycle and travel westward looking for him, it might be the very instant that he was flying eastward looking for me. We might miss each other altogether.

When Jason was an adolescent and disappearing and reappearing, I often went out on the street to try and find him and, after searching for an hour, would return to the apartment where he'd be sitting straddle-legged on the kitchen chair, gobbling a vienna sausage sandwich. "Where the dickens have you been?" I'd shout at him, angrily. He'd smile beatifically and shrug. "Don't come looking for me," he'd advise, "It's a waste of your time. I know where you are. I'll find you when you need me."

Jason, I am going to trust in that.

As I walked back toward the church, I thought I heard a sound—the street appeared to be deserted and so did all the shops. The mannequins in a store window hung with cobwebs and on this hot day, there was no breeze to chase the dustballs which crouched like ghosts of rats on the floors of the open stores. I could see no movement anywhere. I walked another block.

I heard the sound again—this time closer. I paused to listen. It was coming from a bookshop. I stepped to one side of the display window and peeked around as a lean young man tiptoed from the back of the shop, scurried to the display window, scooped up an armful of books and hastened to disappear behind black drapes. There was silence for several seconds and a young woman tiptoed out from behind the drapes and set about to do the same thing. As she reached hungrily into the display window, I stepped into full view. She squeaked with surprise. Terror filled her eyes.

"Are you one of them?" Her voice shook.

"I'm a friend," I assured her. "May I come inside?"

She was not immediately gracious. In fact, she stepped in front of the door as though to bar me. "Who wrote *Moby Dick?*" she asked.

I answered and she smiled. "That's the kind of information they've forgotten." She stepped to one side and ushered me into the shop.

She led me toward the back of the store and past the heavy black drapes. There, in a blue haze of cigarette smoke, sat six people around a wooden table. They were reading, eyes devouring each page like college students cramming for an exam. There was a young man, two young women, two gray-haired ladies and a middle-aged man, leaning so deeply into the pages of his book, I couldn't read his face.

"Read," he bellowed, without looking up. "Absorb it all. Never stop learning!"

I recognized the well-trained voice of a minister who was an actor. I screamed with joy. "George!"

He peeked above the pages of his book and stared at me a full half-minute before he leapt to his feet and bellowed, "Josie!"

I threw myself into his arms. He smelled of tobacco and mildewed books, but his arms were strong and comforting around me. I was glad the room was shadowy. I was conscious of my wrinkled clothing, of my unwashed hair— but with the wild hope that love conquers all, I buried my face against George's shoulder and cried, "Oh George, how I've missed you."

He gave me a familiar, though brief, peck on the left side of my forehead. "You've come just in time, Josie. I need you." He motioned to the stacks of books which surrounded the group on all sides. "We have to read all these books, every one. Cram them into our heads," he pressed his knuckles against his temples to demonstrate the fervor with which knowledge must be rammed past the human skull. "People are burning books now, burning books!" His voice rose to a tumultuous level of horror. "We're the only intellectuals left. We have a responsibility to the world." He pounded his fist on a stack of books. "We must suck it up. The future lies in our hands."

"George, how did you get here?"

"Don't you see," he continued, "the human brain will soon go fallow."

I jerked on the lapel of his herringbone suit. "George, how did you get here? I thought you were in California."

He shuffled me to the side of the room and whispered feverishly, "I got a summer stock job in Connecticut and I was coming back to New York on the ferry. One of those Jasonites got on the ferry on his cycle and by the time we got halfway across the Sound, the crew and passengers were lolling in the sun. I had to dock the boat myself. I believe I was the only one who got off."

"It was your intellect," I whispered, "knowledge and curiosity make you immune to serenity."

But George wasn't listening to me. He put his finger to my lips. "Now don't tell anybody that I was an actor. It ruins my credibility. I'm a minister," and he took out his mail-order diploma and flashed it at me, "and I'm forming a new church here. You always wanted to be a minister's wife."

"Do you still love me, George?" I whispered softly against his lapel.

"I certainly could use you. We need somebody to set up housekeeping for us, prepare meals, do the laundry. Our work is too important to be interrupted by the petty necessities of survival."

"Georgie," crooned one of the young girls, shaking her long blonde hair from her shoulders, "I don't know what this word here means."

George hurried to her and has he explained the definition of *lecherous*, he tickled her earlobe with his finger.

It's late afternoon now. The sea breeze has cooled the air. The sun is lowering itself behind the Queen Anne house across the street. Spikes of gold flicker in an arch against the blue sky, making it appear that a sunburst is occurring in the widow's walk of the old house. Shadows are falling toward the east and the house casts such a large one that the rococo of its front porch is creating a pattern of black lace across my bare feet. The grass is waist high in the front yards of houses for as far as I can see but I'm sitting in the parking lot of the church and it is sandy here, as one might expect it to be, so close to the sea. The church shelters me from the road on one side and a massive locust tree, against which I'm leaning as I write, on the other. Solomon has climbed to the first limb and sits just above my head, peering at my pen as it moves across the page. Any moment he is going to leap, claws out, into my lap and seize my fingers, just for fun.

"Put down I caught a mouse this afternoon," he orders.

He did. And brought the head to me.

I've thought a lot this afternoon about my friend, Dr. Binbaum, my husband, George, and my son, Jason. I understand what Dr. Binbaum's doing. In a world fraught with chaos, he is organizing a religion. And although Jason told us that Godliness is not found in groups and God does not appear within manmade walls, Dr. Binbaum, convinced that no man is fit keeper of his own soul, has set himself the task of bringing God down to human size.

"I can't accept that, Solomon. If God devised human life as a game with rules, he's just a sportsman. My God is greater than that."

"I'm a sportsman," Solomon smiles and licks his chops. "In the brush," he adds, "I am definitely an omnipotent presence. I'm pretty good in a tree, too. Watch this!" He eyes a bird's nest several branches above his head.

"Solomon, don't."

But Solomon, spurred by scent and instinct, has already begun to climb.

I understand what George is doing, too. George is a Seeker, a questioner. The pursuit of knowledge always has its roots in spiritual soil—but Jason said that facts and theories muddy the naturally clear reflection of one's own soul.

Solomon pauses in his climb. "I'd hate to spend the rest of my life cooped up in the stacks of some old library. I can't live on a diet of bookworms." And having stated that, he focuses his glittering eyes on the bird's nest above his head.

As for Jason—I want to believe Life is but a stream; All time is now; Death is not a headless horseman; She who dances also sings.

I look up and see Solomon's rump and tail hanging over the limb. He is doing what he should be doing, I suppose. He is following nature.

I am going to leave this book beneath this tree where

Solomon is conquering his prey, and walk in the direction of the sun until I need to rest. I will search for food. The world is torn asunder, waiting for a new beginning.

I'll be walking westward where Jason is rumored to have been seen. I'll cut off the legs of these slacks and, like the Jasonites, take a salt bath in the waters of the Sound. I'll scrub my hair with sea-weed, stand bare-breasted in the sun. Perhaps the strong breeze from the Sound will wipe out my knowledge, my expectations. When I again see Jason—if I see Jason—I will be innocent and new.

Jason never said he wanted to be a leader or form a group. He always maintained that each Seeker must come alone. He was passing out serenity the way pretty girls used to pass out samples of chewing gum on New York City street corners, "Try some free, courtesy of the manufacturer"—but serenity, unlike Spearmint, was addictive and completely at odds with the demands of civilization. Jason's free samples resulted in a world-wide nightmare. When Jason was a tyke, he often said that he'd be happy when this dream ended. Maybe it has ended now. Perhaps the bronze-bellied Jasonite seen on the beach this morning was not him at all. Perhaps the woman who saw him was hallucinating.

On the other hand, perhaps we're only at the beginning of Jason's dream.

"Solomon?"

I look up but he's not listening to me. He's listening to his nature.

I envy him. I no longer know what is my nature and what is not. I have no idea what kind of creature God originally meant for me to be.

"Solomon?" He's not listening. Like George, Solomon seems to feel that expressions of love make him somehow vulnerable. I speak softly so he may continue to feel free. "Solomon, wherever I go, I'll remember you. I'll wish you fat rats and nests of tender mice. I'll dream for you a mate who's strong by day and warm at night, who'll present to you a kindle of sweet kittens, handsomely marked. And though I know that you'll sneer at this last thought, I wish for you, serenity. Jason always said that Seeking is a lonely business and though you hunger for adventure, Solomon, you'll have to find your own."

Perhaps Dr. Binbaum's judgment was more binding than I thought: "She shall be sentenced to the final and everlasting state of humankind, forevermore."

I expect to live my days now, chasing Jason.

JANE CHAMBERS (1937-1983) began her career in the late 1950s as an actress and playwright, working Off-Broadway and in coffeehouse theatre. Her plays have been produced Off-Broadway, in regional theatres, community theatres and on television. She has been the recipient of the Connecticut Educational Television Award (1971/ *Christ in a Treehouse*), a Eugene O'Neill fellowship (1972/*Tales of the Revolution and Other American Fables*), a National Writer's Guild Award (1973/ *Search for Tomorrow*, CBS), the Dramalogue Critics Circle Award, the Villager Theatre Award, the Alliance for Gay Artists Award and the Robby Award (1981, 1983-4/*Last Summer at Bluefish Cove*, N.Y. and L.A. productions) and the Fund for Human Dignity Award (1982), among others. She was a founding member of the New Jersey Women's Political Caucus and of the Interart Theatre in Manhattan, and a member of the Planning Committee of the Women's Program of the American Theatre Association. She was also a member of the Writer's Guild East, the Dramatists Guild, the Author's League, Actors Equity and the East End Gay Organization for Human Rights. On February 15, 1983, she died of a brain tumor at her Greenport, Long Island home; she is survived by her mother, Clarice, her two step-brothers, Henry and Ben, and by her life's companion, Beth Allen. New York's Meridian Gay Theatre has named its International Gay Playwriting Contest in her honor, and the American Theatre Association has created the Jane Chambers Playwriting Award to encourage the writing of new plays which address women's experiences and have a majority of principal roles for women.

ALSO AVAILABLE FROM JH PRESS

Jane Chambers' **BURNING**   (ISBN 0-935672-10-9) $6.95

A lesbian gothic suspense novel! Jane Chambers has written a tale of love that transcends time: Cynthia desperately needed a break from the city and took the offer of a vacation home, sight unseen. Hiring Angela, a young woman who lived in the same apartment building, to help with the children, Cynthia took possession of the New England farmhouse. And then, from an earlier century, Abigail and Martha reached out to possess the living.

> "Burning *brings the past persecution of lesbians into the present in an illuminating tale that is both an affirmation of a way of life and a good suspense story. I loved reading it."*
>
> — SANDRA SCOPPETTONE

Jane Chambers' **WARRIOR AT REST**   (ISBN 0-935672-12-5) $5.95

Jane Chambers was widely known as a playwright and novelist, but she was also an accomplished poet. The poems in this collection were written from 1958 to 1983, and cover experiences from her life at Goddard College and working in the Job Corps in Maine and New Jersey to the impact of terminal illness in the last months of her life. These poems are personal responses to specific events and feelings, expressed in imagery often too enigmatic to be incorporated into a novel or play.

> "Whimsical, sad, often funny, always affecting ... treasured glimpses into the heart and humanity of this gifted woman."
>
> —THE ADVOCATE

ALSO AVAILABLE FROM JH PRESS

Jane Chambers' **LAST SUMMER AT BLUEFISH COVE**
Paperback: (ISBN 0-935672-05-2) $6.95
Special hardcover limited edition; numbered, signed and with an
introduction by the author relating her own experience with
cancer: (ISBN 0-935672-04-4) $25.00

Heralded by audiences and critics alike as the "breakthrough
lesbian play," Jane Chambers' *Last Summer at Bluefish Cove* is
a tender and moving but still hilariously funny portrait of a
tightly knit summer community of long-time lesbian friends.
For one of the women, it is her last summer there, because of
her struggle with terminal cancer. She meets and falls in love
with a woman to whom she can bequeath her special gifts of
warmth, spirit and independence.

*"A funny, touching, surprisingly upbeat and enlight-
ened portrait of female homosexuality . . . a land-
mark event."*
                                        —OTHER STAGES

*"A tight, truthful script, by turns wonderfully
funny and painfully sad, that holds its own with
the best writing around town today."*
                                        —N.Y. DAILY NEWS